"Can you see me?" Bolan asked.

"Oh, yeah. You look like a good target to me," Grimaldi responded.

"Then you know what to do."

"Yeah. On the count of three. You ready?"

"I'm ready. On the count of three."

"One..."

Bolan took a deep breath. He looked at the armed men as they moved in, surrounding him. He had to leave. Now. And this was the only way.

"Two," Grimaldi said.

The Executioner braced himself.

"Three!"

Suddenly the chopper's engine roared. A split second later Bolan felt the straps of the harness bite into his chest and shoulders. He was whipped away from the ship's deck at what felt like the speed of light.

He felt himself losing consciousness.

MACK BOLAN ®
The Executioner

#190 Killing Range
#191 Extreme Force
#192 Maximum Impact
#193 Hostile Action
#194 Deadly Contest
#195 Select Fire
#196 Triburst
#197 Armed Force
#198 Shoot Down
#199 Rogue Agent
#200 Crisis Point
#201 Prime Target
#202 Combat Zone
#203 Hard Contact
#204 Rescue Run
#205 Hell Road
#206 Hunting Cry
#207 Freedom Strike
#208 Death Whisper
#209 Asian Crucible
#210 Fire Lash
#211 Steel Claws
#212 Ride the Beast
#213 Blood Harvest
#214 Fission Fury
#215 Fire Hammer
#216 Death Force
#217 Fight or Die
#218 End Game
#219 Terror Intent
#220 Tiger Stalk
#221 Blood and Fire
#222 Patriot Gambit
#223 Hour of Conflict
#224 Call to Arms
#225 Body Armor
#226 Red Horse
#227 Blood Circle
#228 Terminal Option
#229 Zero Tolerance
#230 Deep Attack
#231 Slaughter Squad
#232 Jackal Hunt
#233 Tough Justice
#234 Target Command
#235 Plague Wind
#236 Vengeance Rising
#237 Hellfire Trigger
#238 Crimson Tide
#239 Hostile Proximity
#240 Devil's Guard
#241 Evil Reborn
#242 Doomsday Conspiracy
#243 Assault Reflex
#244 Judas Kill
#245 Virtual Destruction
#246 Blood of the Earth
#247 Black Dawn Rising
#248 Rolling Death
#249 Shadow Target
#250 Warning Shot
#251 Kill Radius
#252 Death Line
#253 Risk Factor
#254 Chill Effect
#255 War Bird
#256 Point of Impact
#257 Precision Play
#258 Target Lock
#259 Nightfire
#260 Dayhunt
#261 Dawnkill
#262 Trigger Point
#263 Skysniper
#264 Iron Fist
#265 Freedom Force

DON PENDLETON'S
EXECUTIONER®
THE
FREEDOM FORCE

A GOLD EAGLE BOOK FROM
WORLDWIDE®

TORONTO • NEW YORK • LONDON
AMSTERDAM • PARIS • SYDNEY • HAMBURG
STOCKHOLM • ATHENS • TOKYO • MILAN
MADRID • WARSAW • BUDAPEST • AUCKLAND

First edition December 2000
ISBN 0-373-64265-2

Special thanks and acknowledgment to
Jerry VanCook for his contribution to this work.

FREEDOM FORCE

Revenge is the poor delight of little minds.

> —Juvenal
> *Satires* XIII.

What I do is not revenge. But there are gaps in the written law which sometimes allow the guilty to go unpunished. That's where I come in. It's not revenge, it is justice.

> —Mack Bolan

For
Bid and Peg

PROLOGUE

Vladimir Syvatoslav let the cool breeze tickle his face as he looked out over the Black Sea. In the corner of his eye, he could see the glimmering night lights of Odessa. But his primary vision was focused intently on the ship anchored just off shore. Behind him, a dozen men were wheeling two large crates toward the loading area along the docks. As the moon moved behind a cloud, he could see only their silhouettes, and they reminded him more of ants than of men.

Squinting, Syvatoslav made the men's images even more indistinct, and in his mind's eye allowed the shadows to take on the forms of ants rather than human beings. "Ants," he said quietly under his breath, and the thought brought a smile to his lips. "Little worker ants, serving their queen. Or in this case, their king."

A chuckle escaped Syvatoslav's lips but was carried off on the wind. Like his quiet words, it went unheard by any of the men. Ah, he thought silently, the parts working for the whole. Such thinking was what the Soviet Union, indeed the entire concept of Communism, had been built upon. And these human ants he saw working before him now were accustomed to such thinking—leftovers from the days when Communism had united Russia, Ukraine, Moldavia and all of the other countries that had been known as the Union of Soviet Socialist Republics. Many of the men along the shore tonight, like himself, had been KGB officers. Some had been GRU—Soviet Military Intelligence. A handful had come from the elite Soviet special forces units known as Spetsnaz. But regardless of their backgrounds, they all had at least three things in com-

mon. They were all good men. They had been out of work
when the Soviet Union fell. And they all now worked for
Syvatoslav's oldest and dearest friend, Leon Kishinev.

Syvatoslav watched the men wheel the two dollies up the
long plank to other men waiting on the ship. These were *his*
men, who waited to receive the crates. And they all bore similar backgrounds with Soviet military and intelligence units.
All except for the very few who were of Polynesian extract,
and they were along only as observers.

One of the shadows broke away and began walking toward
Syvatoslav. The former KGB man couldn't make out the
man's face but he had no doubts as to who it was—he would
have recognized the shadow's gait blindfolded. His smile widened.

Vladimir Syvatoslav and Leon Kishinev had been friends
for far more years than either man could remember. Syvatoslav valued that friendship, and he knew Kishinev did, as well.
They had saved each other's lives on several occasions during
the old KGB days, then worked together at a variety of tasks—
from espionage-for-hire to drug smuggling—after the USSR
had turned from Communism to capitalism. Syvatoslav trusted
none like he did Kishinev. And he knew the feelings were
returned.

Kishinev stopped at arm's length just as the moon drifted
out from behind the cloud. The soft rays caught his face, and
Syvatoslav saw Kishinev was also aging. "You're getting old,
Leon," he said with a chuckle.

"Ah, yes," Kishinev said. "But not you, Lasso?"

Syvatoslav's chuckle became a laugh at Kishinev's use of
his old nickname. Kishinev had given it to him while they
watched an old American western movie years ago. But the
symbolism went far deeper than that, and the name hadn't
come from any rodeo abilities on Syvatoslav's part. "Yes, I,
too, am aging," he said. "Who would have thought it for
either of us? Who would have suspected we wouldn't both
have been killed years ago?"

"I win bets with each new birthday," Kishinev said, nodding. He reached up, scratching the gray beard that covered

his face. Behind him, Syvatoslav saw that his friend's men had reached the ship. The men on board were taking possession of the crates. "But I think we are both growing too old for this sort of thing."

"How so?" Syvatoslav asked. "We're just standing here, and we both can still do that. It is easy enough."

"Yes, this time it is easy enough," Kishinev said. "But that's only because we're dealing with each other. Other people who I—and I'm sure you, too—are forced to deal with these days can't be trusted. Just last week I supplied a mideastern contact with a shipload of AK-47s at this very same spot. I was forced to bring three times the men, and post snipers at every possible location." He indicated the hills on both sides of where they stood. "And still, I didn't breath easily until both the money was in my pocket and they had sailed out of sight."

Syvatoslav nodded his understanding.

"I saw someone the other day," Kishinev said, his tone lighter. "Someone I hadn't thought of for many years."

"Who?"

"That time in London," Kishinev went on. "The Czech whore we tried to set up with the British Prime Minister. Do you remember her name?"

"Ivanna, I believe?"

Kishinev turned toward the ship. He nodded. "Yes. She is running a house now in Kiev."

"You are a dirty old man, Leon." Syvatoslav laughed.

Kishinev returned the chuckle. "Perhaps," he said. "But why shouldn't I be? After all, I was a dirty *young* man. In any case, she said to tell you hello."

"Please return the greeting when you see her next. And I am sure you will see her again."

"Yes, you may be sure of it," Kishinev said. "She didn't come by her nickname the Human Vacuum Cleaner by accident."

Both men laughed softly as another dark shadow approached them. Syvatoslav recognized one of Kishinev's former Spetsnaz soldiers. "We're finished," the man said simply.

Kishinev nodded. He turned to Syvatoslav. "Shall we return to your room and conclude our business?" he said. "Then, I have an excellent bottle of Stolichnaya that is begging to be consumed."

Syvatoslav nodded. He turned toward the black automobile parked on the road behind them. Kishinev followed. As always, he would ride back with his old friend while Kishinev's men followed in their own vehicles.

The men rode in silence until, halfway back to the small tourist court on the edge of Odessa where Syvatoslav was staying, Kishinev broke the silence with a laugh.

"Yes?" Syvatoslav said.

"I was thinking of the time in Moscow when you recorded Khrushchev with the two prostitutes, then anonymously sent him the film. Eight millimeter in those days—long before videotapes." He paused, then added. "I have never decided which I liked more about you, Lasso. Your professionalism when we were working, or your practical jokes when we weren't."

Syvatoslav smiled in the darkness. "Little Nikki had cut our budget," he said. "He deserved a practical joke and a good scare at the same time. And his wife was the only person he feared."

"I feared her myself," Kishinev said, and both men laughed again. "Her arms were bigger than my legs. In any case, I saw him the next day, and he didn't look like a man who had slept the night before."

Syvatoslav turned into the tourist court with the cars of Kishinev's men pulling in behind. They got out and started toward Syvatoslav's door, but the other men remained in their vehicles. Syvatoslav turned to his friend. "Invite them in for a drink," he said. "They did their job well and deserve it."

Kishinev frowned as Syvatoslav stuck the key in the door. "I have only the one bottle," he said.

"I have three more. Polish vodka. We will save the Russian for after they have left and it is just the two of us."

Kishinev turned and waved the men forward. Car doors

opened and then slammed shut as the eight men who had accompanied him responded.

As soon as he was inside the room, Syvatoslav walked to the cabinet and pulled out the three bottles of vodka. He didn't have enough glasses to go around but these men wouldn't care—they had passed bottles between them many times in the past, and in some ways it was a more fitting way of toasting their comradeship than the usual method. He began uncapping the vodka as the men found seats around the room. "Cheers!" he said as he held up one of the bottles and turned to them.

Syvatoslav let the bottles make a full round before moving to the bed and pulling a briefcase out from under it. He took it to the table, waving one of the men away and toward the bed. With his back to the wall, he worked the combination on the lock, then lifted the lid. "So, it's time for the money to exchange hands," he said.

The men stared at the lid of the briefcase anxiously.

Syvatoslav smiled, then looked down. Instead of the money they all expected, he saw a 9 mm Uzi submachine gun in the briefcase. A sound suppressor had been threaded onto the barrel. "What is this?" he asked, his face a mask of surprise. "I have forgotten the money!" He pulled the weapon from the briefcase, then dropped the lid in place. "But I did remember this. So, as the Americans say, this is a stickup."

There was a moment's pause as the men's faces went blank. Then Kishinev laughed out loud and soon the other men joined him. "I'm sorry to ruin your fun, old friend," he said. "But your reputation for practical jokes precedes you."

One of the bodyguards, a tall, stocky man sitting on the bed not three feet from Syvatoslav, nodded. "Colonel Kishinev has told us many stories about your pranks," he said. "But you did have us going for a moment there."

Syvatoslav smiled at the man.

Then he shot him in the face.

The former KGB colonel swept the Uzi around the room, quickly firing three-shot bursts into each target. As he neared the end of the massacre, the last two men had recovered from shock and were reaching for their own weapons. But not in time.

A few seconds after the first rounds took out the man who had spoken, only Leon Kishinev and Vladimir Syvatoslav were still breathing inside the room. Syvatoslav turned the Uzi to where his old friend sat in one of the chairs by the table. "I am sorry," he said.

Kishinev just nodded, as if he might have known all along this was always a possibility. "I suppose it is better to die at the hands of a friend than by those of a stranger," he said.

Syvatoslav pulled the trigger a final time, then returned the Uzi to the briefcase, snapped the lock into place and walked out of the room toward his car.

"Ants," the former KGB man said under his breath as he slid behind the wheel. "And one can't afford to let ants leave their trails. Their dens must be stepped upon when their work is complete."

1

The man wearing the long coat over his skintight black combat suit had come for one reason, and one reason only.

He intended to kill another man.

Mack Bolan, who for years had been known to the world as the Executioner, sat motionless behind the wheel of the nondescript late-model Pontiac. Through the window of the Cadillac parked along the curb on the other side of the grade school playground, he could see a head. The hair covering that head had been skillfully manicured and swept off the man's forehead to create a carefully planned windblown look. The eyes below the hair were hidden by three-hundred-dollar designer sunglasses. Beneath the man's head, the Executioner could see the white collar of an Oxford shirt buttoned at the neck. The tie that fell from the collar had cost more than most men's best suits. It drew a line down the open lapel of a gold silk sport coat, which had come at a price higher than the yearly income of the average American worker.

Bolan's eyes narrowed. Cecil Osburne dressed well. He could afford to—the Mafia paid him well. And while he wasn't actually in the Mafia, he was definitely a connected guy.

A divergent thought crossed the Executioner's mind as he waited. Yes, it was the Mafia who paid Cecil Osburne. The *old* Mafia; the *real* Mafia. Not any of the new breed of punks who had stolen the word and gave themselves appellations like the Dixie Mafia or the Black Trench Coat Mafia. Osburne contracted to men with actual Sicilian blood running through their veins. Men who had names like Guido and Giuseppe and Paulo and Mario and used titles like Don. Osburne wasn't

Sicilian, or even Italian. But the old Mafia today was a new breed, too. They no longer restricted acts such as Osburne performed to their own family. Today's Mafia did its best to disconnect themselves from overt street violence and hide behind the facade of legitimate business. But getting dirty was often part of that business, so they contracted to skilled masters of mayhem, from whatever race was available, to get such jobs done.

And Cecil Osburne had proven, many times over, that he could get the job done.

A sudden vibration against his side broke Bolan's thoughts. He jerked the pager from his belt and looked at it. Unlike many such pagers, in which a return phone number would have appeared on the screen, he saw only the digit three. He wasn't surprised. Only one phone ever used this pager, and he knew that number by heart. The code entered was simple: three meant low priority, no rush to return the call. Finish what you're doing first.

The Executioner turned his attention to the man in the other car.

Cecil Osburne had been a contract killer working for the Mob for years. Conventional law enforcement had known it but, like was so often the case, there had never been enough evidence to bring Osburne to justice. That had changed several weeks before, the day after the killer-for-hire had pumped two rounds of 12-gauge buckshot into a bank president who was late on his gambling debts. Osburne had killed the man on the sidewalk outside a New York City candy store. But he had made a mistake.

The sun had been reflecting off the store's window, and he hadn't seen the woman who had watched him commit murder as she sat at the soda counter eating an ice cream cone.

Marilyn Saucier Little had been horrified, she later told police. But not so horrified that she didn't want to get involved, like so many people. Marilyn's father had been a cop who had died in the line of duty—gunned down on the street by a man not much different than Osburne. But before he had died,

NYPD Officer John Saucier had taught his little girl to do the right thing.

Bolan shifted slightly in his seat. Marilyn Saucier Little was no longer a girl. Now married to an NYC cop, she was a middle-aged schoolteacher who had children of her own. She had come forward to the police without hesitation, picked Osburne out of a mug shot book, then identified him in a lineup. And none of the threatening phone calls she and her family had endured had dissuaded her from testifying at the grand jury, either.

Marilyn Saucier Little might not like it very much but she was going to do the right thing until the bitter end. Why? Because of an old-fashioned idea that seemed lost on many people in current American society. It was the right thing to do.

And the Executioner intended to help her do it.

Bolan glanced at his wristwatch, then at the school building. Osburne still hadn't moved inside the car. But he would. Soon. He was out of jail on bond, awaiting trial. A trial which, if it included Saucier Little's accurate eyewitness testimony, would either send him to prison for life or to the lethal injection table. Bond in a capital case such as this wasn't as rare as many people believed—especially with the Mob behind you and enough money to grease the greedy palms of the right judges and district attorneys.

The vibration buzzed against the Executioner's side and he lifted the pager again. The number two had been entered this time. Whatever it was, it was still not an emergency. But he needed to return the call as soon as possible.

Outside the car, a loud school bell sounded from within the building. A few seconds later, children ranging from roughly six years of age to twelve came pouring through the doors with the gleeful expressions of inmates escaping prison. In fact, Bolan realized as he saw the happy, laughing faces, they seemed to have only one thing in common. They were all delighted that school had ended for the day.

As children ran for parked cars and yellow buses or began walking home, Bolan reached under his coat and double-

checked the thumb snap securing the Beretta 93-R in his
shoulder rig. Satisfied, his hand moved to the big .44 Magnum
Desert Eagle on his right hip. It was securely in place, as well.
He checked the other weapons hidden beneath his coat as he
waited. Cecil Osburne still hadn't moved a muscle. He was
waiting until all the children had left the building. He had
learned his lesson about witnesses.

Which suited the Executioner, too. He had no desire to let
any of the grade school students see what was about to happen.

When the final trickle of children filing through the doors
had ended, Osburne got out of the Cadillac. Slamming the
door behind him, he strolled casually across the street toward
the entrance to the building on the other side of the playground
from Bolan. The soldier exited his own vehicle with the same
relaxed demeanor. He wanted to appear like a father on his
way to a parent-teacher conference. But he left his long coat
open as he adjusted the tails to make sure they hid his weapons
as he started toward the entrance nearest him.

The gray speckled tiles covering the grade school hall floor
looked like they had been there since Bolan was in grade
school. Marilyn Saucier Little's classroom was halfway down
the hall, and as he walked that way, he saw Osburne enter the
building at the other end.

Bolan walked forward, keeping his eyes on the trophy cases
and other school memorabilia that decorated the wall. In his
peripheral vision, he could see Osburne doing the same from
the other end of the school. Otherwise, the hallway was clear.
To anyone watching, there now appeared to be two fathers on
their way to find out why their children were failing math or
English. But the Executioner knew what was racing through
Osburne's mind, even as the two men continued to close on
each other like a pair of unaware old West gunfighters about
to meet on Main Street. Do I kill the big bastard coming at
me? Or wait until he's disappeared down another hall?

The Executioner guessed Osburne would pick the former.
There was always the chance the other father would remember
the gold silk sport coat and the man he'd seen in the hall.

Besides, Osburne didn't just kill people for the money he was paid.

He *liked* his work.

Bolan passed an open classroom door and saw Marilyn Saucier Little bent over her desk, a red pen in her hand as she graded papers. She didn't look up.

When he was twenty feet from the professional assassin, the pager buzzed against his side. He ignored it as he passed an intersecting hallway and caught a glimpse of a little girl, her arms full of books. At least she was headed away from them, walking toward another exit of the building. But if gunfire broke out...

Already Osburne had sensed something amiss and was frowning, his hand starting to move beneath the gold silk sport coat.

The Executioner's strategy changed in a microsecond. Ten feet away from the hitman, he slid the Applegate-Fairbairn combat knife from its Kydex sheath on his belt. In a blur of movement, he lunged forward and thrust the six-inch dagger blade into Osburne's heart, at the same time trapping the murderer's gun hand against his chest.

Eye to eye, Osburne stared at the Executioner—his Executioner—with the same confused expression Bolan had seen on the faces of countless other men in the past. Somehow, murderers always seemed to find it even more shocking than others when they were finally on the other end of a bullet or knife.

Bolan jerked the Applegate-Fairbairn from Osburne's chest. As Cecil Osburne hit the floor, Bolan turned toward the intersecting hallway. He was just in time to see the little girl push open the fire-safety bar on a door and leave the building, oblivious to what had taken place behind her.

Returning to the body on the ground, Bolan wiped the dagger on the gold silk sport coat, then sheathed it on his belt. Another quick glance up and down the hallway assured him there were no eyes watching as he turned and walked to Marilyn Saucier Little's classroom. He paused at the open door and knocked.

The woman's head shot up from the papers on her desk. She had never met Mack Bolan and had no idea who he might be. All she knew was that there was a big, tough-looking man standing just outside her room, and the sight brought terror to her face.

Bolan had no doubt that she had lived in such terror for many months. But that terror had ended. And he wanted her to know it. "Your problems are over, Marilyn," the Executioner said. "And there's no longer any need for you to testify. Osburne is dead."

Before she could answer, he had disappeared.

The pager on his side buzzed again as Bolan walked down the hall. It buzzed a third time as he exited the door and started toward the Pontiac. Pulling the pager off his belt and holding it up in the sun, he saw what he'd expected to see.

The last three calls had all come within thirty seconds.

And all three times, the caller had left the number one.

THEY WERE COMING in armed and dangerous and under normal circumstances would have never gotten through customs. But that was covered—the Learjet 55C had left Los Angeles and had been cleared for landing through the U.S. Department of Justice before it even took off. Officials in Hawaii believed two Justice Department special agents, about to go undercover, would be arriving in the Learjet.

They'd been given direct orders to do nothing that might draw attention toward either the craft or the two men. In fact, they'd been ordered to stay away from the plane altogether.

Two undercover Justice Department special agents, Mack Bolan thought as he opened his eyes. It wasn't the truth, or even a half-truth. The Executioner rubbed his eyes. He hadn't slept for two days as he searched for, found, then stalked the man who intended to murder Marilyn Saucier Little. So he had dozed from his base at Stony Man Farm on the eastern coast of the U.S., then again after the plane had refueled in L.A. As his brain cleared of fatigue, he realized that while the information the Justice Department had given Hawaiian authorities wasn't true or half-true, it was roughly three-quarters true. The Learjet was the property of the Justice Department, all right. And while neither he nor the man seated beside him in the jet were special agents, the Executioner certainly had a long history of working with that agency from an arm's length distance.

Bolan looked down as the plane descended through the sky, seeing the north side of the island of Oahu appear below in the distance. High waves—some at least twenty feet and others perhaps higher—rolled onto the sandy shore near the Koneohe Marine Base. Farther inland stood the high-rise office buildings of downtown Honolulu. Although he couldn't see them, Bolan knew that the downtown streets and sidewalks would be shoulder-to-shoulder crowded like New York, Los Angeles or Paris. The third largest body of land in the Hawaiian chain, Oahu was nevertheless home to three-fourths of the state's population.

Next to him, Jack Grimaldi sat behind the controls of the Learjet. The craft dipped a wing and changed course slightly, and the Executioner watched Diamond Head and Waikiki disappear beneath them. A moment later, the wheels of the 55C hit the tarmac and the Learjet rolled to a halt.

Bolan turned toward the pilot. He and Grimaldi were old friends and had worked together on missions out of Stony Man Farm for years. In fact, their history together went back to a time when the Farm hadn't yet even become an idea or dream. Before leaving for the islands, the pilot had hung his brown leather bomber jacket over the back of his seat and traded his Alaskan bush pilot's cap for a cooler model with an adjustable mesh back. The front read U.S. Department of Justice and displayed the seal of that agency. Again, it wasn't exactly accurate. But it was certainly appropriate for this stage of the mission.

"Jack, who's our contact with the local cops?" Bolan asked.

"Detective Sergeant Susan Ogatu," Grimaldi answered. As one of the pilot's hands worked the controls, the other reached down and pulled a manila file from his briefcase on the floor.

He flipped it open and produced a photograph. "Quite a looker, if you ask me," he said.

The Executioner nodded as he eyed the picture. It showed a woman who looked to be in her early thirties. Susan Ogatu had raven black hair and matching eyes. Her features were a mixture of Polynesian and Japanese—and she'd gotten only the best of both. In the picture, Ogatu wore a navy blue skirt and a white blouse open at the collar. "No argument there, Jack," Bolan agreed. "Not bad at all."

Grimaldi laughed. "Maybe you'll get lucky," he said. "It's about time you broke that celibacy string of yours."

"It's not by choice," he told his old friend. "Some of us have work to do, so we have to leave the romance to those of you who don't."

"Ouch," said Grimaldi. "Point and match to Striker," he said, using Bolan's code name.

"Which brings up how I contact you when I need you." Bolan looked up from the picture at his comrade in arms. The adage about a woman in every port pretty much applied to Grimaldi. All you had to do was add "air" to the "port."

"Lena Largo," Grimaldi said and recited a phone number the Executioner instantly memorized. "Met her a few weeks ago when I flew Able Team down this way. She lives about five minutes from here."

Bolan had turned in his seat to pull his bags from behind him. "Lena Largo," he said. "Please tell me that's not her real name."

"No, it's a stage name," the pilot said. "She's a dancer at one of the local clubs."

"Well. Why am I not surprised?" the Executioner said. "But are you sure about that?"

Grimaldi didn't pick up on the meaning of the question. "Sure I am," he said. "I've watched her dance."

"I'm sure you have. What I meant was, are you sure a dancer is *all* she is?"

Grimaldi nodded a new understanding. "Oh, okay, I see. Yeah, I checked her out with the Bear."

Bolan nodded. Aaron "the Bear" Kurtzman was the computer wizard of Stony Man Farm, the top-secret counterter-rorist instillation out of which he, Grimaldi, Able Team and Phoenix Force worked. If Kurtzman had cleared Lena Largo as nothing more than a dancer, then she was nothing more than a dancer.

Bolan pulled his bags in front of him. "What did you tell her *your* name was?" he asked the pilot. "If she answers the phone I'll need to know who to ask for." Again, for security reasons, he knew Grimaldi would have used an alias.

"Can't remember," Grimaldi said. "It was either Joe or Hank. I'm hoping to just say, 'Hi, Lena' and then she'll say 'Hi, Whoever" back, and jog my memory.

"Well, let me know when you find out. Until then, I'll just ask for the Flyboy." He turned toward the rear of the plane where Dr. Gregory Sielert, one of the top nuclear experts in the United States, sat waiting. "You ready, Greg?" he asked.

Sielert nodded. His face was slightly pale, and his hands clutched the armrests of his seat a little too hard.

"Then let's hit the bricks," Bolan said, and stepped out of the Learjet.

A car had been arranged for them and stood parked where they'd been told it would be. A nondescript late-model Pontiac Bonneville. The keys were hidden on top of the left rear wheel where Bolan had been promised they'd be. The key ring included a remote control, which worked both the doors and the trunk. The Executioner opened the doors and threw his bags on the back seat. On the other side of the car, Sielert did the same. Bolan slid behind the wheel, the other man took the passenger's seat, and a moment later they were leaving the airport and heading toward downtown Honolulu.

As he navigated the Bonneville through the heavy Oahu traffic, the Executioner glanced at the man seated next to him. Sielert had a ring of auburn-turning-gray hair circling his ears, but the top of his skull was bald. He wore a khaki bush vest—the kind worn in the city these days only by photographers or off-duty cops needing something to carry camera equipment or to hide weapons. Either way, it would draw the attention of wary criminals. Bolan made a mental note to get Sielert's looks changed before they hit the field.

"I understand you were in the Army before you went back to school," the Executioner said as he slowed, then stopped at a red light. He had met the scientist only a few hours earlier, and having just come in tired off the other mission, used the flight to catch some sleep rather than get acquainted.

Sielert nodded. "Only a couple of years, and that was a long time ago," he said. "But I've tried to stay fit. Jogging, golf, some Nautilus and free weights." He turned to face the man driving. "A good deal of Tae Kwon Do, and I'm a pretty darn good shot, too. Been to most of the good shooting schools." He ran off a list of the top half-dozen places around the country where civilian defensive shooting was taught.

"That's nice," Bolan said as he turned a corner. "But that's not why you're along." He watched the man's reaction out of the corner of his eye. He didn't want the division of labor getting confused. The last thing he needed was some half-trained wanna-be commando getting in his way when the action started.

Sielert seemed to take the comment without offense. "Oh, I know," he said quickly. "I'm the egghead of this dynamic duo. But I just wanted you to know you could count on me. Just in case..." He let the sentence trail off.

"It's good to know," Bolan said. He turned his full attention toward the line of cars in front of him. Greg Sielert seemed like a good man. He had a job to do in Hawaii that was as important as the Executioner's. But Bolan wanted him to do *that* job, and not get in the way.

A few minutes later, the Bonneville pulled into the main headquarters of the Honolulu P.D. Bolan and Sielert exited the vehicle, and the Executioner used the remote control to lock the doors, then checked each one to make sure it had worked. He trusted electronic and mechanical devices only so far— they had a way of quitting on you when you needed them the most, and he had learned never to rely one hundred percent on such equipment. In fact there was only one thing Mack Bolan relied on a hundred percent.

Himself.

Bolan led the way up a walk to the front door and inside, stopping in front of a glass window that looked very much like a ticket booth at a theater. But this glass was bulletproof. Pulling his Justice Department credentials out of his sports coat, he held them up in front of a black woman in an HPD uniform seated behind the glass. "Special Agent Mike Belasko to see Detective Sergeant Susan Ogatu," he said through the voice hole.

The woman nodded and smiled. "Ogatu is expecting you," she said. She lifted the phone, tapped a number into it and said, "Susan, Agent Belasko is here." Setting it down, she reached for a button mounted on her desk, then stopped, looking past Bolan at Sielert.

The Executioner anticipated her question. "He's with me," he said.

A moment later Bolan heard a buzz and the door next to him swung inward. He led Sielert through the opening and into a brightly lit hallway.

Almost as soon as their feet had left the carpet of the reception area and hit the yellowing tile beyond the door, Susan Ogatu came out of an adjoining hallway. The Executioner had no trouble recognizing the Honolulu detective from the picture Grimaldi had shown him. While it didn't look to be the exact same navy blue suit she'd worn in the photo, it was similar. The open collar of another white blouse could be seen above the lapel, and her almond-shaped black eyes were of almost exactly the same pigment as her shoulder-length hair. Susan Ogatu's high heels clicked to a halt on the tile as she held out her hand.

"Special Agent Belasko?" she said, smiling to show a row of perfect white teeth. "I'm Detective Sergeant Ogatu."

Bolan took her hand, finding the skin soft but the handshake firm. "This is Dr. Sielert," he said, turning to the man next to him.

"Call me Greg," Sielert said.

The beautiful young detective nodded. "Then I'll be Susan." Her eyes flickered toward Bolan. "Belasko?"

"We may be spending a lot of time together," the Executioner said. "Better make it Mike."

Ogatu's smile widened. She started to say something, then her eyes flickered, and the smile waned slightly. Whatever her first response had been, she had decided to edit it. Turning to address both men, she said, "Please follow me." She turned on her heels to click off down the hallway from which she'd appeared.

Bolan and Sielert followed the beautiful female detective through a labyrinth of hallways and into a small office. Pictures, certificates and awards covered the walls; a younger Susan Ogatu in full HPD dress uniform graduating from the academy. Ogatu in another navy blue suit and white blouse shaking hands with the current Hawaiian governor. Ogatu at the firing range wearing ear protectors and shooting glasses. Bolan's eyes skirted the wall that held the pictures and certificates and noted that the woman had received advanced training in homicide and rape investigation and counterterrorism, and been awarded plaques by several civic clubs for her work on high-profile cases.

The detective's desk was stacked high with files and other clutter. Rather than sit behind it, she rolled the chair around to face the small couch and armchair in front of it. Bolan took the chair. Sielert lowered himself onto one end of the couch. The Executioner broke the silence that had prevailed as they walked through the winding halls. "We understand you have an informant inside the Polynesian Freedom Fighters," he said.

Ogatu nodded, then glanced at the ceiling. "He's upstairs in a cell right now," she said. "But I'm warning you, he's low-level PFF. Arrested for a crime totally unrelated to the movement."

"What was it?" Bolan asked.

Ogatu chuckled. "Robbing a convenience store. He got roughly twenty-seven dollars. And with his record, it'll cost him close to that in years. So he's anxious to make a deal."

"Have you interrogated him yet?"

Ogatu shook her head. "I was about to when I got the call to hold off until you arrived."

"Now's a good time to get started."

Susan Ogatu lifted the telephone receiver from the cradle and punched a button. "Jack," she said. "Bring Buck down, will you?" She replaced the phone.

"Buck?" Bolan asked. Somehow the name didn't seem to fit his expectations of what an ethnic-minded terrorist would call himself.

"His name's James Kalakaua," Ogatu said. "But he goes by Buck."

Sielert snorted. "So much for Polynesian pride," he said.

"You're right about that," the detective said. "But like I said, he's low-level. More criminal than freedom fighter." The last two words were heavy with sarcasm when they came out of her mouth.

Bolan studied the woman in front of him as they waited for Kalakaua to arrive. Inside the soft, good-looking exterior that housed the soul of Susan Ogatu there was a toughness he could sense. And respect.

A few minutes later the door opened and two uniformed officers brought a handcuffed man into the room. James "Buck" Kalakaua was a big man. Most Samoans were. Somewhere in the back of his mind, the Executioner remembered hearing or reading that they had the largest average bone circumference of any race on the planet. He had never seen anything to make him doubt it.

Kalakaua sat down on the other end of the couch next to Sielert. He wore a light blue dress shirt with the sleeves ripped off to exhibit huge arms decorated with bad tattooing. His hair was long. It was also as dirty as his khaki work pants and as ragged as the canvas tennis shoes on his feet. He looked to be in his late thirties, and a frightened expression covered his face. The Executioner guessed he didn't want to be ready for Social Security next time his feet hit the pavement outside the penitentiary.

"You can take the cuffs off," Ogatu said.

One of the uniformed men frowned. "Susan, he's, uh…"

"What?" the detective asked.

"Well...big."

The woman smiled. "Go ahead."

The cop shook his head as he stuck the key into the hand-cuffs, then he and his partner exited the room.

As soon as they were gone, Bolan said, "Tell us about the PFF."

Kalakaua's eyes narrowed. "What's this going to get me?" he asked.

"For starters," Bolan said, "a trip back upstairs instead of to the hospital when I'm finished with you."

In the corner of his eye, he saw Ogatu cast a semisurprised look his way. He ignored it.

"After that," the Executioner went on, "we'll see what we can do about getting you a lighter sentence. No promises."

Kalakaua nodded. He knew the drill. Only the judge could make the final decision as to whether or not to cut the man any slack. But a recommendation from Susan Ogatu to the district attorney, which would then be passed on to the court, would go a long way.

Bolan took a second to gather his thoughts before he continued. Aaron Kurtzman had hacked into CIA intelligence reports and learned that the PFF was making a pickup by sea from Russian mobsters somewhere in the old Soviet Union. The spooks from Langley highly expected the contraband was nuclear bombs. The President had decided against sending overt military forces for fear that the Polynesian terrorists would detonate the bombs early if they learned they were being pursued.

The mission called for the most sensitive, low-profile investigation and a surgical strike by the best counterterrorist team available.

And Mack Bolan was the best America had.

"So," the Executioner said. "What do you know about the deal with the Russians? Is it nukes?"

The big man seated next to Sielert nodded. "I think so," he mumbled.

"You *think* so?" Bolan said, leaning forward at the waist

until his face was maybe a foot and a half from Kalakaua's.
"I don't want to hear what you *think*, Buck. I don't want your
assumptions or imagination. What do you *know*?"

The big Samoan leaned back slightly to get away from the
stern face. "Look, I'm not that big in the group," he said.
"They pay me to run errands. Stuff like that. But it's nukes.
At least that's what everybody says."

"Who's everybody?" Bolan demanded.

Kalakaua took a deep breath. "They're going to kill me for
this," he said in a weak voice. It seemed that the possibility
had just dawned on him. "My life will be worthless if they
find out I talked to you."

The Executioner drew back his coat and slid the mammoth
.44 Magnum Desert Eagle semiautomatic pistol out of the holster on his right hip. He saw both Sielert's and Ogatu's eyes
widen. Before either of them could protest, he shoved the gun
under the Samoan's chin and rose to his feet, towering over
the man. "Your life is worth nothing to me," he growled in
a low voice. "So, do you want to die now, or later?"

Kalakaua's whole body seemed to pale. The brownish-
yellow skin on his bare arms turned white, making the poorly
executed tattoos stand out more vividly. "Wait," he whispered hoarsely. "You, uh, you can't do this. You're a cop."

"No," Bolan said in the same menacing voice. "I'm not a
cop, Buck, and that may be the most important thing you ever
learn during your time on this planet. What I am is a man
who doesn't give a damn about the rights of a low-life criminal
when they're stacked next to the lives of millions of innocent
people. And I'm a man who doesn't have a lot of time for
dramatics. In short, I'm the man who's going to blow your
head right off your neck in about three seconds if you don't
start talking." He jammed the barrel of the Eagle harder into
the Samoan's neck. "Talk," he said. "Clearly and precisely
and *now*."

Kalakaua got the message. His voice quivered as he said,
"Benjamin Liholiho runs the show."

Susan Ogatu might have been shocked at the Executioner's
behavior at first but it didn't take her long to get into the swing

of things. "We know that," she snapped. "Tell us something we don't know."

"You know about Vladimir?"

The soldier dropped the Desert Eagle to arm's length at his side but didn't reholster. "Vladimir?" Bolan asked. Must be the Russian contact.

He wasn't surprised when Kalakaua said, "Vladimir is Liholiho's friend."

"Go on." The Executioner frowned. "What's Vladimir's last name?"

"I don't know," Kalakaua said. "I swear that's the truth. But I've heard Liholiho call him Lasso. It's some kind of nickname, I think."

"Lasse?" The Executioner asked. It was a common Scandinavian nickname for Lars and might well be used for any Russian with the same appellation.

Buck Kalakaua shook his head. "No, Lasso. You know, like the rope a cowboy uses?" He twirled his hand in the air over his head.

Bolan's eyebrows lowered. *Lasso.* Curious nickname for a Russian. He'd have to get the Farm busy trying to identify the man. "The nukes are coming by sea?" he asked Kalakaua.

The big Samoan nodded. "I've heard it's a Ukrainian ship."

"What else do you know?" Bolan demanded.

Kalakaua's eyes fell to the floor. "That it's either already in port or will be soon. And that it's carrying other cargo besides the nukes...as cover."

When Kalakaua said no more, Bolan said, "I didn't tell you to stop talking, did I?"

Kalakaua took a deep breath, then looked into the face above him. "Word is, and this is just something I heard, that both bombs are to be off-loaded here in Honolulu."

Bolan paused. That might well have already happened. Just in case, he asked, "Where are they going after they arrive?"

The big Samoan shook his head. "That I *don't* know," he said. "It's the truth. I swear."

Bolan believed him—he was surprised that the low-level PFF man had known as much as he had. But he had to wonder how much of it was true. Kalakaua wasn't going to win the Albert Einstein award for brains and might well have confused some of what he'd heard. Then again, disinformation could have been purposely leaked by the PFF's top dogs in case anyone like the Samoan talked out of school.

Looking from Sielert to Ogatu, the Executioner said, "Let's take a ride to Honolulu Harbor and look for Ukrainian flags."

But they weren't quick enough. Suddenly all hell broke loose.

The electronic alarm seemed to scream.

"What is it?" Sielert asked Susan Ogatu.

The woman had produced a 9 mm Glock 19 from somewhere under her jacket. "One of two things," she said, her eyes alert and all business. "Either the station is under attack or there's a jailbreak in progress."

Bolan looked quickly to Kalakaua. The man would be in their way. He turned back to Ogatu. "You have some cuffs?" he said.

She pulled a pair of handcuffs from under her jacket and handed them to him.

Bolan cuffed Kalakaua's hands behind his back, barely getting the steel ratchets around the Samoan's big wrists but finally locking them closed on the last notch. "Leg irons?"

Ogatu stepped over to a filing cabinet, opened a drawer and withdrew what looked like a giant set of handcuffs with a short chain connecting the two jaws.

"You don't have to do that," Kalakaua protested. "I won't go anyplace."

"I know," Bolan said, closing the leg irons around the man's ankles. "I'm going to make sure of it." Rising to his feet, he sent a right cross into the man's jaw.

Kalakaua stared in surprise for a second, then his eyelids closed. He fell on his side on the couch. Except for the fact that he wore handcuffs and leg irons, he looked like a man taking an afternoon nap.

The Desert Eagle again found its way to the Executioner's hand. He hurried to the only window in Ogatu's office, quickly looking up and down the street. There was no sign of assault from that direction—only a few curious eyes staring at the building as people went about their business. A small child, his left hand gripped securely by his mother, cried in frustration as he tried to cover both ears against the screech of the alarm.

Bolan turned from the window. Just because there was no attack on that side of the building didn't mean there weren't on the others. But his gut instinct told him the threat came from within rather than without. Had he been a betting man, he'd have put his money on a jailbreak. Sprinting to the door, he motioned Sielert and Ogatu to get out of the line of fire from the hallway. As soon as they were against the walls, he held the big .44 Magnum at a forty-five degree angle and jerked the knob with his left hand.

The hallway was clear. But the faint odor of smoke caught in his nostrils. Somewhere in the building there was a fire. His eyes shot to Ogatu. She had smelled it, too. The detective shook her head, answering his question before he asked it.

"Wrong alarm," she said. "The fire alarm sounds different."

The Executioner stepped into the hallway, then crept cautiously toward the smell of smoke. There were times in battle when you were forced to rush in blindly—to take the bull by the horns, so to speak. Other times, it was wiser to move more slowly, keep the matador's cape held in front of you like a shield and wait on the bull. This was one of those times.

Retracing the route they had taken from the reception area, Bolan led the way. A dozen or so cops came out of the offices, weapons drawn, and fell in behind them. Many pairs of curious eyes fell on the Executioner, wondering who he was. But the Honolulu P.D. was too large for everyone to know everyone else. They would figure he had to be some high-ranking officer to be carrying such an unauthorized weapon as the Desert Eagle.

But there was more to the fact that they automatically followed his lead. The Executioner's mere presence bespoke leadership.

When they neared the public waiting area where they'd entered, Bolan turned to the men and women behind him. "Spread out," he said. "Find out what's going on." He nodded to Sielert and Ogatu. "You two come with me." The rest of the officers split into pairs and branched off down the various hallways.

With the scientist and the detective close at his heels, Bolan turned the last corner to the door where they'd entered. To see into the office where the female officer receptionist sat, he would have to swing the door open and enter the waiting area. But before he could do that, he heard the ring of an elevator arriving on the ground floor a few feet down one of the connecting hallways.

The Executioner hurried that way, hearing the slap of Sielert's soft-soled shoes and Ogatu's heels clicking against the tile behind him. They arrived at the elevator just as the door rolled back.

Three men, all dressed in the plain white T-shirts and white painter's pants, stepped onto the tile. Jail trustees.

The man closest to Bolan held a butcher knife. A half-step behind him came a trustee wielding a Glock identical to Ogatu's. The third man was armed with a meat cleaver.

The Desert Eagle screamed twice, and the man holding the Glock took the rounds in the chest. The force threw him back into the elevator where he slammed to a sitting position against the far wall. He was dead before he hit the ground, but his eyes remained open in surprise. The white T-shirt and painter's pants became a solid black-red all the way to the crotch.

Compared to the roar of the Eagle, the 9 mms that exploded to his side sounded like pop guns. Bolan turned to see that Susan Ogatu had stopped the man with the butcher knife. But the third man, armed with the meat cleaver, raised it over his head and began to bring it down at the Executioner.

"Don't shoot him!" Bolan ordered the other two. He needed someone to tell him what was going on, and this was the only source of information left who could speak.

As the meat cleaver came down, the Executioner stepped

slightly to the side. He brought the Desert Eagle across his body, slamming it into the attacker's forearm. Then, checking the remaining momentum in the descending arm with his left hand, he brought the big hand cannon under the trustee's arm and over the man's wrist. The bottom of the Eagle's grip caught the hook in the back of the cleaver, and slid it out of the man's hand to clatter onto the tile.

Bolan moved in immediately, grabbing the trustee's throat with his free hand and jamming the business end of the Desert Eagle into his face. "What's happening?" he demanded. "You've got one second to tell me exactly what's going on."

The trustee tried to answer but all that came out were gasps for air. The Executioner relaxed his fingers enough for the man to speak. "Jailbreak," he sputtered.

Tightening his grip around the man's throat, Bolan said, "I can figure that part out for myself. How many men, how many guns?" He relaxed his fingers once more.

"Two dozen," the trustee said before being hit with a coughing spasm. When he could speak again, he added, "Four...maybe five guns."

By now, Ogatu had recovered the Glock from the floor. Bolan glanced at it again. It was a cop's gun. The trustees had overpowered one of the officers and taken his weapon. How, Bolan didn't know. At any department the size of the Honolulu P.D., there were lockers just outside the jail area where officers secured their guns before passing through the bars. All weapons should have been out of reach of the prisoners. Even the trustees.

But right now how the guns entered the prisoners' hands wasn't important. Getting them back, and the prisoners behind bars once more, was the name of the game.

The Executioner brought the Desert Eagle down on top of the trustee's head and heard a loud crack. "You have another set of cuffs?" he asked Ogatu.

The woman pulled a second pair of handcuffs from behind her back and knelt to roll the man onto his back.

Dr. Gregory Sielert smiled nervously. "Just like the old TV show," he said in a quivering little voice. "Cuff 'em, Dano."

The Executioner didn't respond. The smell of smoke was stronger near the elevator, and as Ogatu rose to her feet, he said, "We can't risk having this thing shut down on us. Where are the stairs?"

Ogatu kicked off her high heels then moved past him and began sprinting down the hall in her nylon-clad feet. Bolan and Sielert followed until they came to a door in the wall. Sielert swung it open, and Bolan raced through to see gray-stepped stairwells leading up and down. He looked down. "Basement?" he asked.

Ogatu nodded. "Storage and firing range. No outside exit. They'll be more interested in getting out of the building."

The Executioner nodded. The smoky smell was coming from above, and that's what they needed to check out first. The upper floors must be beginning to fill with it. He started upward.

Bolan had made the halfway landing between the floors and was about to climb the rest of the steps when he suddenly remembered Sielert. He stopped and turned quickly. With his Colt Gold Cup Trophy gripped in both hands, the nuclear expert was coming up the first flight of steps next to Ogatu, shuffling clumsily in a Weaver stance. He'd been to some of the shooting schools, all right—that was evident. But like most of their graduates, he hadn't put in the time and thousands upon thousands of rounds it took to become proficient in their complex shooting style. When the would-be escapees had come out of the elevator, Bolan had seen him vainly trying to focus his adrenaline-pumped eyes on the front sight. By the time he'd found it, the gunfight had been over.

"Greg, you should get out of here," the Executioner said. "This has nothing to do with you or the nukes, and we can't afford to get you killed."

A nervous grin spread slowly across Sielert's bloodless face. "Probably more dangerous to try to get out than to stay with you, from what I've seen so far."

Bolan nodded. He didn't know the layout of the building, and there was no time to confer with Ogatu about it. There could be, and probably *were*, other ways to reach the public

waiting area and exit from the jail. For all he knew, prisoners
were fleeing out of the building even now, and sending Sielert
off to meet them could be like signing the man's death
warrant.

The Executioner was about to start up the stairs again when
the sound of running footsteps echoed from the hallway above
them. Raising the Desert Eagle, he paused, then suddenly drew
his Beretta 93-R from beneath his jacket. The Beretta held
fifteen 9 mm Glaser safety rounds. Each bullet was hollow
and filled with tiny shot that exploded through the body soon
after entering. It wasn't nearly as likely as a big Magnum to
pass through the men heading toward them, then ricochet
around the concrete stairwell to strike them or some other
innocent person.

But there were other reasons the Executioner had switched
to the Beretta. It was capable of three-round bursts as well as
semiautomatic fire, and it was equipped with a sound suppressor. Most of the time, Bolan used the suppressor for
stealth. But today he'd be relying on it to save his, Ogatu's
and Sielert's eardrums in the narrow confines.

The running feet were almost upon them when the Executioner whispered, "What kind of ammo are you carrying?"

Ogatu frowned, her face reflecting that she didn't understand the purpose of the question. "Semijacketed hollow
points," she whispered.

Bolan winced. The round she had just mentioned was no-
torious for overpenetration. "Hold your fire," he said. "I'll
take care of it."

An understanding of the question suddenly appeared on the
detective's face. She reached behind her and jerked out another magazine for her Glock. "Mind if I join you?" she
smiled, holding the magazine up to show the Executioner the
first round.

Bolan smiled at the same 9 mm Glasers as in his weapon.

"Back me up," he said, as the woman dropped the magazine from her weapon, jacked the slide to eject the round in
the chamber, then slammed the safety slugs into the Glock's
grip. "Don't shoot unless you have to. You still don't have a

sound suppressor, and I'd like to be able to hear when this is over.''

Ogatu nodded as she worked the slide again to chamber the first round. Her timing couldn't have been better. Just as the Glock's slide snapped closed, a flurry of white appeared at the top of the stairs.

Four men, all clad in white, froze in shock. Two had Glocks, one had a kitchen knife and the fourth wielded what looked like the steel arm of an office chair.

With the Beretta set on burst mode, the Executioner pumped a trio of Glasers into the lead man at the top of the steps. Another of the Honolulu P.D. Glocks tumbled down the steps to the landing. The man followed. Swinging the muzzle toward the other gunman, the Executioner stitched three rounds across his chest. The trustee with the chair arm screamed and dived down the steps, his weapon over his head and ready to strike. The Executioner caught him in the face with all three 9 mms of the next burst, and it was an almost headless man who hit the landing at his feet.

The last man's knife came bouncing down the steps, almost striking Sielert in the knee. The lone trustee at the top of the steps had raised his hands high over his head. ''Don't shoot!'' he pleaded. ''I give up!''

Bolan's eyes scanned the part of the hallway he could see. He listened intently for a moment, glad that Ogatu hadn't been forced to fire. If she had, none of them would be hearing well for several hours.

Other than the trustee with his hands in the air, the hall appeared clear. But the smell of smoke was thicker in his nostrils as he finally climbed the second set of steps. Grabbing the man at the top of the steps, he threw him down to the landing where Ogatu and Sielert stood. The man fell on his side with a moan. ''You can't...do that.'' he said. ''I've got rights.''

''Correct,'' the Executioner said as he came down the stairs. ''You've got the right to live or the right to die.'' He shoved the Beretta's sound suppressor into the man's face. ''You decide which you want it to be.''

The expression on the trustee's face told the Executioner he wasn't quite ready to meet his Maker yet.

"Very clearly, and very quickly," Bolan said, "you're going to tell me what's going on. I'm especially interested in why a bunch of trustees are trying to escape. If you were doing a long stretch, you wouldn't be trustees in the first place. It doesn't make sense."

The man was still trying to catch his breath. "One of the guys—the trustees—Mackin's his name—is Big Farley's bitch," he said.

"And we're supposed to know who Big Farley is?" the Executioner asked.

"Farley's a wharf rat waiting on trial," Ogatu said. "He works the docks, loading and unloading. About a twenty-five-time loser for rape, robbery, burglary, you name it. But this time it's a multiple homicide. Killed four on a drug deal."

"And Farley forced Mackin to get this thing rolling?"

The man on the ground said, "Well, I wouldn't exactly say forced. Convinced would be more like it." The man opened his mouth in a leering smirk. Bolan fought an urge to bring the Beretta across his face and obliterate it. Instead, he said, "Go on."

"Mackin got hold of a tire tool when he took out the trash this morning. On the way back in, he sprang the locks on the gun lockers. There was about a half dozen cops inside lockup and he forced them and the jailers into a cell, took the keys and got Farley out."

"That still doesn't explain why you short-timer trustees went along with it."

The man's face turned white. "You don't know Farley," he said. "He'd a killed us all."

"He gave you weapons," the Executioner said. "You could have killed him."

"You don't know Farley," the man said again, trembling.

Bolan rose to his feet. It wasn't as wild a story as it seemed. Prisoners had a pecking order far stronger than that outside. The trustees would be in for minor crimes. They weren't born killers like many of the men who were awaiting trial before being transferred to a state penitentiary. A man like Big Farley might well scare them from the top of their heads down to the bottom of their county-issue canvas sneakers and force them to do anything he wanted.

"How many prisoners are out?" the Executioner asked.

"Maybe twenty, twenty-five altogether…that's including the trustees. But they were gonna open more cells."

"What's the smoke coming from?"

"Hell, nothin' really. Some of the men set their mattresses on fire. It won't spread."

Bolan nodded. That was one less worry, at least. And if the men who had set the fires perished in them, then they had perpetrated their own deaths. He turned to Sielert and Ogatu. "You two stay here and guard this guy."

"No way," Susan Ogatu said. "You seem to be forgetting this is my house. I'm going with you."

Bolan paused, then said, "Okay. Come on then." He turned toward the steps.

"Where you going?" Sielert asked.

"To find Farley," the Executioner answered.

BY THE TIME Bolan and Ogatu arrived at the jail office on the top floor of the building, the situation was under control. Police officers, deputy sheriffs and every other type of law enforcement officer available in the Honolulu area had converged on the jail to put out the mattress fires and return the prisoners to their cells. It seemed that Bolan, Ogatu and Sielert had met the advance guard and were the only ones to have encountered escaping inmates. The other officers had taken different routes to the jail and met no resistance along the way.

Only one of the trustees—an elderly man called Pops—had made it out of the building. He was the chief jail cook and had called in a few minutes earlier to tell them that someone needed to stir the stew he was making for dinner every few minutes so it didn't scald. He had also informed them he'd be back just as soon as they promised him that crazy son of a bitch Farley was back behind bars.

Mackin, the trustee who had helped Big Farley, was no

longer a trustee but confined in one of the maximum security cells. The jailer who had been forced into the cell with the officers had been in a vengeful mood after his humiliation. He had placed Big Farley in a cell directly across from Mackin where the two lovebirds could look but not touch.

Bolan holstered the Beretta under his left arm as soon as he read the situation. He had fallen into the jailbreak and was glad it was over. He had far more important matters to which he needed to attend.

Ogatu followed the Executioner down the steps to where Sielert still had the trustee covered with his Gold Cup. Bolan was about to start toward the top floor to return the man when three officers entered the stairwell.

"Take this clown upstairs for us, will you?" Ogatu said, flashing her badge. "They'll know what to do with him."

The three men nodded. They looked a little disappointed to have arrived too late to get in on the action.

Bolan led the way down the steps and out of the building toward the Bonneville. He glanced at Sielert out of the corner of his eye as he walked. The nuclear physicist had a face as long as the Executioner's arm. Sielert was a good man. But he wasn't a warrior—a fact that distressed him greatly. Bolan could see it in his face. Dr. Gregory Sielert was highly disappointed in how he had reacted when the fighting started.

Thirty feet from the Bonneville, the Executioner sighed silently as he thumbed the button on the remote control to unlock the doors. It took all kinds of men and women to make up a planet. Not everyone was the same. But the worst part of that was that some people—even top experts in their fields like Sielert—wanted to be something they weren't.

"Susan," Bolan said. "I'll need you in the front where you can give directions." He slid behind the wheel. Ogatu got into the passenger's side of the car. That left the back seat for Sielert, and he opened the door with the resignation of a man who viewed his new seating arrangement as some kind of demotion.

Pulling away from the parking lot, Bolan began following

Susan Ogatu's directions toward the harbor. They were the only words spoken until Sielert finally said, "Hey, I'm sorry."

"For what?" Bolan said as he turned a corner.

"I didn't do very well back there."

The Executioner paused for a few seconds. He had hoped to speak to Sielert privately so as not to embarrass him in front of Ogatu. But the man had forced the issue, and now he had no choice. Besides, even though he had only known Susan Ogatu a little over an hour, he could tell she was smart. And he suspected she was the kind of officer who would understand what he was about to say.

"Greg," Bolan said. "Give Susan and I some kind of physics problem. Not too hard but not too easy, either. Something you could work in your head but that would take a little thought."

"What?" Sielert asked. "I don't underst—"

"Just do it, Greg," Bolan interrupted. Ogatu pointed to her left, and the Executioner turned the wheel that way.

Sielert rattled off a string of numbers and letters and words that made no sense at all to the Executioner. When he was finished, Bolan looked at the woman sitting next to him and smiled. "You get all that?" he asked.

Ogatu laughed. "Sorry," she said. "I got distracted discovering a cure for cancer."

"Do you get my point, Greg?" he said over his shoulder.

"Not really." The depressed voice came from the back seat.

"Neither Susan nor I have the vaguest idea as to what you just said. The point is, different people have different talents, abilities and fields of expertise."

A short silence came from the back seat. Then Sielert said, "Yeah, but all I do is work problems like that. You guys save lives."

Bolan pulled up to a red light and stopped. Turning in his seat, he said, "Greg, when we find the nukes, you just do what you do best and you'll be saving more lives than the two of us put together."

It took a moment to sink in but then Sielert nodded. "Okay," he said weakly.

As they neared the harbor, Bolan spotted a convenience store with a telephone booth outside. "I need to make a call," he said, pulling into the store.

"Here," Ogatu said, producing a cellular phone. "Just use this."

"It's long distance."

"The department is paying for it."

"And it needs to be secure." Bolan opened the door and got out. "Be right back," he said as he slammed the door behind him.

The Executioner walked to the phone booth. If he had wanted to speak in front of Ogatu and Sielert, he had his own cellular phone. But he had barely met the Honolulu detective, and while he sensed she could be trusted, it was too early to take chances. A moment later he had dialed the number to Stony Man Farm. He waited while the call was routed to six different dead zones in different spots around the globe before Barbara Price's voice said, "Striker?" on the other end.

The Executioner looked at his wristwatch. "You're working late," he said.

The mission controller laughed. "So what else is new?"

"Must be all that overtime pay."

Price laughed harder. "Oh, right," she said. "What was that old song? Nothing times nothing means nothing?"

"Something like that," Bolan said. "Barb, double-check the scrambler, then connect me to Hal, will you?"

"Sure thing. Just a second."

There were a few seconds in which the Executioner could hear only clicks over the phone. Then Price came back on. "All secure," she said. "Hold for Hal...wait, he just walked in."

In his mind's eye, Bolan watched Stony Man Farm's good-looking blond mission controller hand the receiver to Hal Brognola, the head of sensitive operations. "Hello, Striker."

"We've talked to the snitch HPD had," the Executioner said without preamble.

"And?"

"He doesn't know as much as I'd hoped he would. Ask

Kurtzman to see if he can ID a Russian named Vladimir something. He's Liholiho's second in command. Wait a minute.''
Bolan paused to think, then continued. ''Tell the Bear to open
his search to any former Soviet military or intelligence officer
regardless of nationality. Some people call them all Russians.''

"Will do, Striker. What else?''

"The man's nickname is Lasso.''

"Lasse?'' Brognola said.

"No, I made the same mistake. Lasso, as in lariat.''

"Okay. Got it. Anything else?''

"Just that the bombs are supposed to be arriving on a
Ukrainian ship. It's carrying other cargo as a cover. And that
the nukes are supposed to be off-loaded here.'' He paused to
take a breath, then answered the question he knew Brognola
would ask—the same question he had asked Kalakaua. ''I
don't know whether they've already picked them up or not.
Hope not. Our man didn't know where they were going from
here.''

Bolan could almost see Brognola, cigar stump threatening
to be bitten in two between his teeth, nod. ''There's always
an argument for the possibility they could dock, off-load some
of the other cargo as part of their cover, then shift the nukes
to another ship once they were back out at sea,'' the Justice
man said. ''But I think they'd have off-loaded before entering
the harbor if that was their plan. Before hitting customs.''

Bolan agreed, then said, ''Yeah. On the other hand, they're
under closer watch on the way into American waters than on
the way out. Coast Guard boats would have swooped in on
them like sharks if they'd met up with any local boats or
pulled into shore anywhere else. My guess is they hid them
well on board and plan to take them out right here under our
noses.''

"Okay,'' Brognola said. ''So there's a good chance the
nukes are still on board. That is, if the Ukrainian ship hasn't
already come and gone.''

"We'll just have to hope it hasn't.'' Bolan took another
breath and glanced out through the clear plastic of the phone

booth. "I'm on my way to find out. But now it's your turn, Hal. Anyone received any demands yet from the PFF?"

Bolan heard a chewing sound on the other end of the line and knew Brognola's cigar stump was working overtime. "Not so far," the big man said.

"That's another good argument for the nukes still being on board," he said. "The PFF will want to wait until they've taken possession and are all set up before playing their hand."

"That'd be my guess too, Striker. All of the likely candidates to receive the call—State Department, Treasury, the White House—they're ready to trace the call or try to triangulate it if it comes from a cellular unit."

"Good," the Executioner said. "But there are other means of communication these days. It seems unlikely but they might always use e-mail, some of the Internet chat rooms or something like that. You might suggest to Kurtzman to have Tokaido or one of his other computer whizzes start scanning the screen."

"He's already on it, Striker," Brognola said. "Anything else we can help you with?"

Bolan thought a second, then said, "Not right now. I'll keep in touch."

2

Dusk was falling by the time the Bonneville neared Honolulu harbor. The tropical sun was setting over the soft lapping waves with more color and beauty than even the talented James A. Michener could depict. Although the harbor was known more as a place of commerce than exoticism, no part of Hawaii was completely devoid of romance. Young couples first discovering love and longtime partners finding it anew walked arm-in-arm along the quay as men loaded and unloaded the heavily laden cargo ships.

The Executioner knew they would need a good cover if they were to approach the harbor without drawing attention. He glanced at Susan Ogatu as they got out of the car. The woman looked back and nodded. She knew it, too.

Bolan let his eyes lock with hers for a moment. Although they had been together only a few hours, they were already picking up on each other's thoughts. The Executioner smiled inwardly. That often happened with fellow warriors. But it rarely happened this fast. It seemed almost as if he and Ogatu were locked into the same mental mission control. Which was good. Very good. In the course of the next few hours or days, such communication might very well make the difference between life and death for either or both of them.

Exiting the Bonneville, Bolan used the electronic remote on the key ring to spring the trunk open. From one of his bags, he pulled two colorful and wildly flowered Hawaiian shirts. He tossed one of the shirts through the air to Sielert. Hesitating, he looked at the equipment bag he'd transferred from the plane to the Bonneville. Then, unzipping it, he produced a small backpack and transferred several items, including a cellular phone, to the smaller bag.

Ogatu frowned slightly at the cellular phone, remembering that the Executioner had refused the use of hers and stopped at a phone booth. But the frown didn't last long. The woman was a professional. And she knew there were things about him she didn't know, didn't need to know and wasn't ever going to know.

Bolan and Sielert used the car as cover for their weapons as the Executioner slipped out of his sports coat and Sielert finally lost the telltale safari vest. Both men donned the aloha shirts, leaving them open with the tails untucked to cover the guns.

Sielert looked at the tail of his shirt and a curious expression covered his face. He lifted the edge of his shirt closer to his eyes and smiled as he saw the lead fishing weight safety pinned inside the seam. "Cool," the scientist said. "And it makes sense."

The Executioner nodded. He had added the lead weights to both shirts to make the tails heavier and easier to swing back over a gun on the hip if a fast draw became necessary.

Sielert took a quick look around to make sure no one could see him, then indexed both hands on his chest, wiped the shirt tail away from his Colt Gold Cup and grasped the butt of the .45 pistol. He nodded, let the shirt fall over the gun and turned to Bolan. "Just a trio of tourists checking out the dock scene, huh?"

"You got it," Bolan said. He slid the backpack over his shirt, then held out his arm, Ogatu slipped hers through it, and they started down a set of concrete steps toward the water. "Greg," the Executioner said. "Walk next to me. You're my buddy who's along with us tonight. Maybe you live here and we've come to visit. You're showing us around."

Dr. Gregory Sielert might not have been the world's best gunman but he wasn't stupid, either—he understood the need for a low-profile approach. Pulling a bandanna from his pocket, he wiped the sweat off the top of his head. "Bald guys never get love." He grinned. "Always the fifth wheel."

Susan Ogatu giggled like a school girl—completely out of character. Bolan realized she'd changed characters to conform to her undercover role. ''Third wheel in this case,'' she said.

They strolled along the quayside chatting, Sielert occasionally pointing out items of interest and, all in all, doing a pretty good job of looking like the native or longtime resident of Hawaii showing his visiting friends around. Bolan took on a new respect for the man. Dr. Greg Sielert would do in role camouflage, he decided.

They passed several dockside cranes not in use, then a grain terminal and a series of storage silos. Turning a corner, they saw a floating crane gliding up to a ship. But the ship flew the Union Jack of Great Britain.

The trio walked on, with Susan Ogatu occasionally patting Bolan's arm with her other hand. Every so often, she looked into his eyes with a glazed look of infatuation. The Executioner knew it was part of the act, necessary in case any suspicious eyes from the PFF fell on them. But to say it had no effect on him would have been a lie.

Honolulu Police Department Detective Sergeant Susan Ogatu had already proven she could be a tough, no-nonsense cop. Now she was proving there was a woman inside that beautiful face and body. Bolan wondered how much of it was an act and how much might be real.

Bolan, Ogatu and Sielert reached a long row of docked ships flying flags from all nations. Men on board were busy with crates, sacks and every other imaginable system of packaging products for import and export. As the sun fell lower on the water, the lighthouse light flashed on and a small ferryboat tooted its horn.

They came upon the only Ukrainian ship in harbor near the end of the long row of vessels. A large container ship, Bolan saw the name *Nakinka Melaniya* painted in huge letters on the bow. Men moved busily on deck. A steel bench stood just a few feet off the quayside on a stretch of grass—big enough for two weary lovers and their friendly guide. He led Ogatu and Sielert that way.

Bolan and Ogatu sat at one end of the bench. The nuclear

expert dropped to a seat next to the Executioner. "Don't look directly at it," Bolan said to both of them. "A glance once in a while is fine. But look at the other ships, too. We're just mainlanders eyeballing the tourist attractions."

Sielert nodded.

Ogatu squeezed his arm, then leaned in and rested her head on his shoulder. "I'm not exactly a rookie, you know," she said, laughing softly.

Bolan forced his attention away from the woman against his side. He had recon work to do, and if he allowed himself to be distracted and make mistakes they could all be dead in a few hours. Staring across the water between the ships, he watched as one of the fixed cranes began lifting the huge containers from the ship and setting them on the dock. Men clad in khaki work shirts and blue jeans went to work breaking open the hard plastic containers to expose the wooden crates inside. Other crews waited to transfer the crates to nearby trucks.

Bolan turned his attention to the Ukrainian ship's compass bridge. Through one of the glass windows, he could see a man with binoculars. He appeared to be looking directly at the bench where they sat.

Before he could mention it, Ogatu said, "You see him?"

Bolan nodded. "He might have spotted us. Then again, maybe not." As the words came out of his mouth, the man redirected the binoculars.

"Better make it look good," Ogatu said. "No sense taking chances." Shifting her body slightly, she brought her head to the Executioner's and pressed her lips against his.

Bolan felt a short electric shock race through him. It came from both the suddenness of her action and the female electricity he had sensed emanating from her since they'd first met. But the kiss didn't last long. She pulled away and grinned. "Might as well make work fun when you can," she whispered, too low for Sielert to hear.

But Sielert had *seen*. "Damn," he said. "How come the guys with the hair get the best assignments?" He chuckled.

The Executioner shifted his attention to the ship. Several of

the men who had worked on deck had completed their jobs
and were walking down the plank for shore leave. They whistled and joked, showing the excitement of men who have been
shut up for days at sea and are about to hit land.

Bolan took Ogatu's hand and stood, helping her to her feet.
"We'd better get moving," he said. "We've had our rest."

"So what's the next step?" Ogatu asked. She was leaning
closer to him as they walked on.

"We've located the ship," Bolan said. "No point in hanging around. Now we go someplace and work out a plan for
getting on board after dark." He glanced out at the sea, which
was quickly turning from blue to black. "That won't be long
now."

"And what if they already unloaded the bombs?" the
woman asked. "Or do it now, before we get on board?"

"Then we do what we have to," he said. "You have to
play the cards you're dealt, Susan. You know that."

Susan Ogatu nodded against his shoulder.

The Executioner walked on, very aware of the woman beside him and hoping this was as far as she'd try to take it.

At least until after the mission was over, until America's
fiftieth state wasn't half a second away from being a mushroom cloud.

EVEN THOUGH it was called a drugstore it was really a general
store, selling everything from prescription medication to sou-
venir T-shirts. Two blocks inland from the docks, it also sold
alcohol.

Bolan paid the woman behind the counter for the half pint
of Beefeater gin, twisted the sack around the neck of the small
bottle and exited the store. Ogatu and Sielert stood waiting on
the sidewalk, and he led them quietly into a nearby alley.
Breaking the cap on the bottle, the Executioner poured a handful of the gin into his palm, then applied it to his neck like
aftershave before rinsing his mouth out and handing the sack
to Ogatu.

"Damn waste of good gin, if you ask me," Sielert said,
grinning.

When the bottle had made the rounds, Bolan took it and stuffed the bottle into his pockets. "I see only one major problem," he said.

Sielert nodded. "She doesn't look much like a dockworker, and I'm damned if I can figure out any way to make her look like one."

Bolan turned his eyes to Susan Ogatu. What Sielert had said was the truth. They couldn't hide that femininity simply by dressing her in khakis or denim.

"Let's concentrate on getting ourselves outfitted," the Executioner said. "We'll figure something out."

Walking toward the docks, Bolan spotted a pair of men coming up from the *Nakinka Melaniya*. Both were about Sielert's size. An idea hit him, and he walked up to the men. "Heading ashore, guys?" he asked.

The two men nodded. "What's it to you, pimp?" one of them asked in a gravelly tone. Although he looked to be close to fifty years old, he wore a sparse beard that didn't appear to have ever quite made it through puberty.

The Executioner smiled. "You read me well," he said. He hooked a thumb toward Susan Ogatu. "Want to get started right? Fifty bucks apiece."

The ruse had come on him suddenly, and he hadn't had time to discuss the details with Ogatu. But the seasoned detective took to her impromptu undercover assignment without missing a beat. Stepping up to the man with the beard, she looked into his eyes as she tugged lightly on his belt. "I also accept tips," she purred softly. "And I can make you *want* to tip me."

The man looked at her and licked his lips, ignoring the fact that she was dressed more like a businesswoman than a prostitute, once again confirming the old adage that an erect penis has a brain of its own. "Yeah," he mumbled almost incoherently. "Okay…where?"

Ogatu took his hand and led him toward the alley where they'd washed their mouths out with gin. "They'll wait out here," she said in the same purring voice, indicating Bolan and Sielert with a nod. "Don't worry, honey, we'll have all the privacy we want.'' She smiled at the other man. ''And then it'll be your turn.''

The other man, younger and clean shaven, looked as if he was choking on the incoherent words that never made it out of his mouth.

Bolan, Sielert and the younger sailor stopped at the end of the alley as Ogatu led the older man into the darkness by the hand. A few seconds later, a dull thump drifted out of the shadows.

The Executioner took the initiative immediately, grabbing the younger man waiting with him by the collar. ''Did you hear that?'' he demanded. ''If your friend is kinky, you're both going to pay. If she's hurt...'' He let the sentence drift off.

''Hey, no!'' the younger man said. ''He wouldn't hurt her!''

Bolan dropped the man's collar as a pair of tourists walked by. To them, it looked like any other argument between a dockworker and a local.

''We'll just go see,'' the Executioner said, and pointed toward the alley.

''She's okay, I know it,'' the younger man said in a frightened voice as he led the way into the shadows.

A moment later, the Desert Eagle came down on the back of his head.

Bolan lifted the unconscious body and carried it on down the alley to where Susan Ogatu's silhouette stood holding a collapsible ASP baton. The older man lay on the ground, as unconscious as his companion in the Executioner's arms.

As they neared, Ogatu knelt and struck the end of the ASP against the asphalt alley. It snaked back into the handle. Producing two more sets of handcuffs from her purse, she handed one to Bolan.

''Jiminy Christmas,'' Sielert said. ''How many handcuffs do you carry?''

She laughed softly. ''As many as I can,'' she said.

The Executioner pointed to the men on the ground. ''Take your pick of clothes, '' he told Sielert. ''The store is open.''

Sielert pulled the pants and shirt off the younger man and began changing. A few seconds later, he looked like one of

the men who had unloaded the *Nakinka Melaniya.* The real
sailors were cuffed behind their backs and stuffed into a large
white trash container. Tearing strips from the older man's
shirt, Bolan finished the task by tightly gagging both men.

In the dim light in the alleyway, Bolan saw the concern on
Sielert's face. "They'll be awake in a few hours," the Executioner whispered. "They'll both have headaches but they'll
make enough noise someone will find them."

Sielert shook his head. "That wasn't what was bothering
me," he said. "Can your handcuffs be traced?" he asked
Ogatu.

"No, these are *mine,*" she said. "Not departmental issue."
She paused, then grinned at the Executioner. "Just like the
Glocks I'm carrying tonight. They're the same make and mod-
els as the ones I usually carry but I took them off a couple of
bad guys over the years. There's no record of them.
Anywhere."

Bolan returned the smile. The woman was sharp. If she had
to shoot someone, there would be no way of matching the
rifling on the bullets to her issue weapons. "Okay," he said.
"One down, two to go." He glanced at the iridescent hands
of his wristwatch. "And we'd better get moving. Look for a
big guy and a little guy. With any luck, together."

They moved out of the alley.

WITH SIELERT dressed as, and playing the part of, a sailor just
off the Ukrainian ship, reeling in two more men was child's
play. But as usually happened at least once during one of the
Executioner's missions, his old friend Murphy showed his
ugly head, and with that head came Murphy's Law.

Wearing another splash of gin and a goofy, satisfied smile,
Dr. Gregory Sielert took off by himself toward the *Nakinka
Melaniya.* Bolan and Ogatu waited just beyond the harbor.
During that time, they had to turn down two drunken men
from another ship who were the wrong size. And one real
prostitute who liked the looks of both of them.

"Ever think we could make more money doing this for

real?'' Ogatu whispered to the Executioner as the disappointed prostitute walked away.

"You don't strike me as the type," he said. He liked Susan Ogatu. She was not only beautiful, she was tough, smart and had a wicked sense of humor. All of that put together produced a very attractive package, and he reminded himself not to let any of it get in the way of the mission.

The soft evening wind blew up from the harbor, bringing with it the pleasant smell of the salt sea. A few moments after the prostitute left, the Executioner saw Sielert lead a pair of sailors up the walkway from the harbor. One was stocky—almost as big as the Executioner. The other was a short man, although not as short as Susan, and most definitely broader than the petite detective. Again, Bolan glanced at his watch. The two men weren't perfect by any means. But they would have to do. He had no idea how long the Ukrainian ship would stay in port and had no time to search out a tailor-made fit.

"There!" Sielert said, pointing toward Bolan and Ogatu. "There they are!" He staggered a few steps as if about to fall over from drunkenness, then dropped onto another of the steel benches scattered throughout the area. "Boys, I promise you'll get your money's worth."

The bigger man looked at him suspiciously. "You coming with us?" he asked in an eastern European accent.

"Why?" Sielert giggled drunkenly. "You need my help?"

The big man's face reddened. "No, I don't need damn help," he sputtered in broken English. "But a friend of mine got shanghaied here last year. Stole all his pay."

Sielert laughed again, and once more Bolan was impressed with the doctor's acting. "If you lose all your money, it'll be 'cause you want to go again and again with her." He slurred the words, then forced himself off the bench. "But hell, for a fellow deep-sea sailor, I'll walk you to the alley and stand guard." Again, he staggered forward.

Bolan greeted them with a smile and the same price he'd given the other men. But the return greeting from the big man included a wariness he hadn't found in the earlier pair. A wave of caution swept over the Executioner. He didn't like the feel-

ing he was getting. But there was no time to change courses.
They needed to board the *Nakinka Melaniya* without further
delay.

Ogatu played her part as before, maybe better, as she led
the larger of the two men into the alley. A moment later,
Bolan, Sielert and the smaller of the two men heard the same
dull thud they'd heard before. But this time, it was followed
by a scream of rage.

"What the fuck!" said the smaller man—the first words he
had spoken. Bolan barely had time to note the same foreign
accent he had heard in the larger man's voice before the small
man spun away and took off down the street.

The sounds of a struggle within the darkness of the alley
issued forth. The Executioner hesitated only a second, determining the best course of action. Ogatu's first strike obviously
hadn't knocked the big man out. Could she handle it from
here? He didn't know, but forced to guess between the detective's ability to take care of herself and the chances that Sielert
could run down the smaller man and bring him back, he'd
have to put his money on the woman. He turned to Greg Sielert. "Go help her," he ordered, then took off after the smaller
man.

The sailor had headed inland, into the off-harbor section of
town catering to tourists. As Bolan ran, he thought of Ogatu,
worrying for a moment about the size disparity between her
and the big sailor. Sielert wasn't going to be much help. But
the small man had to be run down and captured before he
created a scene that brought the attention of the cops assigned
along the off-harbor area.

The small man burst onto a street crowded with bars, shops
and vendors. Looking over his shoulder, he saw Bolan in pur-
suit, and a shrill scream escaped his lips. The noise turned all
heads in the area toward him, and the Executioner cursed
softly under his breath. As if that wasn't bad enough, the man
lost his footing as he turned. A moment later, he fell headlong
into a stand selling coral jewelry.

The rickety stand came down on top of the running sailor
and the young Polynesian woman operating it. Rings, neck-

laces, pendants and other jewelry flew through the air. The squeals of surprise and fear from the stand's proprietor added to the confusion. Bolan reached the site, dug under the fallen canopy and jerked the short sailor out from under the mess.

At the same moment, he felt strong fingers grasp his wrist from the side. He turned to see a huge uniformed Honolulu P.D. officer staring at him. The man's other hand was on the Glock 21 pistol holstered on his hip.

"Justice Department," Bolan whispered as two more uniforms arrived at the scene. The words brought the brief moment of hesitation he had hoped for, and the officer released his wrist. Pulling his credentials from a pocket of his slacks, he held them up for the big cop to see. Still whispering, he said, "We've got an undercover deal going down at the docks. I need this guy *now*."

"I can't just—"

"Yes, you *can*," the Executioner said. It was more the force of his personality than the credentials he held before him that convinced the Honolulu officer to cooperate. "Give me your cuffs."

Bolan hauled the small sailor to his feet and took the big man's handcuffs. Quickly, he secured the sailor's wrists behind his back. He needed to get the uniforms busy. Give them something to do to think they were helping him so they didn't think too hard *about* him. Then he needed to get out of their sight before they started to second guess the whole situation.

"See if you can get these people calmed down," the Executioner said in an authoritarian tone. "This deal we're doing may lead back up here again before the night is over. I don't need the subjects getting cautious because the natives are restless. And I'd appreciate it if you guys made yourselves scarce as soon as you've got things calmed down. Uniforms aren't going to help me, either."

The big cop turned toward the tourists and sailors who had gathered around to gawk. "Okay, folks, show's over," he said. "Go on about your business. Have a good time."

An elderly couple, both wearing Bermuda shorts and sporting cameras around their necks, turned away. "Drugs, Martha," the man said. "Had to be drugs. What's the world coming to?"

The woman's gray head shook, telling her husband she didn't know.

Bolan dragged the sailor's cuffed wrists toward his head and prodded him toward the alley where he hoped Sielert and Ogatu had been able to subdue the big man. Each time the smaller man tried to speak, the Executioner twisted the cuffs slightly and induced a screech. It took only a couple of twists for the sailor to realize that silence was what was being asked for.

A few moments later, Bolan glanced over his shoulder to make sure no one had followed, then drew the sound-suppressed Beretta and pushed the smaller man into the alley. What he saw made him feel better.

The big sailor lay unconscious on the ground. Ogatu and Sielert were busy removing his shirt and pants.

"Any problems?" Bolan asked.

Sielert shook his head with animation. "No," he said, obviously trying to keep a check on his excitement. "I caught him with a spinning kick in the back of the head. He had hold of Susan." The words might have been contained but they came out proud nevertheless.

Bolan nodded. Now was not the time to explain to Sielert how lucky he'd been. The spinning kicks and other fancy techniques the doctor had so diligently practiced over the years were fine for karate tournaments. But nothing but luck, and the fact that Ogatu had obviously seen him coming and been able to hold the big man in place, had made his kick successful.

The Executioner turned to the little man he had brought to the alley and jammed the Beretta under his chin. "You say a word or try to run again, and I'll put three rounds through your head before you have time to say your prayers," he threatened. As the man gulped, Bolan began changing into the khaki and denim the big man had worn, sliding the shirt over his shoulder rig and leaving the tail out to hide the Desert Eagle on his hip. He noted the fresh blood on the shoulders of the shirt. He'd have to come up with a story on how it got there when they boarded the *Nakinka Melaniya*.

"I hit that big bastard with everything I had," Ogatu whispered as Bolan finished dressing. "He must have a skull like a dinosaur."

Bolan nodded and finished dressing. He turned to the little man. "Take off your clothes," he ordered.

"What?" the sailor said. "Here?"

"Do it," the Executioner said, pulling the Beretta from beneath his shirt and sticking it into the man's face once more.

The little man didn't need to be told again. He began unbuttoning his shirt and slid out of his khaki work pants.

A few seconds later, Susan Ogatu's skirt, blouse and jacket were hung over the side of the Dumpster. Bolan kept his eyes on the sailor. Sielert, however, gawked at the nearly nude woman like a kid viewing his first *Playboy* centerfold. "Damn," he said. "This makes the whole mission worth it in itself."

Ogatu grinned at him as she began dressing in the small sailor's clothes. "Always happy to do what I can for morale," she said.

Even though the small man still had his underwear on, his hands had fallen self-consciously to cover his crotch. "What...er, what am I supposed to wear?" he asked.

Ogatu stopped dressing long enough to pull her skirt from the side of the trash container and toss it to the man. "You look good in blue?" she asked.

"I can't wear this!" the man said.

"You don't have to," Bolan assured him. "For where you're going, you look fine as you are." Before the man could speak again he brought the butt of the Beretta down on top of his head.

Ogatu had finally run out of handcuffs, so the Executioner tore strips from the clothing in the alleyway and used it to bind and gag the two men on the ground. He and Sielert lifted the smaller man over the side of the Dumpster and dropped him on top of the two men already inside.

"Thing's filling up," Sielert said. "And trash pickup isn't

until Friday.'' He was still excited about the part he'd played in the alley earlier, the Executioner could tell.

The bigger man took a little more lifting but he, too, was soon inside. Bolan rearranged arms and legs and closed the lid over them.

Susan Ogatu was fastening the last button on her shirt when Bolan turned to her. Sielert had been right. Even in the dim light of the alley, she still looked like exactly what she was— a woman trying to look like a man.

''Think I'll pass?'' the female detective asked.

''As is? No,'' Bolan said. ''But I've got an idea.''

''A good one, I hope.''

''I hope so, too,'' said the soldier as he led the way out of the alley. ''Because it's the *only* one I've got, and we don't have time to come up with another.''

THE ACTIVITY on and around the *Nakinka Melaniya* was in full swing as Dr. Gregory Sielert led the way toward the boarding plank with his exaggerated drunken roll. Bolan had sent him into the store again to buy another bottle of gin, and as they came in view of the man at the top of the plank with the clipboard, he pressed the bottle to his lips as if finishing it off, then threw it on the ground before stumbling onward.

Bolan walked behind him. Susan Ogatu was over his shoulder in a fireman's carry, her hair pinned up and hidden inside the collar of her shirt. Her pretty face was buried in his back as if she were unconscious. The ruse served a double purpose. It not only hid Ogatu's very feminine features, it covered the blood on the shoulder of the Executioner's shirt.

The man checking boarders to the ship wore a full beard and held a clipboard in one hand, a pen in the other. As they neared, Bolan saw that the beard had been grown with the hopes of hiding facial scars from some long-ago fire. The sparse hair fell far short of the mark. The man stopped them as they reached the top of the running plank. ''What happened to him?'' he asked.

''Fight with some locals,'' Sielert said in what Bolan hoped would pass for the eastern European accent he had heard the other men use. The story, however simple, would explain the unconscious man he was carrying. If it worked.

It seemed to. "Names?" the man asked, looking at his clipboard.

Sielert gave the man the three names they had found on the ID the sailors had carried. Bolan held his breath.

The scarred man nodded, checked off the names on the list and waved them through the gate. They were halfway across the deck when they heard his voice again. "Hey, wait a minute!"

Bolan and Sielert froze in their tracks. The Executioner's hand moved under Ogatu's legs toward the Beretta beneath his shirt.

The man with the fire-scarred face walked to them. His twisted features exhibited a lecherous grin. Reaching out, he placed a hand on the posterior sticking up off Bolan's shoulder and squeezed. "That ain't no sailor's ass, boys," he said.

Sielert was quick, proving once more he had a flair for role camouflage. "How'd you know that?" he asked in the same accent he'd used before. "You telling me you could spot a female ass through those baggy khakis?"

The scarred and bearded man continued to squeeze Ogatu's rump. "No, but I can damn sure tell when a woman's hair comes undone and falls out of her collar." He grinned. With one final squeeze, he dropped his hand. "Sorry, men," he said. "Cap'n would have my ass if I let you on board with her. Considering our cargo, and all."

If Bolan had any remaining doubts that they'd found the right ship, those doubts disappeared with the man's words. At the same time he realized that the crew had to be aware of what they were carrying—or at least that they were involved in something illegal. They were not just innocent sailors unwittingly transporting the nukes.

The Executioner waited for Sielert to reply—the doctor was doing fine so far, and there was no reason to change horses in midstream. But when no words were forthcoming, he took the cue himself. "Hey," he said in the same accent. His hand

went into his pocket and pulled out several twenty-dollar bills.
"Take this and look the other way."

The scarred man looked across the deck several times to
make sure no one was watching. "I don't know," he said
nervously.

Susan Ogatu took the situation in hand. She looked into his
eyes. "Take the money," she purred in the same sexy voice
she had used on the other men. "Then come around later and
I'll have something else for you."

That cinched the deal for the man with the burned face.
"What cabin you guys in?" he asked as the money went into
his pocket.

"It's on the clipboard," Bolan told him briskly. "Now, if
you don't mind, we're in a hurry."

"I can see why," he said.

"Give us a couple of hours before you show up," Sielert
said, getting into the game. "Not before, okay?"

"All right." The scarred man returned to his checkpoint.

Bolan let Sielert continue to lead the way across the deck
to the starboard side of the container storage area. They
walked briskly to the first set of steps leading downward. Once
they were out of sight on the deck below, Bolan dropped
Ogatu to her feet. He led the way beneath a set of beams into
what appeared to be a storage area for cleaning equipment.
"The way I see it," he whispered, "we've got two major
problems. First, we don't know where the nukes are hidden
or even if they're still on board at all."

"And I still don't look like a man."

"No, you still don't look like a man," Sielert agreed.

Bolan nodded. "But down here, if we run across someone
who sees you're a woman they aren't going to care about you
being on board for the same reasons the guy up top was. In
fact, they're going to be *happy* to see you. A little *too* happy
would be my guess."

Ogatu tapped her kidney where Bolan had seen her hide a
Glock beneath her shirt. "We'll solve that problem when we
come to it," she said. "I'm not worried. I've got two big

strong he-men taking care of me.'' She glanced at Sielert with amusement, then winked at Bolan.

Sielert didn't see either gesture and beamed with pride.

Bolan took the lead, feeling his way beneath the main deck through the bowels of the ship toward where he guessed the most likely hiding place for the nukes would be—the rear cargo area. Most ships like the *Nakinka Melaniya* hauled their goods from the point of disembarkment to many shores, packing those that would be off-loaded last toward the rear to avoid rearranging the cargo at each stop. Unless he missed his guess, it would be here, hidden among other trade goods and probably disguised as such, that they would find the nukes.

Susan Ogatu, her hair again pinned up and hidden inside her collar, walked directly behind the Executioner. She kept her head down, using Bolan's bulk to hide her face. Sielert brought up the rear, shielding her from view. They passed through several lower cabins—some allotted for storage and ship's maintenance but a few rooms that contained bunks bolted to the walls. The few men still onboard were asleep or reading and barely took notice of them.

But as they neared the aft of the ship, one man looked up from his bunk, dropped the skin magazine he'd been ogling and whistled. ''Purtiest damn man I ever seen,'' he said in a deep Southern accent.

Bolan turned toward him in the narrow passageway. But before he could respond, he saw Ogatu raise a finger to her lips. ''Calm down, cowboy,'' she whispered. By now the other pair of men, lying on their bunks, had looked up. ''There'll be plenty left for you guys when I'm finished with these two.'' She smiled the same seductive smile Bolan had seen her use so many times already that night. ''I'll come back. As long as you each have fifty bucks, that is.''

The three men were digging into their pockets as Bolan led them past the cabin.

The rear cargo area was just as the Executioner had imagined it. Stacks of crates reached almost to the deck above them. Some were marked for easy identification, others were not. Which meant nothing. Only a fool would transport illegal nuclear weapons without masking them as some other commodity, and Bolan held no misconceptions that the men of the PFF and their cohort in terrorism—this Vladimir—were fools. Each crate would have to be checked.

But there were two problems that had to be solved before they could start. And both those problems wore khaki slacks and pants and carried sidearms on their hips.

The first of the rear cargo hold guards approached Bolan aggressively. "Who the hell told you to come back here?" he asked. He was big and looked Samoan, which didn't surprise the Executioner. While the ship appeared to utilize an international crew—probably made up of mercenary seamen—Benjamin Liholiho wouldn't have been likely to trust the safety of the nukes to anyone outside his most loyal PFF circle.

The other guard stood at the side of the room, watching from a distance. He, too, was of Polynesian extraction.

Bolan smiled sheepishly at the man who confronted him. He needed to take these two out without noise, and there was too much distance between them. Speaking loudly, hoping that his gin breath would waft into the closest man's nostrils, he said, "We were looking for a little privacy, that's all." He started to walk past the man, hoping the movement would draw the other guard closer. It didn't.

Instead, the big Polynesian took a sidestep to block his path. "What do you want privacy for?" he asked suspiciously.

"For this, you stupid son of a bitch."

Bolan heard the voice behind him and turned. Visible in front of Sielert stood Susan Ogatu. The female detective had opened the front of her shirt and unhooked her bra, exhibiting a firm set of breasts to the eyes of the cargo guards.

Such unexpected exhibitionism has a startling effect on any man, any time. But the cargo guards, who had been shut up at sea without seeing a woman in any state of dress, were virtually paralyzed.

Bolan drew the Beretta and pumped two quiet 9 mms into each man. "Drag them out of sight," he ordered Sielert. The nuclear expert nodded and grabbed the closest man under the arms. Turning to Ogatu, the Executioner said, "Let's get started."

Against the wall to his right, Bolan spotted a toolbox. Inside, he found a pry bar and a claw hammer. Handing the pry bar to Sielert, he turned to Ogatu who was hooking her bra. "Watch the door for us," he said. "We'll start at the very back."

Ogatu nodded. "What do you want me to do if someone shows up?"

"You seem to have your own system," he said. "No sense in changing until it stops working."

Bolan and Sielert moved to the rear of the cargo area and began cracking open crates marked with Cyrillic lettering. Under the lid, he found planting soil bagged into ten- and twenty-pound plastic bags. He picked out random containers, plunging the blade of his Applegate-Fairbairn through the plastic and digging around. He encountered nothing but soil.

Not that it meant the bombs hadn't been broken down into pieces for shipment. They might have been. But if so, some of the elements would be too large to hide inside the bags. If he encountered any pieces, he could always return to check each bag.

Bolan and Sielert continued to search the planting-soil crates with nothing more interesting than a false alarm when Sielert's knife struck a large stone that had found its way inside one of the bags. They moved on to crates containing Ukrainian ceramic ware with no better luck.

The crates in the third section of the cargo area were stamped as containing Moldavian handcrafts. And on the fourth try, the Executioner struck pay dirt. "Greg!" he whispered across the room as he stared into the container. "Come here!"

Sielert moved to his side as Bolan opened another crate. Instead of another nuke, he saw pile upon pile of homemade dolls. But the third crate held another of the devices like the one Sielert was examining.

"Is this it?" Bolan asked.

Sielert nodded, frowning. He pulled a pair of reading glasses from his shirt pocket and lodged them on the brim of his nose. "Damn sure looks like it to me," he said.

"Well, get busy making sure they aren't armed," Bolan ordered. "Then make sure they can't *be* armed before we figure out what to do with them. I'm going to tell Susan to—"

He was interrupted by a loud, Southern-accented voice on the other side of the stack of crates. "Hey, baby!" it said. "Where did your friends go?"

Bolan peered around the crates to see that the three men they had encountered earlier had grown tired of waiting. All three stood at the entrance to the cargo area. The one who had spoken squeezed his crotch as he added, "Hey, baby, wanna get down?"

Susan Ogatu's voice had its usual sexy purr. "They had to go take a leak," she said. "You boys go on back to your bunks and get it ready for me. I'll be there before you know it." She reached out and gently pushed the man toward the open hatchway.

But this time, her approach didn't work as well as it had in the past.

"No, baby, we can do our business while you wait for them," said the Southerner. "Right now, right here, down and dirty, baby."

"No," Ogatu said. "I promised them first shots." This time, when she spoke, her voice had lost the barest trace of confidence.

"Shit," said one of the men behind the Southerner. "It don't matter who's first."

Bolan pulled back and glanced at Sielert. The man was still busy inspecting the bombs and seemed oblivious to what was going on around him. That was fine. Sielert wasn't likely to be of any help in this situation, and might well prove to be a liability. The Executioner drew the Beretta and began to edge around the crate once more. He'd wait and see if Ogatu could handle things herself. If not....

The Executioner never got the chance to finish the thought. As he cleared the barrier once more, he saw all three men grab Susan Ogatu and begin ripping at her clothes, laughing and jeering and taking her to the floor. Bolan saw her Glock slide out of her pants and skid across the deck, but the excited men wrestling with her seemed not to notice.

An all-encompassing anger threatened to sweep over the Executioner. He hated criminals of all sorts, be they robbers, burglars, drug dealers, or murderers. But rapists held a special place on his list.

Leaning around the corner, Bolan took his time, dropping the Beretta's sights on the nearest rapist as he flipped the machine pistol's selector switch to semiauto. The man already had his pants around his ankles and was working on his underwear as the other two men held Ogatu down.

After the attempted jailbreak the Executioner had switched ammunition, trading the Glaser safety slugs for rounds with more penetration. When he squeezed the trigger a near-silent 115-grain semijacketed hollowpoint left the Beretta's barrel and drilled its way through the would-be rapist's skull. Blood, brains and bone flew through the air, causing the other two men to look up.

Bolan's next round caught the second man squarely between the shoulder blades as he turned to duck through the hatch. His chest shot forward in a jackknife movement as his hands tried to touch each other behind his back. But the third man, the one with the Southern accent, rose from the ground and sprinted out of sight down the passageway.

The commotion had driven Sielert out of his private world and into the one around him. His eyes jerked up in surprise. "Stay here!" Bolan ordered. "Finish with the bombs! Make sure they're inoperable before you leave this room!"

"But they aren't—"

"Just do it!" Bolan shouted as he sprinted around the crates. He glanced at Susan Ogatu as he neared. Her khaki pants had been ripped completely off. Her shirt was in shreds, but she appeared unharmed. And if her eyes were any indication, she meant to find the third man who had tried to rape her and make him wish he'd never been born. She was in the process of grabbing her Glock as the Executioner leaped over her.

Bolan entered the passageway and saw the Southerner ahead of him. He raised the Beretta, but the man ducked out of sight into a side corridor. Sprinting, Bolan made the turn, ducking low in case the man had his own weapon and was laying in wait.

The Executioner followed the corridor and the sound of running footsteps ahead, hoping against hope he could reach the man and silence him before he alerted the rest of the crew and a general alarm went out. If that happened, he could only pray that Greg Sielert would have had time to render the nukes useless. If they were still armed or in a state in which they could be activated, the mission was dead in the water. Bolan, Ogatu and Sielert might very well all be killed with no one on shore ever the wiser. The *Nakinka Melaniya* could sail out of port, drop all three of their bodies into the sea, then go on to deliver the bombs to the PFF at whatever point had been arranged.

Which was exactly what the Executioner realized might already be under way as he heard the ship's horn sound and the vessel began to move beneath his feet.

3

Mack Bolan ran on, hearing footsteps behind him. He glanced over his shoulder as he entered a storage hold.

What he saw surprised but didn't shock him.

Behind him ran Susan Ogatu, clad in nothing but her white cotton bra and matching panties. The soft material contrasted sharply with her saffron-brown skin and startled the eye so much that the Glock in her hand was rendered nearly invisible.

The Executioner entered another storage cabin. There was no time to stop and find clothes for Ogatu. But her seminudity didn't seem to be slowing her down. She had already proven that she was comfortable with her sexuality, and using it as a weapon didn't seem to faze her in the least. The fact was, it was causing a split-second freeze in every man who saw her and might prove to be the only advantage they'd have against an enemy who vastly outnumbered them.

The walls of the storage cabin held brooms, mops and other janitorial tools. Shelves rose to the ceiling and were packed high with rags, detergents and other cleaning items. But the room was empty of human life. So the Executioner ran on.

As he entered a corridor, he saw a flash of khaki as the man with the Southern accent darted into a hatchway. Bolan increased speed, skidding to a halt as he reached the opening. Through the doorway, but out of sight, he could hear the clanging of metal.

The soldier edged around the corner to see the Southerner fighting with the locked hatchway to another corridor. "Hey!" the man screamed frantically. "Hey! Open up!"

"Hey, yourself," Bolan said.

The sailor spun around, jerking a knife from his belt. He raised it over his head and brought his aim back like a baseball pitcher ready to deliver a fastball. Two quick 9 mms from the Beretta ended the man's windup. The Southerner sprawled on his face like a pitcher who had slipped on the rubber and fallen onto the mound.

No sooner had the sailor fallen than the hatchway opened. Through the opening, Bolan saw the open mouth of a sailor. He looked down at the dead man on the deck, then up at Bolan. "Oh, shi—" he had time to say before the Executioner pumped a round through his open mouth.

Behind him, in the cabin he'd just left, Bolan heard three fast explosions from Ogatu's Glock.

The man he had just shot fell backward out of the cabin. An unseen voice somewhere behind him in the passageway shouted, "Shooting! Somebody's shooting!" Several sets of footsteps sprinted away.

Bolan took off after them, knowing even as he went that it was futile. Within seconds, a general alert would go out through the crew. He, Sielert and Ogatu had one chance.

They needed a hostage. Someone of importance the rest of the crew couldn't afford to see killed.

The Executioner waited for Ogatu to catch up, then said, "We've got to find the captain. If we can take him prisoner we can—" He had no time to finish the sentence.

Two men appeared in the hatchway aiming Colt 1911 Government Model pistols their way. But the sight of the beautiful, scantily clad woman next to Bolan caused them to pause a hundredth of a second.

And a hundredth of a second was more of an edge than the Executioner had ever needed.

Bolan had already flipped the selector switch from semiauto to three-round burst. He turned slightly. Bringing the Beretta up to eye level, he pointed the barrel as if pointing his finger and pulled the trigger. The man on his right—a disheveled creature whose body odor could be smelled even above the stench of cordite in the air—caught two rounds in the chest and one between the eyes. The man on the left wore a long, thick goatee. He took a double tap of 9 mms through the hair into his throat. A geyser of crimson was shooting from his neck when the third round disappeared in the chin hair.

Grabbing Ogatu by the arm, Bolan pulled her behind him as he darted into the hallway, the Beretta ready. Down the corridor, pandemonium reigned, but none of the enemy were still in the immediate area. Using the opportunity to reload, Bolan dropped the partially spent magazine from the grips of the 93-R and replaced it with a full box. Turning to Ogatu, he said, "You have extra ammo?"

The woman shook her head, then grinned. "I'm a little short on pockets at the moment, Mike," she said.

"Then grab one of the Colt pistols," the Executioner said. As soon as she had, they started down the corridor.

The ship's horn sounded again and the vessel began to pick up speed as it left port. As he moved on through the dimly lit hallways, Bolan knew it had to be an unscheduled departure. The *Nakinka Melaniya* had arrived at Honolulu harbor with a full crew—they had seen that. But they had also seen a good number of the mercenary sailors go ashore. Bolan and Sielert were wearing the clothes of two of them. A lot of the men wouldn't yet have returned. That could only mean that news of intruders had reached the captain and he had abandoned the men ashore in order to save his cargo.

Bolan took a deep breath as he continued to evaluate their situation. Even though the ship was lightly manned, he, Ogatu and Sielert were still vastly outnumbered. Yes, he was taking the right course—the only course they *could* take. Their only hope would be to take the captain hostage. That would give Bolan a chance to slow down and come up with the best plan to destroy the nukes, the ship and its terrorist crew.

The sounds ahead seemed to indicate that a lot of men were moving through the passageways. But the men were still trying to get away from the shooting. Even though it was a criminal enterprise undertaken by the *Nakinka Melaniya,* Bolan reasoned, the Ukrainian ship probably worked off the same philosophy as most seagoing vessels. Only a few trusted men were armed, with the majority of weapons secured behind lock and key. Those arms weren't broken out unless the ship fell under attack.

On most voyages, it was far more likely that men kept cramped in tight quarters for long periods of time would use any weapons they had on each other, rather than an outside party.

But the fact that the majority of men were unarmed would change. Soon. Word was out, and he could imagine someone unlocking shotguns, pistols and rifles and handing them out.

Speeding up, Bolan led Ogatu down the corridor, through empty cabin after empty cabin, until they spotted a ladder leading up to the main deck. Turning halfway around, he said, "My guess is that the captain will have headed for the bridge. Which means we've got to go topside, make our way across the deck into the superstructure, then up."

Ogatu mounted the steps with the Executioner following. She stuck her head through the opening, then turned to Bolan. "I can see a couple dozen men," she whispered. "They're all armed now."

Bolan nodded. "Whenever you're ready," he said.

Susan took a deep breath, then mounted the last few steps to the main deck. Bolan followed, transferring the Beretta to his left hand and drawing the Desert Eagle with his right. He kept both pistols low, against the sides of his legs as they began walking toward the superstructure and the aft of the ship.

So far, none of the men seemed to have noticed them. Bolan wanted to keep it that way. The closer to the superstructure they could get before all hell broke loose, the better chance they had of making it inside. The shock Ogatu produced would only last for a second or so on each man. After that, it would be combat as usual.

The 93-R sputtered a trio of hushed hollowpoint rounds into the chest of the man with the shotgun. As he fell to the deck, Bolan swung the weapon to his right, firing another three-round burst. The first 9 mm took a man in the nose. The second two fell through the face of a seaman with a mop handle.

A man holding a jackknife screamed and lurched forward in panic. He was five feet away when three 9 mms took him to the deck, making him writhe in the last pain he'd ever know.

The two men still standing suffered from the combined shock of Ogatu's appearance and the fact that their comrades had fallen. The Beretta 93-R spat two more bursts of death before they had a chance to recover.

By then, other men on deck had noted the commotion. All heads turned toward Bolan and Ogatu. But the sailors' first reactions, as both Bolan and Ogatu had known they would be, were to the beautiful woman walking across the deck wearing next to nothing.

Exclamations of "Shit!" and "Damn!" rose from the deck as the *Nakinka Melaniya* continued to sail out of port.

There was no point in silence. Bolan opened fire with the Desert Eagle as both he and Ogatu broke into a sprint. A burst of 240-grain Winchester .44 Magnum jacketed hollowpoint rounds sailed from the Eagle at 1,330 feet per second, exploding into the chests and heads of the men hired by the Polynesian Freedom Fighters to deliver the nukes. A red thunderstorm of blood flew through the air. The men's outcries of lust and surprise were replaced by dull moans of pain and screams of terror. Susan Ogatu opened up with the Glock in one hand, the Colt pistol in the other.

Bullets fired wildly in panic by the mercenary seamen flew toward Bolan and Ogatu as they raced across the deck. As they passed a raised lifeboat, return fire struck the stilts supporting it, and the boat toppled off its platform to strike the rail, then splash loudly into the sea.

Bolan followed the cop through the hatch into the superstructure as bullets and shotgun pellets pelted the steel. Taking the lead, Bolan sprinted past the woman and up the ladder to an empty second level. Above him he could hear excited voices.

With the Beretta and Desert Eagle leading the way, the Executioner mounted another set of steps to the compass bridge. A sailor in khaki slacks and a blue and white striped T-shirt—

a shirt the Executioner recognized immediately as old Soviet Union Spetsnaz special forces issue—had drawn a Makarov pistol from the holster on his belt. He got it halfway up and into play before a .44 Magnum round turned the blue and white into a solid red.

Two other men stood in the room, unarmed. Neither looked like they ran the ship. Bolan trained a gun on each of them. "Where's the captain?" he demanded.

The PFF hadn't paid these men enough to risk dying from a lie. Without hesitation, they both pointed toward the entrance to the chart room on the same deck.

He didn't see or hear her, but when the eyes of the men in the compass room widened Bolan knew Ogatu had arrived behind him. "Search them for weapons, then keep them covered," he told the detective, then made his way to the chart room.

The captain was hiding, unarmed, beneath a table covered with maps, charts and other navigation equipment. The Executioner holstered the Beretta, leaned down and grabbed the man's sleeve. He jerked him out from under the table and lifted him to his feet.

The man looked almost like a caricature of a captain—he wore a full gray beard and a navy blue cap. A matching pea-coat had been discarded in the mild tropical temperature and hung haphazardly over a chair on the other side of the table.

A quick glance through the window told Bolan they were a few miles out at sea. He could see Honolulu harbor in the distance. For a split second, his mind raced to Greg Sielert, still alone with the nukes, he assumed. He had to hope the scientist had been able to neutralize the bombs. The ship was not far enough away for the island to escape even a small nuclear blast.

Bolan walked the captain over to a chair and threw him on top of the peacoat. Quickly, he shook the man down for weapons, finding nothing but a small folding knife, which he pocketed. "Sit there, don't move and keep your mouth shut until I tell you to talk," he said.

The gray beard bobbed up and down in understanding.

Bolan started to turn toward the compass bridge, then turned back. He needed to leave the captain alone for a few moments. But there might be any number of weapons hidden around the room. He didn't have time to check, and he didn't have time to tie the man up.

A right cross solved the problem, leaving the captain unconscious in his chair.

The Executioner walked to the doorway leading to the compass bridge. Susan Ogatu had the men in her charge facedown on the floor with their hands clasped behind their necks. A .357 Magnum Smith & Wesson Model 66 had replaced the Colt in her left hand. The .45 pistol lay empty on the floor at her feet, the slide locked back after the last round had been fired.

The Honolulu detective showed Bolan the revolver. "This is the only weapon I found on them," she said.

Bolan nodded, then walked over to a chubby sailor stretched out on the deck and dug a toe into his flabby ribs. "You," he said. "On your feet."

The man promptly obeyed.

"You go down and tell the other men the captain said to lock their guns back up. Tell them if anyone tries to come up here, their fearless leader is going to become shark food."

The sailor shook his head. "Begging your pardon, sir," he said, acknowledging Bolan's new role as ship's commander. "But nobody is really going to give a shit whether the old man lives or dies." In an obvious attempt to gain favor with Bolan and Ogatu he had traded sides in a heartbeat.

Bolan paused. He had no doubt the man was right—this was a crew of hired mercenaries, hardly loyal seamen. He needed another incentive to keep them in line. And they would care about only one thing.

"You been paid yet?" he asked the man. It was a rhetorical question. Considering the kind of men the PFF had employed, if they'd been paid in advance none of them would have showed up for work.

"No," the sailor said.

"Know where the money is?"

"No."

"Does the captain?"

"Yeah."

"Want to get paid?"

"Sure."

"Then I'd guess you have reason to keep the captain alive."

The sailor frowned. "Hadn't thought of it that way," he said.

Bolan shook his head. He wasn't exactly dealing with a genius. So he spoke as simply as possible. "Well, think about it that way. And go tell the other men to think about it that way. Tell them I'll not only kill the captain, but there won't be any money if they try to interfere with us. Then tell them if they cooperate, we'll be off the ship before they know it, and they'll get what they deserve."

The sailor nodded.

"Take off," the Executioner ordered, and the man disappeared out of the compass bridge.

Bolan glanced at the man on the floor. He was twice Ogatu's size—she'd never keep his pants up and be able to move at the same time. "You," he said. "Stand and take off your shirt."

The man rose to his knees. Bolan covered him while he complied. Ogatu set her Glock and the S&W revolver on the deck next to the Colt, and took the shirt when the man held it out. She slipped into it. It hung over her like a circus tent. "Give me your belt, too," she told the man.

The mercenary seaman slid the belt out from the loops and tossed it to her. Ogatu wrapped it around her waist and tied it in a knot. She picked up her guns.

"Keep him covered," Bolan told her, then returned to the chart room.

The Executioner took a seat across from the captain, leaned forward and slapped the man's face back into consciousness. As soon as the eyes above the beard opened, Bolan said, "I want to know everything you know, and I want it now."

The man nodded. Bolan could tell he was willing to cooperate—more than willing. He and his crew—with the few exceptions Bolan had encountered who he suspected were members of the PFF—were nothing more than hired help for Liholiho; they felt no allegiance to the organization. But that also meant that the captain wasn't likely to know very much.

"Where are you taking the nukes?" the Executioner asked.

"Nukes?" the captain said, his face genuinely shocked. "What nukes?"

Bolan reached across the table and slapped the man's face. "Don't play games with me," he said. "I don't have the time or the temperament. I'm talking about the nukes in the aft storage cabin."

The captain's face whitened over his beard. "Nobody told me anything about nukes," he whispered. "I wouldn't have transported nukes if I'd known that's what they loaded. They said it was dope. Heroin."

"*That* didn't bother you, of course," the Executioner said. The trace of sarcasm in his voice was lost on the man.

"You sure they're nukes?" the captain asked. His voice sounded truly surprised.

Bolan ignored the question. "Just tell me where you're supposed to meet Liholiho."

The bearded man's face looked surprised, and Bolan guessed it came from the fact that he knew the name of the ship's contact. "There's no definite place," said the captain. "We're heading back out to sea. He's supposed to radio us."

Bolan frowned. There were holes in a plan like that. Big holes. For one thing, the Coast Guard carefully monitored all maritime radio traffic near the islands. It didn't fit into the professionalism the PFF had shown setting up the rest of the deal with the Ukrainians.

The Executioner stood and walked to the window, staring at the sea. The island of Oahu was barely visible, and it wouldn't be long before they'd be far enough away that even if the nukes went up little damage would be done to Hawaii. But he wanted to avoid detonating them if possible. Such an explosion would kill an untold number of sea creatures, and there was always the possibility of creating a tidal wave that moved farther than expected before it played itself out. Squinting through the glass, his thoughts returned to Greg Sielert, and he wondered again whether the nuclear expert had been successful in neutralizing the threat. There was no way to know without going to the storage cabin where he'd left the scientist.

Bolan was going to have to do that sooner or later. But right now he wanted to give the crew of the *Nakinka Melaniya* time to listen to the sailor he had sent.

The Executioner mulled the situation around in his mind a few more seconds, then turned away from the sea. He knew what he had to do. There was only one plan of action that stood any chance of getting rid of the nukes and at the same time insuring the safety of Susan Ogatu and Greg Sielert.

Walking swiftly to the chart table, Bolan searched through the maps and other papers until he found a grid map of the South Pacific. He picked a spot far enough from land that a nuclear explosion would do minimal damage and memorized the coordinates. Then, dropping his index finger to the map, he turned to face the captain. "Chart a course here," he demanded. "Toward these coordinates. Full steam ahead."

The captain looked at the chart. "There?" he asked incredulously. "There's nothing there."

"Do it," Bolan said.

The Executioner didn't have to say it twice—the captain hadn't forgotten either the right cross or the more recent slap. Hunching over the table, the bearded man picked up a pencil and went to work. A few seconds later, he looked up and said, "I've got to use the instruments in the compass bridge now."

Bolan nodded, stepped back and shoved the Desert Eagle's barrel into the captain's ear. "Then let's go do it," he said.

Escorting the man into the next room, the Executioner saw that Ogatu still held the other sailor at gunpoint. He followed the captain to the instruments and waited. When the man had finished, he pulled a base microphone across the table and pressed down on the key. His voice boomed loudly across the ship's intercom system, and a few seconds later the crew had been advised that everything was under control and given new sailing orders.

Bolan stepped back and pulled his cellular phone out of his backpack. He tapped in a number, and a soft feminine voice answered the phone on the other end.

"Is this Lena?" Bolan asked.

"Why, yes it is. Who's this?"

"Let me speak to your flyboy friend, Lena," the soldier said.

A few moments later, Jack Grimaldi's voice said, "Yeah, Striker, this is Hank."

"Glad you figured out which name you'd given her," Bolan said. He gave Grimaldi the coordinates to which the ship was sailing. "You'll need something that can land on deck," he said. "Got a chopper handy?"

"I'll get one," Grimaldi said. "But it'll be slow getting to you."

Bolan's eyebrows lowered in concentration. "We don't have time to waste but I don't see any other way. You're going to have to pick us up at sea. We've found the nukes but I want to go after Liholiho, this Vladimir character and the rest of the PFF. They aren't going to lie down and play dead just because we stopped them this time."

There was a pause on the other end, then Grimaldi said, "How many of you am I picking up?"

"Three. Counting me."

"Okay, Striker," the pilot said. "I'll come up with something. See you soon."

The line went dead.

THE EXECUTIONER glanced at his watch, then at the instruments within the compass bridge. They were nearing the coordinates he had given Grimaldi and would be there in less than fifteen minutes. He glanced to the floor at his side. As soon as he'd hung up from talking to Grimaldi, he had bound the hands of the man Susan Ogatu had held at gunpoint with silver duct tape. The sailor's ankles were trussed together with the same tape, and a wide strip had been wound around his face and the back of his head to serve as a gag. He lay on his side on the floor.

The captain—John O'Haggerty, Bolan had learned was his name—sat quietly in a chair. O'Haggerty's eyelids drooped. Bolan had told him half an hour earlier what was to happen. His eyes were sleepy, as if his unconscious mind were trying to block out the fact that he might not live to see another sunrise on the South Pacific. But Bolan hadn't told the man the entire plan. If he had, the captain would've had no doubt that he was spending his last hours on Earth.

The Executioner turned to face the man. "It's time," he said.

Ogatu held the roll of duct tape, and she handed it and the short-barreled .357 Magnum to Bolan.

Bolan shoved the revolver into the waistband of the khakis and moved behind O'Haggerty. "Lean forward and put your hands behind you," he ordered.

The captain complied.

Quickly, the soldier taped the man's wrists, then said, "Now lean back again."

As soon as the captain's head was within reach, Bolan tore a long strip of duct tape from the roll. He centered it on O'Haggerty's forehead, then brought the ends around the sides of his head. Drawing the S&W from his belt, he pressed its short, stubby barrel into the back of the man's head beneath his cap. He pressed the tape over the sides of the cylinder, then wound more tape around the man's head and the gun to secure the weapon in place.

When he was finished, he cocked the revolver.

O'Haggerty laughed nervously.

"If I were you," Bolan said, "I'd keep in mind that single-action trigger felt like it took about two pounds of pressure when I tried it earlier. You might want to quit laughing or moving at all."

The captain started to nod, thought better of it.

"Stand up," the Executioner ordered. He helped the man to his feet by pulling up on the grip of the revolver.

The captain stood gingerly, and the Executioner steered him toward the door. He nodded to Ogatu and the cop fell in behind him.

Slowly, Bolan, Ogatu and O'Haggerty started down the steps to the main deck. The Executioner glanced once more at his wristwatch. He had done his best to time things so they wouldn't have to wait on deck longer than necessary for Grimaldi's arrival. He had one job left to do before he went to pick up Sielert, and he wanted to get it done, get the man and arrive on deck as close to the time that Grimaldi got there as possible. The time they spent waiting, surrounded by the crew, would be the hazardous period. That was the time when things could go wrong, and O'Haggerty could get the back of his head blown off.

Bolan didn't want to see that happen. A dead hostage was useless.

As they reached the main deck, Bolan pushed O'Haggerty to the opening of the superstructure, then pulled back on the grips of the revolver to stop him. His hand still on the gun, he leaned around the captain to look through the hole. The crew of the *Nakinka Melaniya* had ignored the orders to lock their guns up, as Bolan had suspected they would. He hadn't given the order expecting it to be carried out. He had done so to emphasize the gravity of the situation.

And that he had accomplished. In all the faces on deck now turned his way, he saw a combination of fear and hatred. But most of all, he saw that the men were taking the situation seriously.

Bolan twisted the revolver's grips to turn O'Haggerty's head to the side. "Can everybody see this?" he called.

A few of the heads bobbed. Most remained frozen in place.

"Then I hope you're smart enough to keep your distance. And I hope I don't have to tell you that if the captain dies, you can say goodbye to the money you were promised."

An unseen man near the back of a cluster of sailors along the rail called out, "If the captain dies, you die!"

Bolan leaned around the captain and into view. He let a hard smile cover his face as he turned in the direction of the voice. "I've been ready for death for years," he called softly. "Have you?"

He got no response from any of the men.

"Here's the bottom line," Bolan shouted. "You cooperate and don't try to interfere. Do that, and I'll make sure you each get what's coming to you. Clear?"

There were a few grudging nods.

Pushing on the grips, the Executioner piloted the captain from the superstructure onto the open deck. "Clear the path!" he yelled at the men. The sea of khaki and denim opened up as the sailors made way, and he pushed O'Haggerty slowly though the throng.

When they had drawn near the closest ladder downward, Bolan leaned toward the back of the man's head. "This lead to the boiler room?" he asked.

Again, the captain started to nod, remembered the hair trigger on the revolver and stopped. "Yes," he whispered.

"Take me straight there," Bolan said. Behind him, he could hear Susan Ogatu's soft steps. With his free hand he waved two of the mercenary seamen away from the ladder, and the three of them went below.

Bolan half-expected to find some of the men hiding beneath the main deck, but they encountered no one as Captain John O'Haggerty escorted them to the boiler room. When they stepped into the large area, the Executioner turned to Ogatu and said, "Take over for a minute. And watch the hatchway behind you."

The woman nodded as the Executioner dropped his hand from the gun taped to the back of the captain's head. She replaced his hand with her own.

Bolan moved quickly, shrugging out of the backpack and unzipping it. He dug through the contents, producing several ignition caps and a supply of C-4 plastique. As Ogatu continued to watch the corridor outside the cabin with her hand on the revolver, he went about the room applying the charges next to the boilers. When he was finished, he connected a small rectangular battery pack to one of the charges, double-checked to make sure it was programmed to the same frequency as the remote detonator still in his backpack, then stuck his arms through the pack's straps once more. "Let's go," he said, taking the revolver's grips from Ogatu.

Bolan, Ogatu and O'Haggerty made their way along a starboard passageway toward the storage area where they'd left Sielert with the nukes. Bolan wondered briefly if the man was still alive. They had been gone a long time, and he might very well have been found by members of the crew. Even if O'Haggerty was telling the truth and the mercs thought their forbidden cargo was heroin rather than nuclear bombs, they would likely have gone to check on it. They'd have suspected that theft was the reason the intruders had boarded the ship.

They neared the aft of the ship and Bolan began to recognize things he'd seen earlier. The hair on the back of his head seemed to stand up. They had been walking slowly so as not to jar the .357 Magnum. With his battle radar on full alert, the Executioner slowed even more. Things had been too quiet. Things were going too well. And he could feel that something lay ahead.

They entered the large cargo area without incident. For a second, Bolan wondered if the feeling he had might have been his imagination. No, that never happened. What did happen sometimes was that a danger he sensed went away before he encountered it. Had some of the men been lying in wait, then decided against attack before he came across them?

The answer was no.

The first gunshot cracked the stillness within the cabin like a thunderstorm suddenly breaking out on a sunny day. It was followed by dozens of rounds as armed men leaped from behind the stacked crates and cartons in the cargo area.

Bolan pulled his finger out of the trigger guard of the S&W, pushing O'Haggerty to the side as he hit the deck and rolled the other way. Round after round zoomed over his head. Lead projectiles struck the concrete to his sides and created sparks that illuminated the room as if a thousand Fourth of July sparklers had all been lit at once. The Executioner rolled onto one knee, his hand coming up in front of him with the Desert Eagle.

Susan Ogatu, who had been carrying her Glock in her hand, had already pumped off a series of semiauto fire when the Executioner sent a double tap into a seaman wearing a blue and white striped Spetsnaz T-shirt. The man clutched his chest, a childlike look of awe on his face as if he'd never believed that death was meant for him. He fell forward.

Swinging the Desert Eagle to his right, Bolan squeezed off another two hollowpoint rounds, which took a khaki-clad sailor in the groin and lower abdomen. A finishing third round into the nose mercifully put him out of his misery.

Enemy fire forced the Executioner to change positions. He rolled to his right into Captain O'Haggerty, who lay prostrate on the ground. The hammer on the revolver had fallen, jarred loose when the man hit the deck. But the back of O'Haggerty's head was intact. He'd been saved by the internal transfer bar, which blocked the firing pin unless the trigger was pulled. But O'Haggerty had heard the metallic click as the hammer fell, and his face was the color of freshly fallen snow.

Rising to one knee, Bolan saw Greg Sielert as the nuclear expert suddenly hopped out from between two crates. The man's hands had been bound behind his back, and his ankles were tied with thick rope. "Get back!" Bolan yelled as he pulled the trigger of the Desert Eagle. Another of the deadly .44 slugs found its mark, and another man in khaki went down.

Rounds ricocheted off the concrete walls to zoom around the cargo area like angry bees. As he watched Ogatu fire her Glock dry, then stoop to pick up a shotgun dropped by one of the fallen sailors, Bolan felt a thump against his back. The skin beneath the captured khaki shirt began to burn, but he ignored it. One of the ricochets—he could only thank God it had slowed to the point where it had lost all penetration before it found him.

The Executioner dropped one more man, then ejected the near-empty magazine from the butt of the Desert Eagle and replaced it with a load from his pocket. By the time the hand cannon was up and running again, Ogatu had blasted a 12-gauge hole through another of the attacking seamen.

Well-placed rounds dropped four more men. Bullets continued to fly through the air, rebounding off the walls to finally find homes in the wooden crates or lose momentum and fall to the ground. Bolan continued to fire, picking off more of the sailors. He was strangely thankful that the ship was carrying nuclear devices rather than dynamite or some other explosive that could be ignited by gunfire. The nukes had a completely different setup, and the chances that they'd be detonated by a stray round were practically nonexistent.

Sielert continued to stand in the open, hopping around madly and trying to free his hands. Bolan was about to yell at him to find cover when the man screamed. He dropped as if he'd been hit between the eyes with a baseball bat. Blood began to drip from the side of his head.

Only two armed sailors seemed to be still operative within the cargo area. Both had taken refuge behind crates not far from where Sielert lay. Seeing that their comrades had fallen, one of them shouted surrender. "Please!" he yelled in a French-tinged accent. "Do not shoot any more! We give up!"

"Drop the guns," Bolan ordered. "Come out with your hands up!"

A Remington pump and an AK-47 rifle skidded out from behind the crates. Bolan heard a quick, whispered conversation, then a SIG-Sauer pistol followed.

"Let me see your hands!" Bolan reminded them.

Slowly, probably expecting a bullet at any second, first one and then the other surviving gunmen stepped from behind the crates. The Executioner didn't hesitate—he had no time to waste on the men, and there was nothing of value they could tell him. Stepping forward, he brought the Desert Eagle down on top of the head of a sailor wearing a blood-splattered T-shirt. As he slumped unconscious to the deck, the second man grimaced and closed his eyes, awaiting the inevitable.

He got it a moment later and went to sleep on top of his friend.

The Executioner turned to Ogatu. "Stick your head up top," he said. "See if you can spot my pilot."

The tails of the oversize shirt the cop wore flapped as she pivoted away.

Bolan knelt next to Dr. Gregory Sielert. The man lay on his side, a pool of blood beneath his face. Rolling him over, Bolan breathed a sigh of relief. A huge bruise was forming around the scientist's temple, but the skin had barely been broken. The bullet had struck, then, following one of the unexplainable paths bullets sometimes take, had skidded across his cheek to open a bloody but non-threatening wound.

The fates had smiled on Greg Sielert. Like the Executioner, he'd been hit by a velocity-spent ricochet rather than a direct round.

Sielert's eyes fluttered open unseeingly as Bolan moved him.

"Greg!" the soldier said, patting his face. "Did you get the nukes disabled?"

Sielert stared at the deck above them, his eyes glazed.

"Greg!" Bolan tried again. "Did you disarm the bombs?"

For a brief moment, Sielert's eyes cleared. "Didn't…need to," he said. Then his eyes glazed over again and his eyelids closed once more.

Again, Bolan breathed a sigh of relief. Evidently, the nukes had never been activated. That task had been left to Liholiho and his PFF terrorists after they received them.

Grabbing Sielert under the arms, Bolan lifted him to his feet and dropped the man over his shoulder in the same fireman's carry he had used when trying to pass Ogatu off as a man. He was starting toward the door when he heard the detective's bare feet running toward him. A moment later, she stood in the hatchway to the cargo area.

"He's here!" Ogatu said, half out of breath. "The pilot you called—he's hovering now. But they're shooting at him!"

Bolan looked at Captain O'Haggerty, who still lay petrified on the deck. "I can't take him and Greg both," he said. "Get the captain on his feet and lead the way."

Ogatu nodded and reached down to assist O'Haggerty. Bolan saw her frown at the revolver's fallen hammer. But she knew how weapons worked as well as how to use them, because her eyes lit with understanding as she figured out what had happened. She nodded but didn't waste time with questions. Instead, she cocked the Smith & Wesson.

With O'Haggerty again in the lead, Ogatu pushed him along using the duct-taped revolver as a steering mechanism. They climbed the ladder to the main deck and were greeted by a host of rifles and pistols aimed their way.

The Executioner heard the whopping sound of rotary blades overhead and looked up to see an AH-1 Huey Cobra helicopter. Even under the circumstances, he couldn't help but smile. As always, Jack Grimaldi had come through. The ace pilot was almost as good at finding the right aircraft for a mission as he was flying them. The Huey Cobra had to have come from Koneohe or one of the other bases on Oahu.

Turning his attention to the men on deck, Bolan shouted, "Okay, listen up! It's like I said before. All the three of us want is off the ship. The captain's a little shook up but he's fine. As long as you don't try anything else stupid that gets him hurt, he'll stay alive and you'll get what you need!"

A few of the men nodded. But none of them lowered their weapons.

Bolan had the cellular phone in a back pocket and pulled it out. "Come on in, Jack," he said a few seconds later. "We're ready to get out of here."

"Yeah, me, too," Grimaldi said. "I've already taken a couple of hits."

"Anything serious?"

"No, this bird is hard to hurt."

Bolan watched the Huey Cobra drop through the sky. A few seconds later, it hovered over the ship and a line began to descend. Bolan turned to Ogatu. "Keep your finger on the trigger," he said, loud enough for the men on deck to hear. "Anybody fires, or tries anything else to stop us...pull it." To the sailors, he added, "If the captain dies, your money dies with him."

When the line from the chopper was within reach, Bolan strapped the still-unconscious Sielert into the harness attached to the end. He gave the line a tug and heard the sound of the hydraulic generator kick in. Sielert's limp form began to rise toward the helicopter.

Bolan took the grips of the revolver from Ogatu as another line and harness came down. He stared at the men around him as the detective followed Sielert into the air to disappear inside the Huey Cobra.

The Executioner took a deep breath as the third harness descended. The tricky part was coming up. As soon as he let loose of the pistol grip, he'd be fair game for the armed sailors. There would be a few seconds where he would be as easy to hit as a duck in a shooting gallery. Awkwardly, with one hand still on the revolver taped to O'Haggerty's head, he shrugged into the harness and buckled it. Then, tapping a number into the cellular phone once more, he pressed it to his lips. "Susan and Sielert inside, Jack?" he asked.

"That's affirmative, Striker," Grimaldi replied. "Safe and sound."

"Sielert still unconscious?"

"Affirmative again."

"Can you see me."

"Oh, yeah. You look like a good target to me."

"Then you know what to do."

"Yep. On the count of three. You ready?"

"I'm ready."

"One…"

Bolan took a deep breath. At the same time, he pulled his index finger out of the trigger guard of the revolver, hiding the movement from the seamen with the back of O'Haggerty's head.

"Two," Grimaldi said.

The Executioner braced himself

"Three!"

Suddenly, the Huey Cobra's engine roared like the start of the Indianapolis 500. A split second later Bolan felt the straps of the harness bite into his chest and shoulders. He was whipped away from the deck at what felt like the speed of light. For a moment, he felt as if the G-force might make him as unconscious as Greg Sielert. He had to fight to stay awake. When he regained his senses, he saw he was at least two hundred yards from the ship, flying behind the Huey Cobra at the end of the line. In the distance, he could see a few of the men on deck impotently firing their weapons. Most had been too surprised to fire.

The hydraulic system kicked in again, and Bolan felt himself being pulled up. The helicopter slowed, and he fell directly below it as it hovered. Seeing no reason to wait, he pulled the remote detonator from his pocket. With a final look at the ship, he pressed the button.

A second later, the port side of the *Nakinka Melaniya* burst into flames.

Bolan reached the Huey, and the sound of the hydraulic lift halted. Ogatu reached out, doing her best to help him inside the craft. He had just closed the door behind him when an explosion rocked the chopper, causing it to sway in the air.

The Executioner looked through the glass to see that the ship below them was completely engulfed in fire. In a seat directly behind him, Greg Sielert was beginning to stir.

"That was no nuclear explosion," Grimaldi said.

Bolan shook his head. "No, C-4 to the boilers. The nukes will sink a couple of thousand feet with the ship. They'll never be seen again."

"And you kept your word to the sailors," Ogatu said. "I noticed you kept saying things like, 'You'll get what you deserve,' and, 'You'll get what you need,' instead of, 'You'll get your money.'"

Bolan nodded.

Sielert sat up in his seat and rubbed his head.

"No chance the nukes could go off underwater?" Grimaldi asked.

Again, the Executioner's head moved back and forth. "No. They didn't even have to be disarmed. They'd never been activated."

"You sure?" Grimaldi asked, frowning.

Bolan understood why the man asked. Grimaldi was no nuclear expert. What's more, he knew Bolan wasn't, either.

"Sielert came alive down below long enough for me to ask him," the Executioner said. "Welcome back to the world, by the way, Greg."

Sielert continued to rub his head and face as his eyes struggled to focus. "Thanks," he said. "It's nice to be back." He paused a second, then added, "But that's not exactly what I said."

Bolan turned to face him. "What's not exactly what you said?"

"I said I didn't have to disarm them. But that wasn't because they'd never been activated. They *couldn't* be activated. They weren't real."

The implication hit the Executioner squarely between the eyes. "They were dummies?"

Sielert nodded.

Bolan stared at him as Sielert continued to rub his head. "Decoys," he said under his breath. The word came out softly, too low to be heard by anyone other than himself. The nukes, the captain, the crew—the whole ship—had been nothing more than a diversion.

The Executioner turned to the front of the chopper and sat back in his seat.

Grimaldi kicked the Huey Cobra into gear, and they began to fly toward Oahu as the *Nakinka Melaniya* sank into the sea behind them. There was no need to state the obvious. So Bolan didn't bother.

Neither did Detective Sergeant Susan Ogatu.

But Dr. Gregory Sielert was new at this game. And he seemed to have to put the reality of the situation into words to understand it. "That means the real nukes are still out there," he said.

No one answered.

4

A kaleidoscopic South Seas dawn had broken minutes before Jack Grimaldi set the chopper down near the docks. It was an unauthorized landing, to say the least. But the ace pilot and his passengers had scattered in different directions long before authorities heard about it.

As Mack Bolan had suspected, Grimaldi had procured the helicopter from a Koneohe Marine Base. As he, Sielert and Ogatu—who, in addition to the oversize shirt taken from the mercenary seaman, wore a pair of USMC sweatpants she had found on board—walked toward the Bonneville, the Executioner's mind raced to plan the next course of action.

Where did he go from here? He didn't know. Their one and only lead—the *Nakinka Melaniya*—had proven false. They had been carefully guided toward the ship by the skills of this Vladimir, Bolan knew, and the decoy had proven effective. If nothing else, it had wasted their time while the PFF took possession of the real nuclear bombs.

As they neared the Bonneville, Bolan reached up and rubbed his face. In doing so, he pushed such negative thoughts from his mind. There was another lead somewhere. Something he had overlooked. Something he couldn't think of in his present state of mental fatigue. But his mind would clear. It would come to him.

It always did.

The Executioner reached into his pocket as they neared the Bonneville, pulled out the key ring and tapped the door lock button. He heard a click as the driver's side door disconnected, pushed the button again and heard the other three doors unlock. Sliding behind the wheel, he watched Ogatu get in next to him as Sielert took a seat in the back.

A dark silence permeated the car as the Executioner drove away from the docks. It was a time for thinking rather than talking. Thirty minutes later, he pulled into the parking lot of the Honolulu Police Department and threw the transmission into park. He turned to Ogatu.

Her voice was weary. "Where will I locate you?" She reached for the door handle.

"We've got reservations at the Hilton Hawaiian Village," Bolan said. "What do you have to do now?"

The cop had obviously been considering her next course of action during the drive. She answered immediately. "I'm going inside, taking a shower and changing into something a little more presentable," she said, glancing at the soiled khaki shirt and sweatpants. "I keep an overnight bag packed in my locker." She paused, took a deep breath, then added, "And I'm going to fill out the necessary paperwork for taking a few days off." She paused again. "I've got the feeling we're going to be doing all kinds of things that don't exactly fall within the guidelines of the HPD policy manual. If I do it on company time, I'll be easier to trace."

"Any of this bothering you?" Bolan asked.

"You mean violating the rights of everyone we bump into or running around naked?" she asked, smiling.

"The first."

"Shooting a few bad guys doesn't bother me," the female detective answered honestly. "Not if it means keeping a million innocent people from getting blown to hell." She hesitated a moment, then added. "It's not like the people we've shot just stepped out of Sunday school."

"No, it's not," Bolan said. "We'll call you when we get settled at the Hilton. I need to do a little planning."

Ogatu nodded, opened the door and disappeared into the building.

Another half hour and Bolan was pulling the Bonneville into a slot in the parking garage at the Hilton Hawaiian Village. He and Sielert—who had dozed in the back seat most of the way—exited the vehicle. The Executioner popped the trunk with the remote, then dug through the contents. Transferring several items from bag to bag, he condensed what he needed, then slid his arm into the strap of a nonconspicuous soft-sided leather suitcase. Sielert pulled out his bag and the Executioner slammed the trunk.

Bolan led the way through a labyrinth of tourist shops selling everything from overpriced Aloha shirts to jewelry and Beanie Babies. The shops formed the outer perimeter of the village, and they crossed a street toward the tall towers where the rooms were located. A huge bar with wicker furniture and every imaginable Hawaiian trapping beneath its hundred-foot-high ceiling had to be traversed before they reached the lobby.

The soldier glanced around at the seemingly endless luxury as he set his bag down in front of the desk. He rarely stayed in such places, and the extravagance meant nothing to him. But he and Sielert were playing tourists on this mission, and their choice of accommodation had to fit the part.

"Belasko," Bolan said as soon as the hotel clerk asked if he could help them. "Two rooms." He handed the man a credit card that bore the alias.

As soon as the paperwork was complete, the clerk handed Bolan one key and gave the other to Sielert. The two men followed the bellhop to the elevator, then exited on the sixth floor. Bolan entered his room, tipped the man who had carried his bag, then walked to the window as soon as the door had closed. He pulled the curtains open and looked onto the beach.

It wasn't even midmorning but the tourists were already in full swing. Men, women and children covered the white sands of the beach, lying on towels or reclining chairs. Others played Frisbee or badminton while a few windsurfed in the waters beyond. High in the air, the soldier could see a parasailer beneath the brightly colored canopy that held him aloft.

The Executioner took a rare moment to appreciate the beauty before him. But a rare moment was all he had for such things. He had work to do. And if he didn't get to it, *no one* would be appreciating such beauty much longer.

Leaving the curtains open to let the sunshine in, Bolan

moved to the bed where the bellhop had left his suitcase. He took out his shaving kit and fresh clothes, then opened the door to the bathroom and turned on the shower.

The soldier had just finished his shower and was halfway through shaving when he heard a knock from the bedroom. Wrapping a towel around his waist, he walked to the door to the adjoining room.

"Mike?" A voice came through the door.

Bolan threw back the lock and twisted the knob. Dr. Gregory Sielert entered and took a seat at the table by the window. The scientist had covered the side of his head with disinfectant, then covered all but the edge of the red-orange paint job with white gauze and adhesive tape. The ricochet wound hadn't been deep, and Bolan knew the bandage could be removed soon.

"Nice digs, huh?" Sielert said.

Bolan nodded silently. "Give me a second," he said, then returned to the bathroom and hurriedly finished his shave.

Returning to the bedroom, the soldier slipped into a clean pair of blue jeans but left the colorful Hawaiian shirt he had taken from the suitcase on the bed. He produced a gun-cleaning kit and several rags from the suitcase and set them on the bedspread next to the folded shirt. Quickly, he slipped the Beretta 93-R's shoulder rig over his bare skin, then picked the Desert Eagle up off the desk where he'd set it earlier.

"Good idea," Sielert said, his eyes on the gun-cleaning kit. He rose, disappeared to his room, and returned carrying his Colt Gold Cup. As the scientist sat down, Bolan saw him staring at the scars that covered the Executioner's chest between the Beretta under his left arm and the spare magazine carrier under his right.

"Yeah, I'd say you've seen a little action in your time," Sielert said respectfully.

Bolan saw no reason to answer. He dropped the magazine from the Desert Eagle, then worked the slide to eject the chambered round. With his thumb, he snapped the other eight rounds from the mag and let them fall onto the bed. He left the Beretta where it was, as it was. It was an old habit. The

Executioner never cleaned one of the weapons without leaving the other with a full load of rounds.

As he went to work cleaning the Desert Eagle, Bolan let his thoughts drift around the problem at hand. Okay, there was another lead to follow. What was it?

He began again. The Ukrainian ship had been a red herring. The real bombs—

He was interrupted by Sielert. "Mike, let me see if I can get all this straight in my head," the scientist said.

Bolan looked up to see the man wiping down the frame of his Gold Cup. "Go ahead," he said.

"The Ukrainian ship was just to throw us, or anybody who might have heard about what was going on, off. Right?"

The soldier nodded.

"So that means the real nukes are still out there somewhere? In the hands of the PFF?"

Bolan lifted the empty Desert Eagle magazine and began cleaning off the residue that had built up at the lips. "If not already in their hands, they soon will be."

The scientist stood, crossed the room, picked several items from the cleaning kit and returned to his seat. "So," he said. "I guess the sixty-four-thousand-dollar question is, what do we do next?"

"That's what I've been trying to figure out, Greg."

"Oh...sorry," Sielert said sheepishly.

The soldier shook his head. "Keep talking. Maybe it'll jog something."

"Well, as I see it," Sielert began, "if they used a ship as a decoy, does that mean they used another ship for the real nukes?"

"Not necessarily," Bolan said. "Could be a plane, but I doubt it. My money is on another ship."

"Why?" Sielert asked.

"Because a plane is too risky," he said. "There are a limited number of places to land. And even the remote islands are monitored by radar."

"I don't know that much about radar," Sielert said as he folded a small white patch, then slid it through the eye at the end of the cleaning rod. "But can't they monitor the ships, too?"

"Yeah. But not as easily. There are hundreds of craft coming in and out of these islands every day."

Somewhere on the perimeter of his conscious mind, a thought suddenly struck the soldier. It floated there to tantalize him, as yet unwilling to surface and allow itself to be defined.

"So you think the nukes came in by boat?" Sielert said.

"That's my guess. I'm not ruling anything out at this point." The unformed abstract thought continued to float with maddening elusiveness through his unconscious mind.

"Well, it's just too bad that guy—Buck whatever his name was—didn't know more. If he'd been higher up on the PFF's ladder—"

Suddenly, Bolan's mind cleared. That was it. The key the Executioner's mind had been trying to identify.

Buck Kalakaua. He was *not* some low-level errand boy for the Polynesian Freedom Fighters. He was a carefully planted decoy, placed so he'd further the ruse of the Ukrainian ship and keep any suspicious minds busy at the harbor while the real nukes were unloaded elsewhere.

Quickly, Bolan finished cleaning the Desert Eagle, reassembled it and loaded it. He jerked the Beretta from his shoulder holster, pulled back the slide for a quick inspection, then let it fall forward. It was good for a few hundred rounds. More if necessary.

The Executioner stood as he replaced the 93-R under his arm.

"You think of something?" Sielert asked.

"I did," Bolan said. He pulled the Aloha shirt over his head and jammed the Desert Eagle into his belt as he hurried toward the door.

"Where are we going?" Sielert asked, following.

"To talk to Buck Kalakaua again."

"But he doesn't know anything he didn't already tell us," Sielert said as Bolan opened the door.

"I think he does."

BENJAMIN LIHOLIHO tapped the huge wooden club lightly against his thigh. There were ancient shark's teeth embedded in the wooden weapon. A soft breeze tickled his legs beneath the faded denim shorts he wore. Across the gently lapping waves, he could see the anchored yacht. A huge eighty-foot luxury craft, it had been stolen by Vladimir Syvatoslav and his men off the coast of France and was manned by Syvatoslav's Ukrainian and Russian mercenaries during the voyage to the islands.

Liholiho let his eyes drift. A rough asphalt road had been cut through the jagged lava shore, with a short T turnout extending into the water. The T was a launching site for small boats. But this was a remote area of the Hawaiis' largest island, Hawaii, and difficult to get to, even on the rugged road. The lava beds were a tempting location for tourists, and an interesting blowhole—shooting its stream of seawater straight into the air every few minutes—stood a hundred yards in the distance, just inland off the sea. But there were similar and far more accessible sites a few miles away. During the six months his men had kept this area under surveillance, it had been used only twice. By them. On practice runs.

The leader of the Polynesian Freedom Fighters could see his own shadow and the moving silhouette of the shark-tooth club. The shadows formed zigzag patterns on the ground. For perhaps the thousandth time, the leader of the PFF wondered briefly who had made the primitive weapon he tapped against his leg. The shark tooth club had been in his family for close to two hundred years, and while its history hadn't been forgotten, it had been embellished to the point where it might as well have been. There were at least a dozen versions of the story of its origin floating around within Liholiho's extended family. Each account portrayed the club's maker as a direct ancestor of that branch of the family, and each account claimed the creator had used the club to kill both members of rival Polynesian tribes and the white invaders who infested the South Seas like cockroaches.

Liholiho smiled. The true history of the weapon was there— somewhere. That he know precise details was not important.

What was meaningful was what the club signified. Freedom. Independence. Autonomy. Not only for him but for all his fellow Polynesians. The club was symbolic of the rejection of all things that had come from Europe and America. It represented a rejection of all things white and a return of the islands to those who rightfully owned them.

The tall Polynesian heard a soft cough next to him. He turned to see Vladimir Syvatoslav. The Ukrainian, a high-ranking former Soviet KGB officer, had walked silently up to him. Syvatoslav wore the brown slacks from his usual suit but had doffed his jacket and tie. Instead, a short-sleeved white shirt, open at the collar, covered his protruding belly. Sweat ran down the sides of the old man's neck, soaking the underarms of his shirt. The tails of the shirt were tucked into his waistband, and just above it, Liholiho could see the grip of a small AMT backup .45 pistol.

Liholiho turned slightly and smiled at his shorter friend. "Lasso," he said. "I have never seen you carry the same gun twice."

Syvatoslav chuckled, then glanced to the revolver on Liholiho's hip. "And before today, I have never seen you carry a gun at all," he said.

The PFF leader shrugged. "The time has come," he said offhandedly.

Syvatoslav nodded. "I have always been forced to view weapons—guns, knives, whatever—as a perishable commodity," he said. "Once used, they should be discarded. It is a mistake to grow too attached to any one." He paused, pulled a handkerchief from his back pocket and mopped his forehead. "At least that has always been my philosophy—and that has allowed me to grow old."

Liholiho nodded. "Yes, Vlad," he said. "But there are exceptions." He held the shark-tooth club in front of him.

Syvatoslav smiled beneath the handkerchief above his brows. "That is not a weapon," he said. "It is an icon."

Liholiho agreed. "True. A symbol. A symbol of the culture my people once had here. And a symbol of freedom. A freedom we are about to take back." He paused, turning to face the man squarely. "Much as your own people took back their long-lost freedom which the Russians had stolen."

"I have never doubted that you would," Syvatoslav said. He stuffed the damp handkerchief into his pocket. "But I'm happy to see you won't try to do so with the club. It was just such discrepancy in weaponry that allowed the Americans to steal your homeland in the first place."

The leader of the Polynesian Freedom Fighters moved his hand to the huge revolver hanging from his belt. A double-action Taurus Raging Bull with a five-inch recoil-compensated barrel. "Yes. We'll use the Americans' own weapons against them." He paused, then grinned and looked toward the anchored yacht. "But compared to the weapons we are about to take possession of," he added, "this, too, is merely an icon." He tapped the Taurus.

Syvatoslav smiled as he glanced toward an incoming raft. "Indeed it is," he said.

Behind him, Liholiho heard the roar of a large engine. He turned to see a flatbed truck with a crane bolted to the bed coming down the road. The driver followed the rugged road, finally grinding the gears to a halt just behind where Liholiho and Syvatoslav stood.

The leader of the PFF walked up to the window as the driver rolled it down. "Back in as close to the shoreline as you can," he ordered.

The driver rolled the window up, turned the truck around and began backing it toward the water. Liholiho assisted, waving the driver on with a hand, then finally holding it up, palm out, to signal him to stop. As the man killed the engine, the PFF leader walked to Syvatoslav.

"Aha!" the Ukrainian said. "Look." He pointed out to sea.

Liholiho followed the man's finger and saw what appeared to be a large fishing boat appear on the horizon. As the incoming raft neared them, the fishing boat sailed toward the anchored ship.

"What is it the Americans say about chickens in a basket?" Syvatoslav asked.

"It is not chickens, Lasso, it is eggs," answered Liholiho.

"The saying is, 'Never put all of your eggs in one basket.' That way if one basket falls to the ground and they break, at least the others are saved."

"Well," said Syvatoslav, smiling, "here comes our other basket." He pointed toward the fishing boat, then turned his attention to the incoming raft. "As soon as this device is unloaded and on its way, we will be free to meet the men in the fishing boat and oversee the installation of the smaller bomb."

Liholiho nodded. But a feeling of uneasiness had crept through his soul. "Vlad?" he asked. "You have done this sort of work far longer than I have. So I would like your opinion. Do you think it will be necessary to detonate the smaller bomb?" Again, he looked at the fishing boat, which hadn't slowed as it approached the yacht.

Syvatoslav didn't hesitate. "Oh, yes," he said, in the tone of a man about to yawn. "Of that I have no doubt. When the Americans receive your demands there will be much posturing on their parts. There will be declarations that they never deal with terrorists, which is what they will call you. But of course they *do* deal—they do it every day—all over the world. They won't capitulate to your demands, however, until they have seen that you have the capability to carry through with your threats." He mopped sweat from his forehead again, then spoke. "It is somewhat like their own traffic lights and stop signs."

Liholiho frowned, confused. "I don't understand," he said.

Syvatoslav returned the handkerchief to his pocket once more. "I have heard it said by Americans that their government never installs traffic lights or stop signs where they are needed until after several people have been killed there in car wrecks."

Liholiho grunted. "That is more of a dismal joke than a reality," he said. "But I see your point." He watched the fishing boat close on the anchored yacht. A line was thrown. "But what we have planned will kill more people than a few simple car wrecks. So let's hope it doesn't come to that."

Syvatoslav shrugged. "It may not. The first bomb will kill only a few people, if any. And once the Americans see that you are serious, perhaps they will listen to reason. As you yourself mentioned a moment ago, even the Soviet Union finally gave in to our own demands.''

Liholiho nodded as he watched the raft touch shore. Several of his men began working straps beneath a heavy wooden crate. Other men attached the straps to the crane. The PFF leader glanced at Syvatoslav.

Until six months ago, Liholiho would never have dreamed that any white man could understand how he and the other members of the Polynesian Freedom Fighters had been enslaved ever since the first missionaries arrived on the islands. But Syvatoslav, a Ukrainian, had grown up under Soviet rule—Russian rule, to be accurate. Like all Ukrainians, he had resented the takeover of his homeland by Ukraine's age-old next-door enemy, just as Liholiho and his comrades still cursed every white who had landed in the South Seas since the arrival of Captain James Cook. But Syvatoslav had taken a different route to free his people, working his way up through the KGB until he reached a level of influence. Then, when the time had become right, he had played a major part in the fall of the Soviet Union. He and other men like him from other countries enslaved by the Russians had killed the enemy from within.

The PFF had chosen a more direct approach. They would kill the enemy from without. But the result would be the same.

"We'll see what happens," Liholiho said. "Either Washington will accede to our demands, or millions of people will die. Regrettable, but necessary." The sound of the crane lifting the crate onto the truck made conversation impossible. Both men took one final look out to sea and saw the fishing boat speeding away from the yacht. "Come!" Liholiho shouted. He turned and started toward the line of cars that had brought the PFF men to this isolated spot. He stopped one of his men as they crossed paths, grabbed his shoulder and shouted into his ear. "Get rid of the raft! Take it away—far away. We have no further need of it but I don't want it found."

The man nodded his understanding and went on.

Liholiho and Syvatoslav opened the doors to a late model Chevrolet. Syvatoslav took the wheel and started the engine.

The cranking of the crane was only a dull roar through the windows. "There are American agents in Honolulu," the former KGB man said.

Liholiho turned to face him, draping an arm over the seat. "Then you were right," he said. "The American intelligence network somehow got word of what we were doing."

Syvatoslav's head bobbed lightly. "As I warned you, that was to be expected. Something this major can never be completely hidden—the Americans may be evil but they aren't stupid. The agents boarded our decoy ship last night, forced it into open waters, then sank it."

"Did they learn that the bombs on board weren't real?" Liholiho asked quickly.

Syvatoslav shrugged. "I don't know at this point. But we should operate as if they did." He paused, wiped sweat from his face one final time, then reached to turn the air conditioner on high. Blasts of frigid air blew from the vents. "The fact that the bombs weren't announced to the public leads me to believe that they know they were fakes. If they believed they had actually captured two nuclear weapons, it would have been on the news. The Americans are never slow to take credit for their victories. But they are never quick to admit when they have been made to look like fools."

Liholiho had laid the shark-tooth club across his lap when he got into the car. He gripped the handle. "What do you think will be their next move?"

Syvatoslav's heavy eyebrows lowered. "They interviewed your man—this Buck Kalakaua. They will return to him."

"He won't say anymore," Liholiho said.

Syvatoslav turned in his seat. "Why are you so sure? I attempted to learn the identities of the three agents who sank the ship. One is a local female police detective. My guess is that she is only the local contact for the other two."

"And the other two?"

"One is a nuclear scientist. Dr. Gregory Sielert. But the

third I couldn't identify. Neither my contacts in Ukrainian nor Russian intelligence have any record of him.''

Liholiho gripped the club tighter. ''What does that mean?'' he asked.

''It means that he is probably a free agent.''

''And that in turn means...''

''That he won't play by the usual rules that keep the hands of American interrogators tied. He may beat, or otherwise torture, more information out of Kalakaua.''

The last comment brought a smile to Liholiho's face. ''I don't think that will be a problem,'' he said. The smile widened. ''You're very good at what you do, my friend,'' he told Syvatoslav. ''But do you think you're the *only* competent man?''

Syvatoslav's eyebrows furrowed even more.

''Kalakaua wasn't the only man I planted in the Honolulu jail.''

A sudden excited shout from outside the car turned both men's attention to the windshield. They saw that the crate had been loaded onto the flatbed truck and covered with a canvas canopy. The truck was pulling away. A pickup, towing a boat trailer, had backed into the slot where the truck had been. The speedboat that had towed the raft was tied to the trailer and being pulled out of the water.

But that wasn't what had brought the exclamation.

Along the shore, all the men who had helped load the truck and speedboat were staring across the water. In the distance, Liholiho could see a U.S. Coast Guard vessel sailing toward the anchored yacht.

Syvatoslav reached across the seat and patted the big Polynesian on the knee. ''Don't worry, my friend,'' he said. ''The fishing vessel with the other bomb is long gone.''

''But they will capture the crew on the yacht,'' Liholiho said. ''I am *certain* that Kalakaua won't talk. But what of your men?''

''The Americans already know that the bombs are on the islands,'' Syvatoslav said. ''And my crew knows nothing more of value to them.'' He chuckled, waited for the flatbed truck to pass them on the road, then threw the Chevrolet into gear.

Liholiho stared at the man as they fell in behind the truck and started away from shore. "How can you be sure none of them overheard something? Or picked up on some small detail that might lead the Americans to us?''

Syvatoslav twisted the wheel slightly. "They might have,'' he agreed. "It is not only possible, it is likely. Which is why I took other precautions.''

Liholiho frowned, waiting for further explanation.

"None of my crew will live long enough to be questioned.'' Syvatoslav said. "I joined them on board the yacht for breakfast this morning. Before you and your men arrived.'' A wicked smirk curled the corners of his lips as he drove on. "Of course I, myself, wasn't hungry.''

DETECTIVE SERGEANT Susan Ogatu's hair was still damp by the time Bolan and Sielert returned to the Honolulu P.D. headquarters building. She was dressed in another of the stark, nononsense blue jackets and skirts that did little, if anything, to hide her femininity.

The same female officer was at the reception window. She recognized Special Agent Belasko and buzzed Bolan and Sielert through the door with a smile. Ogatu sat tapping the keys of a computer keyboard when they entered her office.

Bolan quickly explained what he and Sielert had discussed after checking into the Hilton.

She nodded. "Reinterviewing Kalakaua is about all we have to go on at this point,'' she agreed. She glanced at the computer. "I'm now officially off duty for the next two weeks. But I've just requested notification if any—'' She quit speaking as footsteps sounded just outside the door in the hall. A young man in his mid-twenties wearing stiffly starched blue slacks and a lighter blue sports coat stepped into the office. Ogatu's face showed relief, and she continued. "This is Detective Mark Sastre,'' she said, then introduced Bolan as "Mike Belasko'' and Greg Sielert as himself. "Mark just recently got out of uniform. Like I was about to say, I've requested notification of any entry into the islands by air or sea that seems suspicious. Mark will be checking the screen for me while we're gone, and I'll stay in contact with him.'' She paused.

Bolan took the opportunity to glance at Sastre. The younger man's face beamed with delight, and it wasn't just the aftermath of his recent promotion. His eyes were glued to the beautiful woman at the computer like those of a lovesick teenager. The soldier smiled to himself. The kid had it *bad*. And he couldn't blame him.

"Glad to be of help," Sastre said without taking his eyes off Ogatu. "You have a number where I can reach you?"

She shook her head. "I'll call you, Mark," she said. Then, lowering her voice to a deep, husky whisper, she added, "And I don't guess I have to repeat that this is just between you and me." She winked at the younger man.

Bolan hadn't thought it possible, but Sastre's face glowed even brighter.

Turning to Bolan, Ogatu said, "So, let's go back upstairs and get our man out of his cell, shall we?"

Bolan, Sielert and Ogatu passed the stairs they had climbed during the attempted jailbreak the day before and took the elevator. Just outside the bars in front of the jail office, they stuffed their weapons into the lock boxes and pocketed the keys to the small cubicles.

The head jailer sat at a green metal desk inside the office. An older man, he might as well have had "retired cop" written across his forehead.

"Help you, Susan?" the head jailer asked, his eyes riveted to her breasts the way Mark Sastre's had been glued to her face.

"Yeah, Leo," Ogatu said. "Can you get Kalakaua out again? We'd like to see him in the interview room."

"Sure thing," the man said. "He's in one of the ten-man cells." He swiveled in his chair toward a bank of video screens along the wall next to the desk. Punching a button on the console just below them, he stared upward.

Bolan, Sielert and Ogatu watched the camera attached to

one of the screens zoom in closer to several prisoners seated
around a steel table bolted to the concrete floor of their cell.
They were all dressed in ill-fitting bright orange coveralls and
looked to be playing some kind of card game.

"Huh," Leo said. "Can't see him." He turned back to the
desk, lifted the telephone receiver, and tapped a button. A
moment later he said, "Brownie, did you lock the door to the
bunk room in cell fourteen this morning?"

Bolan understood the question. Most multiprisoner jail cells
across America were divided into two sections separated by a
set of bars. One side was the day room, with tables and
benches, where prisoners were housed during the day. This
kept them from sleeping all day, then raising hell all night
when the jail staff was light.

Leo frowned, said, "Okay," into the phone, replaced the
receiver and stood. "He must be sitting on the floor in the
dead zone."

"That's an area in each cell just below the camera's eye,"
Ogatu explained.

Leo picked up the phone again. "Keep an eye on things,
will you, Brownie? I'm going to take Susan and her friends
up and get Kalakaua out for a few minutes."

After hanging up, Leo turned and stuck one of the keys into
the lock of a barred gate that led from the office into the
trustees' quarters. He led them past the kitchen to a set of
steps, where he unlocked another door to the cells. Behind
him, Bolan, Sielert and Ogatu mounted the stairs to another
locked set of bars, then emerged into an open area that led to
the cell runs.

The door leading to the ten-man felony cells was solid steel,
rather than barred. A small window, shielded by an opaque
cover, was set in the upper half of the entry. Leo swung the
cover back on its hinges and stared down the run for several
seconds. "Can't be too careful with these guys," he said over
his shoulder.

Satisfied that the run was clear, the head jailer unlocked the
door. He led them down the run amid the hooting and hollering of the men caged behind the bars—a hooting and hollering

that increased when Susan Ogatu came into view. Rude suggestions of sex acts the prisoners would like to perform on the beautiful female detective flew through the bars like swarms of predatory birds.

Ogatu seemed not to notice, but at one point Leo stopped and said, "Randall, you, Babcock and the rest of you other filthy bastards keep talking like that, you'll find yourselves in maximum security without any blankets or mattresses."

The cells quieted. At least partially.

Cell fourteen was at the end of the run, and Leo reached it a few seconds before the Executioner. Bolan almost ran into the elderly man's back as the head jailer froze in place.

"Oh, my God." The words came from the old man's lips.

"What?" Susan Ogatu said behind the Executioner.

Bolan pushed Leo gently to the side and stepped around him. Through the bars, he could see the men seated at the table playing cards he had just seen on the video screen downstairs. The Executioner's eyes moved past them to the corner of the day room, where bars separated the tables from the steel bunks on the other side. Just this side of the bars, in the corner of the gray concrete wall behind the men and protected by a steel screen, Bolan saw the lens of the camera that transmitted the picture to the jail office.

And directly below the camera's eye, in the dead zone, was James Buck Kalakaua. But the Polynesian Freedom Fighter wasn't sitting on the floor, as Leo had guessed.

He was hanging from the top of the bars, suspended in the air with a strip of blanket tied tightly around his neck.

5

Leo pulled a small walkie-talkie from his belt, held it to his lips and pressed the button on the side. "J-1 to all J units. Code red." Although his voice remained relatively calm, his face turned red as he repeated the words into the radio.

A few seconds later, quick footsteps sounded at the end of the run. Excited voices could be heard, and then a dozen or so men, all wearing uniforms like Leo's, crowded in front of cell fourteen.

By then, the head jailer had regained most of his composure. "You men!" he yelled through the bars. "On your feet."

The prisoners on the other side of the bars stood up from around the tables. Without being told, they shuffled toward the front of the cell.

Beyond the bars, between the men and the open run, was a gate that led to the bunk side of the divided cell. Leo stuck a large key into a steel box mounted on the bars, swung open the door, then pushed another button. A buzzer sounded, then the door to the bunks opened. The prisoners shuffled through.

"Hurry up, damn you!" Leo called. Bolan could see that he wanted to get into the cell as quickly as possible, on the off chance that the man hanging from the bars could be revived. But the soldier could see from Buck Kalakaua's face that the chance for that had long since passed. As soon as all the prisoners were in the bunk room, Leo opened the barred gate leading inside and sprinted toward the rear of the cell.

Bolan followed. Had there been a chance to save the hanging prisoner, he would have been first. No one wanted Buck Kalakaua alive more than he did. Kalakaua's feet were barely off the ground, and his eyes stared wildly into space. His tongue protruded from his lips in a caricature of suicide. The Executioner reached up and grabbed a wrist. What he found confirmed what he already knew.

There was no pulse. The man was dead and had been for some time.

Bolan stepped back and let two of the younger jailers move forward. One had brought a small footstool with him, and he set it on the floor and stepped up. The other wrapped his arms around Buck Kalakaua's legs, lifting the body slightly to create slack while his partner untied the blanket. A few moments later, the PFF man was stretched out on the floor.

"Okay, everybody back," Leo said. He turned to one of the guards. "Better go notify the chief," he said, his face a mask of worry. The man pivoted and took off.

Leo turned to the bunks behind the bars. Most of the men sat or reclined on their mattresses. "Why didn't you stop him?" he demanded. "Why didn't you notify me?"

Some of the men shrugged disinterestedly. Others didn't respond at all.

Leo's gaze fell on a small man with orange hair. "Brick Top, dammit," he said. "What happened?"

The orange-haired man had a Brooklyn accent. "I didn't see nuttin'," he said. "I was takin' a piss." He pointed through the bars toward the steel toilet on the opposite wall.

While Leo continued to ask questions and get evasive answers and blank stares, the Executioner knelt by the body on the floor. James Buck Kalakaua hadn't committed suicide. Of that, he was certain. And the Polynesian man was big—he wouldn't have gone down easily. But a black and blue bruise on Kalakaua's chin was the only mark on his face, and that had been left by the Executioner's own fist just after the jailbreak attempt. There was no other sign of struggle. At least on the front of Kalakaua's body.

Bolan rolled the dead man onto his face. One of the jailers said, "Hey, we ain't supposed to touch them after we cut them down. Not till the chief—"

"Shut up," the soldier said simply. The man did.

Kalakaua's hair was long and fell nearly halfway down his back. Bolan pulled the greasy mass to the side. Beneath the hair, he saw what he was looking for. At the base of the dead man's neck was a bright red splotch. The blow had come from behind and had been delivered recently. It hadn't had time to darken.

Silently, the Executioner nodded. Buck Kalakaua had either been knocked out or knocked silly. He'd been unconscious or semiconscious and had put up no resistance while parties unknown tied the strip of blanket around his throat and hoisted him into the air.

Bolan had seen enough.

A man wearing a gray business suit and steel eyeglasses, somewhere in his mid-fifties, came walking swiftly down the run. He was followed by an entourage of younger men dressed similarly. The jailers in the cell parted as if Moses himself had waved his rod.

The Honolulu Chief of Police stopped next to the body on the floor. "What the hell happened here, Leo?" he demanded.

"Suicide, sir," Leo said sheepishly. "Done it right below the camera where we couldn't see."

The chief turned to glower at the bunks, then at the head jailer. He started to speak, then noticed Bolan and Sielert. "Who the hell are these men?" he asked.

Leo sputtered. Ogatu stepped forward and said, "Justice Department, Chief Johnston. They came in with me to interview the man."

Johnston's eyes softened as they fell on Susan Ogatu. "What about?"

Bolan took the lead. "Just some cases back on the mainland," he said. "Looks like they're cleared up now." He glanced at the body.

Chief Johnston whirled toward one of the men who had followed him into the cell. "Get the medical examiner up here," he barked. "And assign the investigation to someone." He glanced at the bunks once more. "Every one of you sons of bitches knows what happened in here, and we're going to find out."

Bolan watched the noncommittal stares of the prisoners. They knew what had happened, all right. And through either threat or reward, at least one of them would probably eventually talk. If the Executioner could have gotten them alone privately...but that wasn't going to happen now—not with the chief personally interested in the investigation. What would take place would be a long, tedious and possibly fruitless series of interrogations.

Yes, the important thing, Bolan thought sarcastically, would be that the miscreants on the other side of the divided cell didn't get their rights violated.

The chief turned to Leo. "Get all of these bastards loaded up and throw them in the hole," he said.

Groans, curses and a few threats issued from the other side of the bars.

"Shut up!" Johnston yelled. "We'll take you out individually. Whether or not you go back depends on how cooperative you are." Whirling on his heels, he strode out of the cell and down the run, once more tailed by his convoy of nervous sycophants.

Bolan took Ogatu's arm and looked at Sielert. "Let's get out of here," he said. He led the scientist and detective out of the cell and started to walk past the bunk area, stopping suddenly. Through the bars, he saw a large Polynesian man sitting on a bunk. He was one of the men who had been seated at the table when they'd arrived, but Bolan couldn't remember seeing him when he'd viewed the scene through the video camera in the jail office.

The man stared at the Executioner without emotion. He was sitting on his hands, hiding them between his thighs and the mattress. And he was big enough to have delivered a blow such as the one that had rendered Kalakaua helpless enough to be hanged.

"You know that guy's name?" Bolan asked Ogatu.

The detective shook her head. "But that's easy enough to find out."

"Not now," Bolan said. "Downstairs. In your office."

Ogatu gave him a quizzical look but didn't say anything more.

The soldier turned and led the way out of the run, down the steps and through the jail office. They retrieved their guns from the lockers and got onto the elevator. Not until the doors had closed did Bolan speak. "The big guy I pointed out," he said. "The one whose name I want you to find. He's the one who killed Kalakaua."

Ogatu frowned. "How do you know that?"

"He was sitting on his hands," Bolan said. "My guess is that was to hide a scrape or bruise he got when he hit Kalakaua in the back of the head."

"Then why don't we grab him right now?" she asked.

The Executioner shook his head. "We thought there was one PFF plant. Now we find out there were two—one to kill Kalakaua if we figured him out."

"And if there were two, there could be three?"

"Or more," Bolan said. "Wait until they're all isolated in max. Until then, anything could happen."

Sielert had remained quiet since seeing the hanging body. His face was as pale as the Sheetrock in Ogatu's office. He spoke as if he felt it was his turn and he needed to join in. "So...what do we do until we talk to this...new guy?"

The elevator doors opened. Ogatu started to step off. A figure appeared in her way. Mark Sastre.

The unexpected sighting of his fantasy woman caused the man to stop as if he'd been hit in the face. But he recovered quickly. "Glad I caught you, Susan," he said. "I was afraid you'd left."

Ogatu stepped off the elevator, followed by Bolan and Sielert. "What have you got, Mark?"

The young detective had been holding a sheet of printer paper at his side. He lifted it and handed it to Susan Ogatu.

Bolan looked over her shoulder to read it with her. Ogatu glanced at him, smiled, then went on reading. When they were both done, she handed the page to Sielert so he could take his turn.

Sielert glanced at the page quickly, then looked up. "The

Coast Guard found an abandoned yacht anchored off the Big
Island?'' he said.

Bolan shook his head. "Not actually abandoned. Read on.''

The scientist looked at the paper. His face had been pale.
Now it seemed to turn translucent. "Well.'' He managed to
choke the word out. "I guess that answers my question about
what we do next.''

The Executioner nodded. Hurrying past the love-stricken
Sastre, he led the way out of the building to the Bonneville.
The notification Susan Ogatu had received said the Coast
Guard had found a crewless yacht just off Hawaii's largest
land mass, the island of Hawaii. But the yacht wasn't crewless
because it had been abandoned.

All of the men on board were dead.

Bolan tapped the remote, opened the Bonneville's door and
slid in behind the wheel. It would take a doctor to tell for sure.
But Coast Guard officials said it looked as if the crew had
been poisoned.

THE LARGEST of the land masses that made up the Hawaiian
chain was known as Hawaii, although most natives and tourists referred to it as the Big Island. Sparsely populated compared to Oahu or Maui, it was far superior to the more inhab-
ited islands in pastoral variety. Volcanic craters, silently
suggesting the mysteries of the ages, covered the island. A
visitor to one of the large cattle ranches, complete with cow-
boys known as *paniolo,* might well have mistaken his global
position for Texas. Orchid farms were prevalent, and Hawaii's
shorelines were a near psychedelic combination of white coral,
black lava and green olivine beaches.

No, Bolan thought as Jack Grimaldi brought the AH-1 Huey
Cobra down on an asphalt road that had been sheared through
the black lava coastline, the Big Island was almost a different
world altogether than the Hawaii he, Sielert and Ogatu had
left. Oahu was for the tame tourist who wanted beauty but
also needed constant reassurance that he was still safely en-
compassed by civilization. Honolulu and Waikiki were for vis-

itors who needed to see the golden arches of a McDonald's to
be comfortable.

The Big Island was for the adventurous wayfarer. It was for
the men and women who wanted to leave civilization behind
and see the South Pacific that had been there long before any
man had set foot on its rugged shorelines. The Big Island
catered to people who wanted to camp on isolated beaches,
hike into volcanic craters or explore the Kau Forest Reserve
and Ola'a rain forest.

The Big Island attracted those who had no interest in watching Don Ho sing "Tiny Bubbles" and for whom the daily
grind of modern life had already forced too many Big Macs
down their throats.

Grimaldi set the skids of the helicopter smoothly on the
asphalt. "Want me to wait?" he shouted over the whirl of the
overhead blades.

Bolan opened the door and nodded. "Don't know how long
we'll be," he yelled. "Depends on what we find."

"You got it," Grimaldi shouted. He pulled a paperback
novel from the canvas bag at his feet as the chopper's blades
began to slow.

Ogatu and Sielert dropped from the Huey Cobra carrying
equipment bags. Bolan grabbed his own bags and stepped
away from the helicopter. Several hundred yards out across
the gently lapping blue waves, he could see the yacht. A half
dozen Coast Guard boats were tethered to the rails and had
been joined by several Hawaiian state police craft. Moving
forms, tiny in the distance, roamed the deck. The Executioner
dropped his backpack to the ground, bent at the knees and
retrieved a pair of binoculars. Through the lenses he could
make out the Coast Guard uniforms and dark blue raid coveralls worn by the state police.

Sticking his head into the chopper, Bolan said, "Jack, get
on the horn and have them send a boat in for us."

Grimaldi dropped the paperback and reached for the radio
mike mounted in front of him. "What's your cover story?"
he asked.

"The usual," Bolan replied. He waited while Grimaldi found the Coast Guard frequency.

His transmission was finally answered by a Captain Abbott. "Captain," Grimaldi said. "I've got two Justice Department agents and a Honolulu detective who need to come onboard. I don't think they like the idea of swimming."

Static peppered the airwaves for a moment, then Abbott came back. "We've already got too many people out here," he said. "Including more DEA and BATF agents than I can shake a stick at. We're in danger of trampling out any trace evidence we might find. Tell them they'll have to wait."

Grimaldi looked to the Executioner and smiled. When he spoke into the microphone, his voice had taken on a quality of authoritative irritation. "Captain, you're going to want these people with you," he said. "If not, then give me your full name, your government G-level rating and the name of your immediate supervisor."

There was a longer pause while the static jumped over the radio. Finally, Abbott's voice came back. "We'll find room for them," he said. "It'll also give me a chance to get rid of some of this other dead weight out here."

Grimaldi couldn't resist one last dig. "Make it fast, Cap," he said. "These are busy folks I fly around."

Bolan smiled, returned his binoculars to his bag and picked it up. Jack Grimaldi had always been a maverick who had never had much patience with the pecking order of bureaucracy. Such ass kissing slowed and often nullified successful results. But, over the years, the ace pilot had learned to make it work against his own enemies within, playing the game when the situation called for it and aiding the Executioner in cutting through the red tape he often encountered.

Thirty seconds later, a small speedboat bearing the logo of the Coast Guard sped toward the shore. The man behind the wheel of the boat cut the engine twenty yards out, then expertly navigated the craft into the slip cut through the reef beneath the water. Bolan, Sielert and Ogatu boarded without a word, and the speedboat started toward the yacht.

The Executioner reached to the tool pocket of his brown

heavy canvas Carhardt jeans. The folding version of the knife
he had used to save the life of Marilyn Saucier Little—the
Applegate-Fairbairn combat folder—was clipped inside the
long narrow pocket, and he repositioned it slightly. The Beretta was in place under his left arm, balanced by a double
magazine holder and the same blade he had used on Cecil
Osburne. The .44 Magnum Desert Eagle was on his right hip
with the grips riding snugly against the white T-shirt he'd
tucked into the Carhardts. The same Aloha shirt he had worn
before, this time worn more like a jacket with the lapel un-
buttoned, hid all his weapons except the folding knife.

As the salt spray of the ocean struck his face, Bolan glanced
across the boat to his two partners for the mission. They had
all changed clothes during the chopper flight to the Big Island,
with Ogatu exhibiting her lack of modesty once more as she
traded her dark blue suit for khaki cargo jeans, a matching
shirt, multipocketed vest and floppy canvas hat. Changing
clothes in front of him and Sielert probably seemed no more
embarrassing than showering with the girls after gym class. It
was something the Executioner could respect. During the
course of a mission such as this, there was no time for timidity
or demureness.

Bolan's eyes turned to Greg Sielert. He was getting to know
the man fast, and well, under the conditions they'd encountered. Sielert had finally found a good use for the khaki safari
vest he'd wanted to wear in town and was dressed similarly
to Ogatu in the male version of what the well-clad safari
hunter might wear this year. If the truth were known, he
looked like he'd ordered all his clothes from the *Travelsmith*
catalogue as soon as he'd heard he was to accompany Bolan
to the islands. But the scientist was a good man, in spite of
his naive views of combat and espionage. He was willing to
risk his life to locate the nuclear bombs.

And that, Bolan thought, as the speedboat neared the yacht,
might well be the biggest problem Sielert faced personally. If
the scientist got killed during the course of the mission, there
would be no one who could safely neutralize the nukes when
they were found.

A few minutes later, Bolan and Sielert were on board the yacht and the soldier was extending a hand over the rail to pull Susan Ogatu up. In the corner of his eye, he saw a man wearing the Coast Guard insignia of a captain approach. As he turned, the man extended his hand.

"Captain Rick Abbott," the short, middle-aged man told the Executioner. "I just got off the radio with your man."

"Belasko, Justice Department," Bolan said. He indicated Ogatu and Sielert with his head. "Susan Ogatu with Honolulu PD, Greg Sielert is with me."

Abbott shook hands with them both, then turned to Bolan. "If you don't mind my asking, Special Agent Belasko," he said, "why's the Justice Department interested in this? It's just another drug or illegal gun shipment we stumbled across."

Susan Ogatu stepped in. "Part of an ongoing joint investigation between Justice and Honolulu," she said. She smiled at Abbott. "I apologize for not being able to tell you more."

Her words might have been what melted the captain. But Bolan's guess was that it had more to do with her sultry eyes and her disarming smile.

"Well," Abbott said, raising both hands, palms up. "Feel free. As you can see, I'm finally getting rid of some of the folks who don't really have any business here." He glanced to both the port and starboard sides of the yacht where men were exiting the craft for the smaller boats. "Everybody wants in when something happens that can make for an easy report," he added.

"Any idea what the yacht was carrying?" Bolan asked. He knew the answer. But he wanted to know exactly how much the captain knew.

"Dope, guns…maybe antiquities, but I doubt it," Abbott said. "Dope would be my guess, but when you go below, you'll find a bunch of ATF guys arguing with the DEA."

Without further ado, Bolan took the captain's suggestion and lowered himself down the ladder to the cabin quarters beneath the deck. The main deck might have been clearing of excess human baggage, but the dead men below were packed in shoulder to shoulder. Most of them looked Eastern European in feature and dress, but a few Polynesians lay among the bodies, as well. Some lay on the floor. Others sat in chairs. But they all had one thing in common.

They had died in excruciating pain. Their faces were frozen in eternal agony.

Bolan saw a couple of men with crime scene kits. They had on blue nylon jackets with the letters DEA printed in white across the back. Others wore jackets that said BATF.

"Until you *prove* it was drugs, we're not going *anywhere*," Bolan heard an angry voice say from across the room. "Besides that, they could have had drugs *and* guns, and that lets us in on the game, too."

The soldier followed the voice. Two men stood in the corner of the large sitting area he had just entered. As frequently happened among law enforcement agencies, it appeared that the men arguing were more interested in who had jurisdiction than they were in solving the crime. Which didn't matter much to him. Let them argue. It would keep them out of his way.

Shouldering his way through the crowd, Bolan flashed his Justice Department credentials to both men.

"Oh, great," said the DEA man. "More problems with you?"

"No," the Executioner said politely. "You aren't going to have any problems with me. In fact, I'm anxious to get off your boat and back to what I'm already involved in." Susan Ogatu stepped to his side and smiled.

The frowns on the DEA and ATF men's faces suddenly disappeared.

"Give us a quick run-down on what happened, we'll be on our way, file our report and stay out of your hair," Bolan said.

Once again, Ogatu's presence and the sexual charisma that leaped from her body had combined with the Executioner's natural ability to take command. The men became cooperative. "My name's Cutsman," the DEA man said. "This is Jake Peterman." None of them bothered to shake hands, and the Justice ID the Executioner had shown him seemed to be all the introduction Cutsman wanted from the trio who had just come on board. "One of the Coast Guard boats happened on this unidentified yacht anchored here. As they came in to investigate, they saw a smaller craft disappear over the horizon. They couldn't go both places at once, so they radioed for assistance and came on in to check out the yacht.'' He paused, drew in a breath of air, then went on. ''When they got here, a flatbed truck was parked on shore. Had some kind of big wooden crate on it. A small motorboat had just been loaded onto a trailer behind another truck, which must have been how they took the stuff to shore.''

''How big was the motorboat?'' Bolan asked.

Cutsman sighed as if the question was the biggest imposition that had been forced upon him yet that day, pulled a small spiral notebook from the hand warmer pocket of his jacket and flipped through the pages. Stopping and squinting at a page, he said, ''Not big. One of the crew guessed it at about a hundred horsepower or so. Said it looked like a ski boat.''

''They couldn't have transferred a very big load of drugs in that.'' Bolan turned to Peterman. ''Even fewer guns.''

Cutsman glanced at Peterman. ''Depending on what kind of drugs they were smuggling, they could have gotten a good day's pay in it. But you're right about the guns. Which is exactly the point I'm trying to make to our friend, here.''

Peterman didn't reply.

''Anyway,'' Cutsman went on, ''the whole convoy on shore took off as soon as the Coast Guard boat got here.'' He glanced at his notebook again. ''Oh, yeah, there were several other vehicles parked along the road.''

''So the drugs—'' Bolan turned from the DEA man to the ATF agent ''—or the guns went two different places,'' he said. ''Part of the shipment on shore, the other in the boat the Coast Guard saw leaving the scene.''

Cutsman gave the Executioner a condescending smile. ''That's what it looks like,'' he said.

Bolan ignored the man's sarcasm. ''Any description on the trucks or other vehicles that were on shore?'' Bolan asked.

Cutsman looked to his notebook again. ''A few common makes and models,'' he said. ''No licences.''

''They were parked too far away,'' Peterman cut in. ''And

they were gone before the Coast Guard could use their binoculars.''

Bolan nodded. He had all he could use. But he still wanted to keep the illusion going that he agreed the cargo had been drugs or illegal weapons. "One last question," he said.

Cutsman raised his eyebrows.

"Any idea what happened to the crew?"

Cutsman pointed to a dead man sitting in a chair. Before death, he had thrown up over the front of his shirt, and a frothy paste was glued to his face. The DEA man's voice dripped with sarcasm once more as he said, "Well, if I were Sherlock Holmes, my deductive reasoning would lead me to guess they'd been poisoned."

"I can see that," Bolan said. "Any idea why?"

Peterman stepped into the conversation again. "Ever read *Treasure Island?*" he asked.

Bolan frowned at the man as if he had no idea what he meant. "What?"

"Don't you remember how in pirate stories they'd always go bury the treasure, then the captain would kill the men who'd buried it so he'd have it all for himself? Fifteen men on a dead man's chest, and all that?"

"Okay, thanks." Bolan nodded. "We'll get out of your way and go write it up. You know how the bosses are with paperwork."

"Do we ever," Cutsman and Peterman said almost in unison. They turned to each other, obviously anxious to return to their argument over who had jurisdiction in the case. Bolan heard Cutsman whispering as he turned toward the ladder leading upward.

"Where does the Justice Department find those guys?" the DEA man asked Peterman. "They're even dumber than you ATF freaks."

The Executioner led the way up from the bowels of the yacht, and they hitched a ride to shore with the same man who had ferried them out. As soon as the boatman had backed away from the shore and started toward the yacht, Ogatu said,

"They've separated the nukes. Now they'll be twice as hard to find."

"One has gone inland here on the Big Island. The other could have gone anywhere."

Greg Sielert seemed to feel a need to help. "And we don't know for sure that the one here will stay here," he said. He stared at the Executioner for a response.

Bolan nodded, more out of politeness than any gratefulness that Sielert had stated the obvious.

"The problem, I'd say," Ogatu said, "is we don't even have any leads to follow toward the nuke they offloaded here."

The Executioner looked at her. "Maybe, maybe not," he said. Without further words, he walked to the edge of the road, then stepped onto the lava. He wore heavy-soled hiking boots. He made his way across jagged shoreline toward a spot where the land fell. Sielert and Ogatu followed.

Roughly a hundred yards from the road, Bolan came to the small blowhole he had spotted while they'd ridden from the yacht in the speedboat. Every few seconds, as the waves hit the underground pocket hidden beneath the land that separated the sea from the water further inland, a misty spray erupted into the air.

"Shit!" Sielert said as he stepped onto a particularly sharp edge of lava directly behind Bolan. "Okay, I'll bite, Mike. What are we looking for?"

"They didn't bring the nuke ashore in a small speedboat," the Executioner said. "Which meant they had to have a raft."

"Cutsman didn't say anything about a raft," Sielert said.

"That doesn't mean there wasn't one," Bolan said. "It just means it was gone before the Coast Guard boat got here. Or they didn't see it. Or the information got lost somewhere in the shuffle." He looked at the small pond around the blowhole. He could see nothing but dark water. Had it been his imagination, or had he really seen what looked like wood bobbing here as they returned from the yacht to shore? He didn't know.

There was only one way to find out.

Quickly Bolan began stripping off his clothes. As he took off his pants, Susan Ogatu said wryly, "I think I'm having an exhibitionistic influence on you, Mike."

Bolan didn't answer. Clad in his underwear, he carefully lowered himself into the water, mindful of the sharp lava he knew lurked below.

"What's he doing?" Sielert whispered to Ogatu.

"Looking for the raft, is my guess," the Executioner heard Ogatu say before his head dropped below the surface.

Underwater visibility in this part of the Pacific Ocean was often unbelievably clear. But the pond surrounding the blowhole had mixed with sand, earth and lava debris to drop Bolan's vision to only a few feet. He worked more by feel than sight, slowly making his way, hand over hand, down the side of the hole. Using his feet, he prodded the area around him, hoping to strike what felt like wood or metal rather than the sharp coral and lava that scraped his skin. Every minute or so, he was forced to return to the surface for air.

It was during his fourth trip below the surface that he found the raft. It had settled diagonally across several sections of lava. As his hands carefully explored it, he found it had been weighted down with bags of sand. Marking the location in his mind, he shot to the surface for air.

Ogatu took one look at the Executioner's face and said, "You found it."

"Yeah. They tied sandbags to it. My guess is it was done hurriedly after they saw the Coast Guard arrive. They probably didn't have time to check for air pockets in the bags, which would account for it bobbing up and down earlier." He took another second to catch his breath, then pointed toward where he'd dropped his clothes. "Hand me my knife," he said.

Sielert hurried to the mound of clothes and pulled the Applegate-Fairbairn combat folder from its nylon sheath. He handed it to Bolan.

The Executioner took a deep breath, then dropped beneath the water again, surface diving and swimming to the raft. He circled the wooden planks, cutting the sandbags away and casting them aside to sink to the bottom. He had to surface twice for air before the job was complete. But as soon as it was, the raft floated him up into the sun.

"Bingo," Ogatu said as Bolan towed the raft to the edge of the blowhole. He pulled himself out of the water as Sielert and the Honolulu detective hauled in the raft. Together, the three of them dragged it onto the lava.

The Executioner began dressing again. Behind him, he heard Ogatu say, "Well, this is sort of like a dog chasing a car. Now that we've got it, what do we do with it?"

Bolan turned to her as he slipped into his pants. "You're officially off duty, right?"

"Right."

"How much trouble is it going to create if you call for a crime scene team out here?"

"Lots," Ogatu said. "People are going to get nosy and wonder what I'm up to."

The Executioner nodded. He had figured as much. "Then I'd better take care of it," he said as he finished buttoning his shirt. "We need a forensic expert to print this thing."

Sielert was an expert scientist within his field. But his field was nuclear fission rather than forensics, and he was out of that field now. "You can get fingerprints off that thing? After it's been in the water like that?" he asked in the incredulous tones of a child.

"Sometimes," the Executioner said. He saw little point in taking the time to explain the particulars to the man. With the raft in the sunshine, he knelt to inspect it more closely. The wood was still wet but had not been in the water long enough to warp or otherwise deteriorate from the salt. And while the hardware holding the forest green painted planks together was scratched from use, it was still in excellent condition and appeared fairly new.

"You know much about the Big Island?" Bolan asked Susan Ogatu.

Ogatu shrugged. "Depends on what you have in mind," she said.

"This raft isn't home made—it's commercial. And I don't think it was brought in from anywhere else," the Executioner said. "I think it was either bought or rented right here." As he spoke, he moved around the raft on his knees.

"What makes you think that?" Sielert asked. He wiped the sweat off the top of his bald head with his hand.

"Just a hunch," Bolan said. "No point in bringing in something this cheap and bulky if you don't have to. And they went to some pains to hide it. They didn't want people like us finding it and tracing it back to them. If the raft had come from Timbuktu, there wouldn't be any point in going to that much trouble."

Ogatu stepped next to the Executioner. "Maybe there's a dealer's tag on the back. Or a brand name. Or something."

Bolan had reached the rear of the raft as the words came out of her mouth. Staring at the wet wood in front of him, he said, "There was. Not any more." He pointed to a pair of empty screw holes separated by a triangular-shaped spot where a tag had once been. The bare wood rectangle stood out sharply, a tiny brown island in a sea of green paint.

"Let's get it back to the chopper," Bolan said. Lifting one end of the raft, he let Ogatu and Sielert take the other. Clumsily, they carried the wooden floating craft across the lava to the asphalt road and set it down twenty feet from the helicopter. Through the chopper's bubble windshield, the Executioner saw Jack Grimaldi lower his paperback book, then get out of the Huey and walk toward them. Bolan continued toward the helicopter, so Grimaldi turned and walked silently with him, awaiting orders.

Bolan's clothes were still wet as he leaned inside the helicopter and dug through one of his bags. He found his cellular phone and tapped in the numbers to Stony Man Farm. A second later, Barbara Price answered. "Hi, Striker. Where are you?"

Bolan leaned out of the chopper into the sunshine. "Between five and ten miles southwest of Kalapana," he said. "Southeast coast of the Big Island." He told the Stony Man mission controller about the raft, then said, "I don't know if any prints can be lifted off of it or not, and I'm not sure they'll do any good anyway. But it's one of the few leads we've got at this point, and it's worth a try.''

"Affirmative," Price said. "Your Honolulu detective can't get people out there for some reason?''

"No. Things got a little sticky. She's with me, but she's officially off duty.''

Price understood. "I can send somebody from here, but if you'll give me a second I'll see who we might be able to trust closer to you.''

"I'll wait.''

Bolan heard Price tapping the keyboard of a computer. A few seconds later, she came back on. "There's a woman on Maui. Did advanced forensic studies here at the Stony Man lab. Becky Foreman. She sound okay?''

"She sounds fine," Bolan said.

"Okay," said Price. "I'll get one of the pilots—"

"No time for all that, Barb. I'll send Grimaldi that way to pick her up.''

"You won't need Jack yourself?''

Bolan looked over the rugged terrain of the Big Island. Somewhere, close by, was one of the nuclear bombs. He could feel it.

And he intended to find it.

"I'll need him for a short hop, maybe," he told Price. "But he can drop us off and still get to Maui and back faster than you can send someone from the mainland.''

"Okay," Price said. "Anything else?''

"Yeah. Patch me through to the Bear, will you?''

A second later, Aaron Kurtzman, the computer genius of Stony Man Farm, said, "Hey, Striker," into the phone.

"Bear, I've got a raft here that was used to tow one of the nukes from a yacht to the Big Island. I think it was bought, maybe rented, locally. Find me any dealers and rental agencies in the Kalapana area, will you?''

"No sweat," Kurtzman said. "I'll do a fifty-mile radial check. If that doesn't turn up what you need, I'll widen it.''

"How long will that take?" Bolan asked. He lowered the phone and looked across the chopper at Grimaldi. "Fire her up, Jack," he said. "Don't know where we're going yet. But we're going *somewhere.*"

Grimaldi started the Huey Cobra's engines.

Pressing the phone to his ear again, Bolan repeated, "How long will it take, Bear?"

"I just did it while you were talking to Jack," Kurtzman said.

Bolan smiled. Kurtzman's magic machines were faster than fast. State of the art. And so was the man who operated them.

"You prepared to copy?" Kurtzman asked.

Grimaldi handed Bolan a notebook and pen, and the information that had been found through cutting edge technology got recorded the old-fashioned way.

"Anything else Barb needs to know?" Kurtzman asked when Bolan had finished writing.

"Just tell her I'll have Jack drop us off, then send him to pick up the forensic woman on Maui."

"Jack will drop you off, then go to Maui?" Kurtzman repeated.

"Yeah. Barb will know what I'm talking about."

"Good," Kurtzman said. "Take care, Striker."

"Always," said Bolan. He turned to Susan Ogatu. "You know much about Hilo?"

"The city or the whole region?" she asked.

Bolan spoke into the phone. "Bear, you talking about the town or—"

"I heard her, Striker," Kurtzman said. "Yeah, the city of Hilo itself. Fifteen to twenty miles north of you."

"The city," Bolan told her.

The detective shrugged. "Some," she said.

"Well, you're about to learn more," the Executioner said. "See you, Bear," he told Kurtzman before hanging up and turning to Grimaldi. "You got this bird warmed up, Jack?"

Grimaldi flipped a couple more switches on the control panel in front of him, then said, "Ready to rise, big guy."

As Bolan leaned in to return the cellular phone to his bag, the explosion of a high-caliber rifle round suddenly broke the peaceful tranquility of the Hawaiian shore.

The round missed him by inches, buzzing like an angry bee behind the back of his head. Had he not stuck his head into the helicopter, it would have taken him squarely in the temple. Instead, he saw a small round hole appear in the open door of the chopper.

As he turned in the direction from which the shot had come, gunfire erupted from every direction.

6

Round after round peppered the area around Mack Bolan, Susan Ogatu and Greg Sielert. "Get down!" the Executioner shouted, dropping to a crouch as the Desert Eagle sprang into his hand. Twenty yards away, he saw a rifle barrel next to one of the taller lava formations.

The lava along the coast was irregular, with many of the groupings tall enough to hide a squatting or kneeling gunman. But they weren't tall enough to allow attackers to sneak in close while they had been on shore. No, the gunmen had either already been in place when the Huey Cobra first landed or they had moved to their positions while the three had been on board the yacht. In either case, they had been hidden there the entire time he had searched for the raft. Which was probably their reason for staying behind after the other Polynesian Freedom Fighters had departed with the nuke.

Benjamin Liholiho didn't want the raft found. And if it was found, he didn't want anyone left alive who had found it. Why? Because someway, somehow, it led back to him.

As more shots rang out, Bolan turned to Grimaldi. "Get her in the air and out of range, Jack!"

Grimaldi nodded and revved the Huey Cobra's turbo shaft engine in preparation to rise into the air.

The Executioner turned toward the rifle barrel, brought the Desert Eagle to eye level and fired. He had aimed at the top of the lava to the side of the rifle, and the big .44 Magnum round struck it squarely. A scream sounded from behind the formation as tiny chips of the age-old rock flew through the air like prehistoric shrapnel. As the dust settled, a face with

Polynesian features, eyes closed in pain, appeared holding the rifle.

Bolan's second round made sure the eyes stayed closed. Forever.

The Executioner turned. Greg Sielert and Susan Ogatu had been standing several yards from the helicopter while Bolan stood next to it using the phone. They had wisely dropped down amid two of the taller lava formations. The rocky growths were more concealment than cover, but the pair were as safe as they were going to get during this gunfight. Far safer, at least, than they would be if they rose to sprint toward the helicopter. That's what the attacking PFF men would expect them to do, and they'd be waiting to pick them off like ducks in a shooting gallery.

Bolan looked closer. Ogatu had drawn her Glock. Sielert had his .45 pistol out. Both were firing at any target that showed itself in the lava bed.

As the Huey Cobra began to rise, the Executioner had a sudden battle strategy enter his mind. As the chopper's skids passed his shoulders, he reached out and grasped the nearest one with his free hand. Hooking an elbow around the skid, he let it drag him off the ground and into the air.

Ten feet above the ground, the rules of the game suddenly changed.

Bolan looked down, able to see many of the PFF men who had been hidden behind the lava only a second before. The Desert Eagle roared in his hand, nearly blowing the head completely off the shoulders of a gunman who had hidden near the man with the rifle. As the chopper rose, the Executioner pointed the weapon. He knew from long experience that when firing downward, the tendency was to shoot high. Centering his vision on the upper thighs of a kneeling PFF man, he pulled the trigger once more.

The big .44 Magnum slug drilled squarely through the center of the man's chest. A 9 mm Uzi submachine gun dropped from his hands to the ground. The PFF man followed it, striking his forehead on the weapon as he fell facedown to the ground.

The chopper had stopped to hover a hundred feet off the ground. Round after round after round flew past the Executioner from the lava beds. Bolan returned fire, taking out two more of the enemy formerly screened by the lava formations. But there were more men who fired into the air. Most of their rounds missed the Huey Cobra completely, but a few struck nonvital areas of the chopper. That kind of luck couldn't last forever, Bolan knew. Sooner or later, one of the high-powered rifle slugs would find an Achilles' heel in the helicopter.

"Take her on up, Jack!" Bolan yelled at the top of his lungs amidst the roar of the continuing explosions. Grimaldi either heard the Executioner or made the decision on his own. The Huey Cobra rose into the air.

As they ascended, Bolan looked to where Ogatu and Greg Sielert lay on the ground. Ogatu was making good use of her cover, leaning around the lava upcroppings only long enough to take aim and fire with one hand, then jerking herself to safety. Each time she repeated the process, she found a new spot at which to expose herself, never appearing where she had the last time. Smart tactics.

Sielert, on the other hand, was completely out of his element. His training had come within a perfect shooting environment—a firing range. He attempted to put into play techniques that didn't apply to combat. As the chopper rose, Bolan watched him lean around the lava growth in front of him. To employ the two-handed grip he'd been taught, he was forced to expose far more of his body than Ogatu did. As Bolan watched, a flurry of rounds narrowly missed him. Sielert was forced behind cover before he could pull the trigger.

Three hundred feet above the ground, Bolan holstered the Desert Eagle, then pulled himself to a squatting position on the helicopter skid. The Huey Cobra dipped slightly as Grimaldi leaned across the seat to open the door for him, and a moment later Bolan had hauled himself into the seat next to the pilot.

"We having fun yet?" Grimaldi asked.

From his new vantage point, Bolan could see the situation below more clearly. The PFF men on the ground surrounded the spot where the chopper had been grounded on three sides. The only open area was between where Ogatu and Sielert hid and the sea. Turning his eyes toward the yacht and the cluster of boats surrounding it, he saw flurries of movement as the Coast Guards and other law enforcement agents tried to crowd into the smaller landing crafts.

Grimaldi laughed sarcastically, following the Executioner's eyes. "They'll get ashore in time to clean up the bodies. That's all."

"Can't argue with you, Jack," Bolan said. "And in the meantime, Sielert's going to get himself killed." Even as he spoke, he saw the scientist suddenly stand. Exposed from the waist up, he raised the .45 with both hands, hesitated, then fired.

Miraculously, the rounds that flew at him all missed. Even more miraculously, a PFF man ten feet away fell forward, impaling himself on a sharp shard of lava.

"He's going to get himself killed trying to be something he's not," Bolan announced. He turned to Grimaldi. "This bird have a beak?" he asked.

The pilot smiled. "Emerson Electric TAT-102A," he said. "Six-barrel machine-gun turret. Want to see how she works?"

Bolan nodded. "You fly, I'll shoot." He leaned toward the control panel between them. "Buzz them, Jack," he said. "We can't afford to lose Sielert."

"And Susan's too pretty to die," Grimaldi added.

The Huey Cobra suddenly dropped through the air, descending at a forty-five degree angle on a group of PFF men to the left of where Sielert and Ogatu hid. The Executioner waited until they were fifty yards off the ground to open fire. But when he did, the six-barreled machine gun opened up and laid a blanket of lead on top of the lava. Sand and chips of age-cooled molten rock rose in the air to form a gray-black cloud of dust.

The Huey Cobra passed over the spot and rose higher, away from the return fire that came from where the PFF men had surrounded the asphalt road. Grimaldi turned the bird in the air and prepared for another pass.

The Executioner set his jaw as he stared at the ground racing toward them. He could barely see Ogatu and Sielert. Both were prostrate within the lava growths where they'd hidden. Whether it was to escape the onslaught of fire from the air or they'd fallen victim to the rounds of the enemy, Bolan had no way of knowing.

To the side, the soldier saw several small boats filled with armed men leave the yacht and start toward the shore.

"Ready for round two?" Grimaldi asked.

The Executioner nodded.

The Huey Cobra shot down toward the PFF men hiding to the right of Ogatu and Sielert. Again, the TAT-102A turned the ground into a burning, churning cloud of floating grayish-black flakes. The chopper rose again, escaping return fire from the last cluster of PFF men who were concealed in the lava behind Sielert and Ogatu.

On the water, the approaching boats were halfway to shore.

"Time for the knockout punch," Grimaldi said and worked the controls.

The AH-1 Huey Cobra descended once more. The men on the ground had seen what had happened to their compatriots and decided that discretion was the better part of valor. They broke ranks, rising from behind the lava growths and running across the spiky ground.

Bolan opened up with the Emerson Electric, firing clusters of rounds into the running PFF men. One by one, two by two and three by three, they fell to their deaths. But several were still running as the chopper passed over.

Grimaldi did a lightning U-turn and flew across the men. Bolan held his fire. They were too close to Ogatu and Sielert, and the chances of taking them out with the six-barrel too great. Grimaldi twisted the chopper once more, and they repeated the flight pattern away from the sea. More men fell to the Emerson's powerful rounds. But a few others kept running, disappearing into the more moderate terrain of palm trees and other vegetation beyond the lava beds.

The Huey Cobra rose without Bolan having to order Jack to do so. A hundred yards inland, the Executioner could see several vehicles parked amid the heavier vegetation. They would be hidden from the ground and were only partially visible from the air.

"Go after them?" Grimaldi asked.

Bolan shook his head. "We've got to check Greg and Susan. If he's dead, we're dead in the water ourselves."

Grimaldi rarely argued with the Executioner's orders. It was more suggestion than argument when he said, "They might know where the nukes went."

"Liholiho's too smart for that. He wouldn't have left men behind who had that information. We could beat them all day and they still wouldn't be able to tell us."

Grimaldi agreed. Turning the chopper from the fleeing men, he flew to the spot where he'd landed before and set the Huey Cobra on the asphalt.

By the time the Executioner had exited the helicopter the first boatload of men from the yacht had arrived on shore. They came forward in crouched combat shuffles, gripping assault rifles in their hands. Cutsman, carrying an AR-15, and Peterman, who gripped a Ruger mini-14, led the way.

Bolan held up a hand. "You're a little late," he said. "Show's over."

"What the hell happened?" Cutsman demanded.

The Executioner ignored the question. Leaving the road, he jogged across the jagged footing to where Susan Ogatu was rising from the lava bed. The detective was covered head to toe with sand, dirt and black lava soot. But she smiled through the grime on her face as soon as she saw Bolan. "Nice shooting," she said.

"Where's Greg?" Bolan asked. The last time he had seen the scientist from the air, the man had been on the ground not ten feet away. But the spot where Sielert had been was empty save for a few spent brass .45 caliber casings.

"He's alive," Ogatu said. "I saw him get to his feet just a few seconds ago."

Bolan found Sielert kneeling next to the lava formation where the man he had shot had fallen, chest first, into the sharp rock. The scientist stared at the man's face.

The dead PFF man stared back with open eyes.

"You okay?" Bolan asked as he approached Sielert from the side.

The scientist didn't answer. He continued to stare.

Bolan stopped next to the man. "Are you okay, Greg?"

Sielert's head swiveled slowly. He gazed at the Executioner with what could only be described as a thousand-mile stare. When he spoke, his words seemed to come from the back of his throat. "I got him," the scientist said. "I actually killed this man."

Bolan nodded.

Then the scientist turned to the side and vomited.

THE EXECUTIONER'S hunch that the raft used to off-load one of the nukes had come from the Big Island began to make more sense as the Huey Cobra took them north toward the city of Hilo. It seemed that Grimaldi had barely gotten them airborne when Hilo Bay appeared in the distance. "That's Banyan Drive you see," Susan Ogatu said. "Where the hotels are."

The Executioner turned slightly to look at Ogatu and Sielert sitting behind him in the helicopter. They had gone down to the shore to wash away the dirt and lava dust with which they'd been showered during the Huey Cobra's aerial attack on the PFF men. But both could have still gone undercover as professional chimney sweeps without creating much suspicion.

"Not many hotels," Bolan said.

"Not many visitors," the cop answered. "At least this side of the island. On the west coast, the Hilton Waikola Village alone has more rooms than all of Hilo put together."

Large droplets of rain began to strike the top of the chopper as Grimaldi dropped them through the air toward the small airport. "See those arched bridges and waterways off to the side?" Ogatu asked.

Bolan nodded, directing his eyes at the structures that were set inside what appeared to be a park built in the same style he'd seen many times in Japan.

"That's Lili'uokalani Garden," the Honolulu detective said. "They built the arched bridges to serve as a safety zone after a tidal wave hit in 1960. Killed over sixty people."

Bolan didn't answer. He cast a quick glance at Greg Sielert, who had been silent during the flight. He hadn't spoken a word after throwing up next to the body of the man he'd killed. The scientist sat staring at the hands folded in his lap. Whether he was in the midst of an attack of remorse, shock or both, Bolan couldn't tell. But the Executioner made a mental note to speak privately with the man as soon as possible.

Having Sielert tag along was necessary to the mission. But the man was a liability, even with all his faculties working properly. The last thing Bolan needed was for the doctor to go zombie on him.

Grimaldi set the Huey Cobra smoothly on the ground. Bolan, Sielert and Ogatu grabbed equipment bags and stepped out. Bolan stuck his head in, the movement reminding him of the last time he'd stood outside this helicopter and spoken on the phone. He fought the impulse to look behind him, to see if there might be more lava beds hiding more PFF gunmen right here in the center of Hilo. "Jack," he said to Grimaldi. "Head on to Maui. Get hold of Barbara on the way. She'll have made arrangements on where you should meet this Becky Foreman."

Grimaldi nodded and smiled. "Have a rum punch for me," he said.

Bolan turned to where Ogatu and Greg Sielert stood waiting, then turned back. In the rear of the chopper, Grimaldi had stored four M-16A2 assault rifles he had scrounged from the Koneohe Marine Base. Rather than leave them in the telltale rifle cases, the pilot had taken them out and wrapped them in blankets, which wouldn't draw attention. Bolan reached in and grabbed them.

It was always better to be safe than sorry.

A few minutes later, they had rented a blue two-year-old Nissan Maxima and were driving away from the airport. Bolan lifted the cellular phone to his ear and tapped in the Stony Man number. He knew Price would have been busy with

Kurtzman during their chopper flight, getting them directions to the establishments that sold rafts, rented them or did both. When Price answered, he said, "We're just leaving the airport, Barb. What's the closest place?"

"Here's the first on your list," the Stony Man mission controller answered. "Randy Rentals and Sales." She gave him directions.

Randy Rentals and Sales was squeezed between two seaside hotels on Banyan Drive. It was a large establishment for this side of the Big Island. Bolan saw both old and new sailboats and power craft as he pulled into the lot. He directed the rental car toward a small white building in the center of the property and killed the engine just outside the front door.

A dark-skinned man wearing a striped polo shirt, khaki Dockers and leather deck shoes came out the front door before any of them could get out of the car. Bolan smiled in spite of himself. The salesman could have stepped right out of any used-car lot on the mainland. But he had a little different opening pitch than the Executioner had heard before.

"Aloha, my friends. The ancient gods of my people spoke to me this morning, telling me you would come. But they didn't tell me whether you sought sail or power." He smiled broadly as he swept a hand across his body to indicate the inventory on the lot. "So I procured both for you. Just in case."

Susan Ogatu laughed. Pulling her badge case from a pocket of her vest, she flipped it open. "Sorry, sport," she said. "But we're here on business."

Had it been Bolan who showed his credentials, he was sure the salesman's smile would have faded. But since it was Ogatu, the smile remained. The catalyst that curled his lips upward changed from greed to lust. "Ah, the gods forgot to throw that part in, too," the man said. He extended his hand and shook Ogatu's. "I'm George," he said. "How can I be of service?" His eyes moved up and down the female detective's dirty clothes. "Want me to give you a bath? No charge. I can—"

"No," Ogatu interrupted him. "We're looking for a raft.

Actually, we *found* a raft. Now we need to find out where it came from.''

"We've got them for sale and rent both," George said. "In the back. Want to take a look?"

"We do," she said.

Bolan and Sielert followed Ogatu as George led her into the small building, through several offices and to the back lot. The cop had taken the lead with George, and Bolan had no problem with that.

His heart skipped a beat when he saw the wooden rafts lined up along the tall chain-link fence at the rear of the lot. They looked identical to the one he had pulled out of the blowhole. Were they going to get lucky for once? Find the lead they needed on the first attempt? He felt his jaw tighten. Life experience had taught him things didn't come that easily.

George stopped at the end of the long row of rafts and said, "You know if it was bought or rented?"

Ogatu shook her head. She turned and looked hopefully at the Executioner.

Bolan circled the raft, his heart suddenly sinking. No, it wasn't going to be that easy. The raft about to be fingerprinted and swept for any trace evidence by Becky Foreman might be identical to the one he saw before him, but he realized the one the PFF had used had not come from Randy Rentals and Sales. Bolan knelt next to the raft. It had a steel plate that advertised the Randy company screwed into it, all right. But the logo was fastened to the side of the raft rather than the rear. And it was round and considerably larger than the rectangular bare area where the plate had been pulled from the PFF raft.

Bolan pointed to the steel plate. "George," he said. "You mark all the rafts with this plate?"

George looked confused. "Well, yeah. Actually, we mark everything with that plate. Boats, rafts, trailers—"

"Ever use a different one?" the Executioner asked. "Smaller plate? Rectangle?"

"Not since I've been here," George said. "Why?"

Bolan didn't answer. Instead, he walked quickly down the row of rafts toward the end, checking both the sides and rear of each craft. There was always a chance, however slim it might be, that George the greedy, horny, glib-tongued boat salesman was part of the PFF.

But the Executioner didn't think so. Every raft at Randy Rentals and Sales was marked identically to the first one. Walking to where they stood, Bolan said, "What other places sell or rent rafts like this one, George?"

George had been engaged in conversation with Ogatu while Bolan checked the rafts, and he didn't seem too thrilled to have it interrupted. But he answered anyway. "You mean *just* like this one?" he asked. "Same make and model?"

Bolan nodded as he pulled the list he'd made during the phone call to Kurtzman from the pocket of his brown jeans.

George squinted in thought for a moment, then rattled off three names that were on the list. "And there's the new place," he said. "Just opened last week. They might have them, might not. I haven't been down there yet."

The Executioner pulled a pen from another pocket and wrote down the name. Then, looking up, he said, "George, we'd appreciate it if you'd keep the fact that we were here under your hat. Okay?"

George nodded enthusiastically. "Always glad to help out the law," he said.

The salesman stayed where he was as Bolan, Ogatu and Sielert started toward the parking lot. Halfway to the building, Ogatu grasped the Executioner's arm and said, "You two go on. I'll be along in a minute."

Bolan was curious. But during the last couple of days he had grown to respect her more and more. As she turned and started toward where George stood, Bolan nodded for Sielert to accompany him on to the car. This was as good a time as any, he supposed, to have his private talk with the scientist.

As soon as they were inside the vehicle, Bolan started the engine and turned the air conditioner up. Sielert had taken his seat in the back, and the Executioner turned to face him, resting an arm over the seat between them. "You okay, Greg?" he said.

Sielert's face was pale, but was capable of speech. "Yeah," he said. "It's just...*different* than I thought it would be."

"Combat?" Bolan asked.

The scientist nodded. "Yes, the various aspects of it I hadn't considered."

"What part bothers you the most?"

Sielert hesitated, then said, "I'm not sure, really. Two things, I guess."

"Which are?" the Executioner prompted.

"Well, first, I guess, is that it wasn't a paper target or a steel plate I shot. Before I pulled the trigger, that was a walking, talking, breathing human being."

"He was walking, talking and breathing," Bolan said. "The human being part is debatable."

Sielert nodded. "I know what you mean. And it was self-defense, wasn't it?"

"He was trying to kill you," Bolan said. "Unless my definition of self-defense is way off the mark, I don't see how it could be any more clear. And don't forget he's part of a group that not only wanted to kill you, but wants to kill several million other people, too."

"I know," Sielert said. "There really isn't any other way, is there?"

"No."

Sielert leaned forward in his seat. "Does it get any easier, though?" he asked. "Killing people?"

"No," the Executioner said. "But that doesn't change facts, either. It has to be done, so somebody has to do it."

"The other thing is still the fear," said the man in the back seat. "I mean, I was so scared back there. Scared beyond anything I've ever experienced in my life."

Bolan was tempted to smile but was afraid it might be misinterpreted. "Only fools and liars never get scared, Greg," he said.

"You've got more courage than anyone I've ever seen."

Bolan hesitated. It was true that he had faced death so many times over the years the emotional aspects of such encounters had dulled. That happened with any emotion that got overworked, and the natural fear that came with combat was no different. But that wasn't what Greg Sielert needed to hear at the moment. It was about fifty levels too deep for his experience and wouldn't make a bit of sense to him.

Looking Sielert directly in the eye, Bolan said, "Greg, courage isn't the absence of fear. It's just the ability to function in spite of the terror."

Sielert nodded. "Okay," he said. "I see your point."

Bolan turned just as Ogatu appeared at the side of the office building, arm in arm with George. Ten feet from the car, she stood on her tiptoes and kissed him on the cheek. Then, opening the door, she got in and whispered, "Get me out of here."

"What was that all about?" Sielert asked her when they were a block away from Randy Rentals and Sales.

"The Big Island is a small island in some ways," she said. "People here love to talk. I knew when George promised not to tell anyone we were here looking for rafts he'd be on the phone as soon as we left." She shrugged. "So I promised to meet him at a bar near here tonight. And I promised if he kept his mouth shut and didn't tell anyone what we were doing, I'd have a big surprise for him."

"And what's that surprise going to be?" Bolan asked, as if he didn't already know the answer.

"That I'm not going to show up."

THE NEXT BOATYARD they checked was less interesting and proved no more fruitful. Located just off the Bayfront Highway, it was smaller and sold rafts like the one they'd found in the blowhole and at Randy Rentals. But they did no rentals. The manager—a female this time, who was more charmed by Bolan than Susan Ogatu—was happy to check her sales receipts.

As it turned out, they had sold no rafts of any kind during the previous twelve months.

Bolan got in behind the wheel of the Nissan. He supposed Liholiho or one of his men might have bought the raft over a year ago. The wet floating device he had pulled out of the blowhole had looked fairly new. But it could be that old—

particularly if it had been stored somewhere rather than used or left out in the open to be assaulted by the salt sea. On the other hand, the Executioner's instincts told him that was unlikely.

By the time they got to the third boatyard the sun was fading fast over the Big Island. It was located on the Wailuku River just outside of town, and a hand-painted wooden sign announced the unlikely and very un-Hawaiian name, Hudson Bay Boats.

The Nissan pulled onto the lot just as the last salesman was about to lock up for the night. He stood on the front porch of an old house that served as an office, a key ring in his hand, his back to the approaching vehicle. The man was in his late fifties. He had a large beer belly that even his baggy Hawaiian shirt couldn't hide, gray hair and skin so white he must have taken great pains to avoid the tropical sun.

He turned to them as Bolan, Ogatu and Sielert walked from the Nissan. Bolan asked about rafts.

"Sure," the man said in an obvious Northeastern U.S. accent. "We've got rafts like that. You folks looking to rent or buy one?"

Bolan and Ogatu showed their credentials, and the man's face lit with delight. "My name's Frank," he said. Bolan introduced Ogatu and Sielert, then himself as "Belasko." They all shook hands.

"My son's a police officer," Frank said. "In Boston. So, how can I help you?"

The Executioner explained that they were trying to track down someone who had used a raft like the ones on the Hudson Bay lot.

"Well, the big boss has already gone home for the night," the man said. "But I don't suppose I'd be in any more trouble with her if I checked through the records than I always am anyway. I forgot to give you my last name. Hudson. Frank Hudson. The big boss is my wife."

They followed Hudson into the old house. The living room was still a living room but it was used by customers rather than family. Couches and armchairs were arranged around the walls, and coffee tables were stacked with boating magazines and brochures.

Hudson walked down a short hallway and into an office that had begun its architectural life as a bedroom. He went to a row of filing cabinets with the other three at his heels. "That's R-dash-four-one-one," he said.

"Pardon me?" Ogatu asked.

"I was just talking to myself," Hudson said as he pulled out a drawer midway down one of the cabinets. "File number for the rafts. R for raft, four-one-one is the model number." Pulling out a manila folder, he turned and set it on a scarred and battered wooden desk. "Want me to look for something, or you want to do it?" he asked.

"Let's all look at them," Bolan said. "You might recognize something we'd miss."

Hudson beamed. "Happy to help," he said. "Worked as a security guard when I was in college. Always wanted to become a cop myself. But somehow I got sidetracked." He opened the file. "Glad my boy got to do it."

Bolan, Ogatu and Hudson began looking through invoices. With the area around the desk already too crowded, Sielert took a seat in a metal folding chair against the wall and picked up a boating magazine.

As they searched for anything of interest, Bolan and Ogatu learned Hudson's life history. Born in Maine, as Bolan had suspected from the accent, he had married soon out of college and been talked into going into the insurance business with his wife's father. The couple had sold the business when her father died five years earlier, moved to Hawaii and bought the boatyard.

Bolan and Ogatu listened politely as they searched the files.

Hudson said, "Now there's one that surprised me." He held up an invoice.

"How's that?" Bolan asked.

Hudson looked at the paper in his hand. "Dicky Haili," Hudson said. "Bought one of those rafts about two months ago. Came in here and paid for it in cash."

"We don't know Dicky Haili," Ogatu said. "So you'll have to tell us why that was such a big surprise."

Hudson turned to her and smiled. "Before that, I'd never seen Dicky with more money in his pocket than it takes to buy a bottle of cheap wine. And as soon as he passed a liquor store, that'd be gone, too."

"What did he do with the raft?" Bolan asked.

Hudson shrugged. "Don't know. Haven't seen him much since."

Ogatu turned toward the soldier. He read her face. The PFF could have used this Dicky Haili to buy the raft, then gotten rid of him so he couldn't get drunk and talk about it.

Hudson might have never realized his lifelong dream of becoming a police officer. But he had the mind of a cop, and he read Ogatu's face as well as the Executioner's. "Oh, Dicky's still alive," he said. "Saw him downtown this morning, matter of fact, when I went to the post office. I said I hadn't seen *much* of him since he bought the raft. I didn't mean I hadn't seen him at all."

"You have an address on the invoice?" the Executioner asked.

Hudson smiled. "General delivery, is what's written down here. Try the Fish Market area."

Bolan had no idea why a drunk would hang around a fish market, and Ogatu, too, frowned in confusion.

Frank Hudson chuckled. "Turn off Banyan onto Lihiwai Street," he said. "You'll pass the Suisan Fish Market. About six blocks further down, you'll come to Hilo's version of the Bowery. If he's got money, he'll be in one of the bars. Probably the Edge of the Island. If he's already spent it, he'll be sleeping it off in one of the alleys."

"Thanks," Bolan said. "We appreciate your time."

"My pleasure," Hudson said, smiling.

Bolan led the way to the Nissan. Night had fallen by the time he slid behind the wheel, and a beautiful Hawaiian moon filled the sky. A gentle breeze blew through the open window as he drove toward Banyan Drive, then found Lihiwai Street. As they passed the Suisan Fish Market, a ship's horn tooted in the distance, and Bolan turned to see a fleet of fishing vessels nearing the harbor. A dozen men wearing bloodstained aprons and armed with butcher and filet knives came out of the market to await the day's catch.

The Executioner drove on, watching the streets steadily deteriorate into a slum. A small commercial area appeared, and cheap neon lights began to announce places with names like Mom's and Hawaiian Paradise and sometimes just Bar. Men, and a few women, walked the sidewalks.

"Where should we start?" Sielert asked from the back seat.

"I'd say one's about as good as the next," Ogatu said. "But Frank suggested the Edge of the Island."

Bolan nodded silently and drove the Nissan slowly down the street.

"There," Sielert said, pointing to the right.

Bolan pulled in against the curb and parked. As they opened the doors and got out, the soldier read the sign above the door—at least the letters over which the bulbs hadn't yet burned out.

Sielert was first to the door, and Bolan watched the man stop long enough to reach under his vest and make sure his pistol was in place. He saw the Executioner watching him and said sheepishly, "Seems like a good place to get shot or stabbed."

Bolan nodded out of politeness rather than agreement. From what he'd seen so far, the vast majority of the inhabitants of this area of Hilo would have long ago dropped below the predator level. In fact, they'd have become prey themselves if they'd had anything worth taking.

Sielert opened the rickety screen door and Ogatu stepped inside. Bolan followed, with Sielert bringing up the rear. What conversation they had heard from the sidewalk had been hushed. Now it stopped altogether. Bolan, Sielert and Ogatu were out of place in the Edge of the Island. They were sober, healthy and clean.

Not so the patrons of the bar.

Bolan took it all in with one glance. He'd seen a million bars just like it all over the world. It was a place where old drunks came to pass time they'd never remember while they kept working toward that one final bender of oblivion from which they would never awaken.

The walls were bare except for the occasional hole where someone in the depths of alcohol had slipped and bumped his head. The furniture was old, and as broken down as the men and women sitting on it. A stench of stale beer, wine, cigarette smoke and urine permeated the air, and cockroaches roamed the floor and scurried across the splintery tables. Some of the inhabitants seemed to regard them more as pets than nuisances.

The Executioner led the way to the bar. Standing behind the counter, openly staring at the three interlopers, was a woman who might have been twenty or seventy. She wore a sleeveless pink housedress covered with faded flowers and stains. Her hair hung in slimy strands to her shoulders. A green eye patch was fastened with dirt-browned white adhesive tape over her left eye.

"Do you know Dicky Haili?" Bolan asked politely.

The woman stared at him.

"I asked if you knew a man named Dicky Haili," the soldier repeated.

The woman's lips barely moved as she said, "You ain't drinking, I ain't talking."

"Give me a beer," Bolan said, reaching into his pocket.

The woman with the infected eye used the other one to look at Ogatu. "How about those two?" she said.

"Bring them a beer, too."

The woman turned, stuck her fingers inside three already filthy glasses on the other side of the bar, then set them on the drain beneath the keg. Pulling the handle down, she filled the glasses with more foam than beer.

She set the glasses in front of them as Bolan shoved a twenty-dollar bill across the bar. "Keep the change," he said. "Then tell us where Dicky Haili is."

"Dicky was in earlier," the woman behind the counter said as she swept the twenty off the bar and stuck it inside the bra that peeked from the neck of her housedress. "Left maybe an hour ago."

"Any idea where he was going?"

"You cops?"

"Of a sort," the Executioner said. "But we don't want to arrest him. We just need some information. If we get it, we'll pay him. And you know where that money will wind up."

The woman behind the counter suddenly grinned—the first change in expression since they'd entered the bar. "What would you say if I told you I thought I could find him for you?" she asked.

Bolan reached back into his pocket and produced a hundred-dollar bill. "I'd let this talk for me," he said.

The woman reached greedily for the money but Bolan kept it out of her reach. "*After* we find Dicky," he said.

The smile became a scowl. "Half now," she said. The woman with the eye patch understood how the game was played.

Bolan smiled, tore the hundred-dollar bill in half and handed one of the pieces to her.

"That wasn't exactly what I had in mind," the woman said. "But try the alley outside the back door. He went out to take a piss and never come back. My guess is he passed out."

Bolan watched Sielert frown. It appeared to be another of those times when he thought he hadn't done anything to help and was determined to say something—anything—that would demonstrate his eagerness to assist. "Why didn't he just use the rest room?" the scientist asked, pointing toward a sign at the rear of the bar.

The woman behind the bar laughed with genuine humor. "Damn thing hasn't worked in two years, that's why," she said.

Bolan showed her the other half of the hundred in his hand, said, "We'll come back through here on the way out," then stuffed the piece into his pocket. He led the way past dozens of narcotized eyes that tried to follow them but couldn't quite focus. But four men managed to rise to their feet and make it to the bar after the untouched beers that stood there.

Something told Bolan to turn as he neared the back door,

and he saw the woman behind the bar staring at him. She had picked up the telephone receiver and pressed it against her ear.

The Executioner turned back, opened the door and stepped into the alley. As the woman had predicted, a small dark-skinned man lay asleep on the ground. He looked like he might well be a descendant of all three of the major races who had come to the Big Island to work the sugarcane fields during the last century—Portuguese, Chinese and Japanese. He wore a ragged shirt whose sleeves had come off long ago, and his emaciated arms were covered with badly illustrated tattoos.

Bolan knelt beside the man and lightly slapped his face. Dicky Haili didn't stir. The Executioner slapped harder with the same result. Reaching down with both hands, he grasped the man by the shoulders and shook him like a rag doll.

"Rita?" Dicky Haili slurred, his eyes still closed. "Rita? Check is in the mail…"

It took a good five more minutes of shaking and slapping before Dicky Haili was seated against the back wall of the Edge of the Island with his eyes open. He still wasn't sure where he was, or probably even *who* he was, but he could talk.

"Dicky," Bolan said, leaning over him. "You bought a raft a couple of months ago."

"Naaaaah," Haili slurred, shaking his head violently. "I never bought no calf."

"A raft, Dicky. A raft. Like you use to float things with."

"Ah, a raft," Haili said. "You got a raft for me?"

"My, this is fun," Ogatu said, her face a mask of total disgust.

Bolan shook the man's shoulders gain. "Dicky, if you don't wake up, I'm going to beat you within an inch of your life."

"Go ahead," Haili slurred and closed his eyes again.

"Then I'm going to take you to detox."

Haili's eyes suddenly shot open wide. "Yeah," he said far more clearly than before. "I do remember buying a raft."

"Tell me where you bought it," Bolan demanded. He wanted to make sure the man was coherent before asking the important questions.

"Hudson Bay," Haili said clearly.

"Why'd you buy it?"

"Some guy gave me the money. Said he'd buy me a six-pack if I bought it for him."

"What guy, Dicky?" Bolan asked. "What was his name?"

"Don't know."

"Okay, Dicky, " the Executioner said. "Get ready for the giant spiders and pink elephants, because detox here we come."

"No! Really!" Haili said. "I never asked his name, and he never told me. I swear!"

"Where'd he find you?" Bolan demanded. "Why did he pick you?"

"I dunno why he picked me," Haili said. "But I met him at the Golden Gates, I think."

The Executioner felt his eyebrows lower. He remembered passing the Golden Gates just as they entered Hilo's slum area. It was in the block before this one. "Had he ever talked to you before?" Bolan asked.

The horror of going through detoxification had sobered Haili up quickly. He was almost human. "Not before that night," he said. "But I know where he works."

"How? How do you know?"

"'Cause I seen him," Haili said. "Seen him plenty of times, going in and out of the fish market."

"He works there?" Bolan asked, remembering the men in the stained aprons.

"Nah. He's on one of the fishing boats."

The memory of the fishing boat the Coast Guard had seen sailing away from the abandoned yacht returned to the Executioner's brain. There was a connection there. He grabbed Dicky Haili by the shoulders again. But instead of shaking him, he hauled the little man to his feet.

"What...?" Haili said as he swayed drunkenly to keep his balance.

"Dicky," the Executioner said. "You're going with us."

The little man's head jerked toward the back door to the

bar. His eyes were terrified. "No, I can't go. I can't go without—"

"We'll pick up a six-pack on the way," Bolan said. "You're going to get one beer every hour, on the hour. No more."

"Well..." Haili didn't look quite as frightened as before. "Gee...that ain't much."

"It'll be enough to keep the shakes away," Bolan said. "And it's that or nothing. One way or the other, you're going with us."

Haili nodded. "You buying?"

Bolan shook his head in disgust. "Yes, Dicky. I furnish the beer." He turned to Ogatu and Sielert. "You ready?" he said.

Sielert had looked nervously up and down the alley, his hand on his gun, the whole time Bolan had talked to Dicky Haili. His answer was direct. "I'm ready," he said.

Ogatu reached out and took Bolan's arm. "You saw that Cyclops barmaid on the phone," she said. "And you know what it meant."

"It didn't happen back here. Which means it's going to happen out front. Either when we get out the door or at the car."

Ogatu nodded.

Bolan turned to Sielert. "I want you to take charge of Dicky," he said. "In case Susan and I get busy. You understand?"

It was clear by his face that he didn't. But the scientist nodded.

"Let's go, then."

7

The attempted robbery Bolan had known was coming since he'd seen the one-eyed barmaid on the phone hadn't occurred when he dropped the other half of the hundred-dollar bill on the bar. The Executioner knew why. He had promised her the other half of the hundred, and she wanted it before the robbery went down. Oh, she'd get her cut of the spoils from whoever lay in wait for them outside the bar. But she wanted the hundred dollars off the top—before it got confused with what the robbers took.

The woman with the eye patch looked nervously at Bolan as he thanked her for her help.

The soldier stopped at the front door and glanced outside. When they had entered the Edge of the Island a half hour ago, the streets and sidewalks had been alive with drunks. Now, he could see no one on the street. Which confirmed his belief that something was going down.

Turning to Sielert, he said, "Remember, you keep Dicky with you. Stay a few steps behind Susan and me on the way to the car."

"What—"

"Never mind, Greg," the Executioner said. "Just do it."

Sielert nodded.

When it finally came, the robbery attempt was enough of an anticlimax to be pathetic.

Two of the three men who had hidden out of sight behind the Nissan looked like they were in almost as bad a shape as Dicky Haili. Like the barmaid, they were probably thirty-five going on ninety. One held a tire tool and had to use both

quivering hands to keep from dropping it. Another grasped a
trash can lid. They were dressed and moved like they'd just
come from the cast party of *Night of the Living Dead*.

But the third man wasn't as alcohol-ravaged. At least not
yet. Looking to be a mixture of Caucasian and Polynesian
blood, he was in his mid-twenties and wore cleaner blue
jeans—at least they were clean by local standards. His tight
black T-shirt stretched over wiry muscles, and his long coarse
hair had been tied in a ponytail. He had no weapon.

At least nothing visible.

He was the last to rise from behind the Nissan, and an evil
smirk covered his face.

Bolan had seen such alliances among the world's scum before. The two older drunks needed money to buy alcohol. They
looked at their younger, stronger leader as, if not a meal ticket,
more of a drink ticket. In turn, the younger man had probably
flunked out of the low-life at every level on his way down to
this one. Here, he could rule. His following might not be
much. But it was a following nonetheless. When you combined the three men with the barmaid inside who had set them
up, the situation made the Executioner think of the old adage.
In the world of the blind, the one-eyed man is king.

The younger man stepped around the Nissan. "Nice wheels,
my man," he said to Bolan. Then, looking past the Executioner, his eyes fell on Dicky Haili. "These friends of yours,
Dicky?"

Haili had frozen in place next to Sielert. "Uh...hi, Dog.
How ya doing?" he asked nervously.

The man called Dog ignored the question and looked at
Bolan. "Okay, let's cut to the chase. We like your car. We
want it. You're going to give it to us, and all your money,
or—"

"You'll kill us?" Bolan interrupted. "Squash us like bugs?
Rip us all a new one?" He paused. "What exactly was your
next line supposed to be?" He couldn't suppress a yawn. What
was about to take place wasn't even going to qualify as a
decent training exercise.

Dog was thrown off guard by the stranger's confidence. But he bounced back. "The first one," he said.

"Can't remember what that was," the Executioner said.

"Kill you."

"Oh," Bolan said. "And exactly how do you plan to do that?"

The big folding knife was cheaply made. But it came out of the man's blue jeans fast and clicked open with a tinny ding. "With this," Dog said. He made several slashing motions in the air as his feet danced. "Now," he said, grinning, and the canine expression told the Executioner what had spawned his nickname. "You want to give us the keys and all your money? Or you want this thing stuck up your ass?" As he continued to dance, Dog began tossing the knife from hand to hand.

Bolan smiled. Dog must have seen the old movie *West Side Story*—not a bad show but hardly a training film on knife fighting. The Executioner made a quick check of the area behind the man juggling the knife and took a half-step to the side. In one lightning motion, the Desert Eagle came out of his holster, into his hand and up. As he felt the barrel fall on the airborne knife, he squeezed the trigger.

The .44 Magnum round struck the knife in midair, splitting the handle into three parts and sending the scraps and the blade flying in different directions. The bullet passed harmlessly over Dog's hand and drilled into the grass between the sidewalk and an abandoned building across the street.

Dog dropped both arms to his side and froze. A second later, a wet spot appeared at his crotch. As Susan Ogatu began to laugh, the spot spread.

Bolan walked forward, raised the Desert Eagle over his head and brought it down on Dog's skull. A sickening crack sounded along Hilo's skid row, and Dog collapsed on the street next to the Nissan.

The Executioner turned to the two drunks who had stood motionless throughout the incident. "You two," he said. "Drag this heap off the street." He paused. "Then I want you to return that tire tool and trash can lid from where you stole them. You understand?''

Both men nodded. "Yes, sir," one of them said. They started to shuffle drunkenly away from the scene, then he turned back and said, "Thank you."

Bolan unlocked the driver's side door, then used the electric button inside to open the others. Ogatu slid into her usual shotgun seat and Sielert helped Dicky Haili into the back. The Executioner didn't see the old drunk get in. But he *knew* he was there. Essence of Haili immediately permeated the vehicle.

As Bolan pulled the Nissan away from the curb, Susan Ogatu's nose wrinkled. "You know," she said, casting a quick glance over her shoulder at Haili, "it's such a nice night. Why don't we turn off the air conditioner and roll down the windows. All of the windows."

Detective Sergeant Susan Ogatu's window was already halfway down by the time she'd finished the sentence.

THE SUISAN FISH MARKET stood at 85 Lihiwai Street, where Hilo Bay narrowed into a small channel leading into the Waiakea Fish Pond. The fishing boats they had seen arriving earlier were lined up waiting their turn to dock and unload the day's catch. The fish would be sold to customers when the market opened at seven-thirty the next morning.

Bolan pulled into a parking lot near the Lili'uokalani Garden, killed the light and the engine and turned in his seat. Dicky Haili sat directly behind the soldier. The little drunk looked happy as a clam with the bottle of Heineken held firmly in both hands. The bottle was further secured between his thighs. Haili wasn't going to spill a drop of the precious liquid; it was worth more to him than gold.

Ever since Bolan had taken the little man into the liquor store to pick out the brew of his choice, Haili had treated the six-pack as if it were a sextet of Hope diamonds. On the way out of the store, he'd been so excited he'd told Bolan all about one of the happiest nights of his life. Shaking and desperate for a drink, Dicky Haili and two other tipplers had broken into a liquor store.

"I drank bourbon out of an Elvis Presley decanter," Haili had said as they got into the car. "The one with the cape—where the King is bent over singing into the microphone. You remember that one?"

The Executioner looked at the broken little man with mixed feelings of aversion and sympathy. He knew alcohol could sink its talons into a man with as deadly a grip as any other drug, and even deeper than most. True alcoholism was a disease—an acquired disease, perhaps, but one for which some individuals were born with a predisposition. That Dicky Haili had inherited that unfortunate gene made the Executioner pity him. But there was help available—help Haili and his drinking buddies in and around the Edge of the Island chose to ignore.

And for that, all Bolan felt was disgust.

"You remember which boat he worked on, Dicky?" the Executioner asked.

Haili took another gulp of beer, then said, "Not for sure. I used to see him up here on the docks. Helping dump the nets."

The Executioner stared across the space that separated them from the docks. From where they sat, they had a clear view of the area in general. But identifying the face of any one man—even if the person trying to make the ID was sober—wasn't going to be possible.

Haili would have to be closer. Much closer. Which presented a problem.

There was a better than even chance that the Polynesian Freedom Fighter who worked on the ship would recognize Bolan, Ogatu and Sielert if they showed themselves. If he saw them before they saw him, he would slip away and never be found. But Bolan couldn't just send Haili to the docks on his own and expect him to come back. That would take far more thought and discipline than the little drunk could muster.

No, Dicky Haili would have to have some incentive to keep all that together in his brain. He needed a carrot hung out in front of him. And the Executioner knew there was only one thing that might make the situation important enough that the man would remember even simple instructions. More alcohol. The trick would be to give Haili just enough beer that he reached his own peculiar state of normal function.

Which would be quite a challenge. With a man in such advanced stages of alcoholism, the line separating the convulsions of too little, and the abyss of too much, was thin indeed.

Reaching down between where he and Susan Ogatu sat, Bolan pulled another Heineken from the torn cardboard holding the remaining bottles. "You about finished with that one, Dicky?" he asked.

"Yeah," Haili said, draining what little remained in the green bottle. "Is it time?"

"No," Bolan said. "But I'm going to give you an extra one."

Haili's eyes lit up like a little boy's on Christmas morning.

"Here's the deal," Bolan said, lifting the bottle in his hand but keeping it out of Haili's reach. "I want you to take this beer and go on down to the docks where you can see better."

"I'll do it," the little man said quickly, reaching up.

The Executioner pulled the bottle out of his reach. "I'm not finished," he said. "There are four beers still up here after this one. Now, if you don't see the guy who had you buy the raft, come back in an hour and I'll give you another one. You come back before, you get squat." He watched the quick calculations going on behind the eyes of the little man. It was amazing how shrewd even the most pickled brain could get when there was a chance of obtaining more pickling juice. Haili was trying to figure out just how to work the situation so he could get the maximum amount of alcohol into his system.

"I know what you're thinking," Bolan said. "If you see him too soon, you lose the rest of the beer. So I'll sweeten the pot. When you find the man, come back. As soon as we're convinced you didn't lie, you get whatever's left all at once. And I'll even give you enough money to go buy another six-pack."

Haili looked like a man who'd just won the lottery. "Deal," he said. He reached for the bottle in Bolan's hand again.

The Executioner continued to hold it back. "One more thing," he said. "You finger the wrong guy so you can win the jackpot early, and my promise to take you to the detox clinic still holds. You got that?"

Haili nodded vigorously. His eyes were still glued to the bottle in the Executioner's hand. Bolan handed it to him. Haili popped the cap and downed half of it before getting out of the Nissan.

Greg Sielert waited until he was halfway to the docks, then said, "Man, that's pathetic." He paused, then added. "Does it bother you at all to give him beer?"

Susan Ogatu answered the question for Bolan. "What's wrong, Greg?" she asked. "You worried that we're leading him astray? Considering the hundreds of gallons of alcohol that have already passed through his liver and kidneys, I don't think another couple of six-packs is going to make much difference."

The Executioner watched the little man disappear into the shadows, then reappear in the moonlight and sit down under a palm tree near the docks. Haili still held the bottle, but Bolan guessed it was empty long before he finished his walk. He kept bringing it up to his lips, however, whether out of habit or the hope he might be able to squeeze out a few more drops, the Executioner didn't know.

Time passed slowly as they waited, watching the fishing boats take turns pulling into the docks to dump their nets. As each boat finished the process, it sailed away from the docks to let the next craft in. But Bolan noticed that many of the men, their work finished for the night, headed from the fish market toward the bars. Throughout it all, Dicky Haili sat under his tree, fidgeting and squirming, still holding the empty Heineken bottle like Linus clinging to his security blanket in a Peanuts comic strip.

Thirty minutes later, Bolan saw the little man stand and start toward the Nissan.

"Just when the stench was about to clear out," Ogatu said.

Haili walked to the driver's side of the car. "Is it time?" he asked.

"Close enough," Bolan said, and handed the man another bottle. "No sign of him?"

The soldier had to wait while Dicky Haili downed half the Heineken. The man choked, coughed, then shook his head and started back to his tree.

Fifteen minutes later, Bolan saw Haili suddenly spring from his seat and stagger toward them again. He clenched his fists. Bolan winced. He hadn't instructed the little drunk to play it cool when he saw the man, knowing he was already taxing a brain that would be coveted by alcohol abuse researchers someday. He would have to pray that the man who had hired Haili to buy the raft hadn't spotted the drunk's sudden burst of enthusiasm and grown suspicious.

Haili stumbled to the Nissan. "It's him!" he whispered excitedly. "He's down there now. Just got off the boat!" He looked past the Executioner at what remained of the six-pack.

"You're sure?" Bolan asked.

"I'm sure," Haili said.

Bolan handed him another bottle of beer. "You get the rest, and the money, when *I'm* sure. Get in."

Haili got in next to Sielert. Bolan dragged what he believed was probably a fairly accurate description of the man out of him. The fisherman on the docks helping unload the catch was Samoan, and like most Samoans, he was big. He wore a short-sleeved blue chambray work shirt rolled up over his powerful arms. Long black hair fell to his shoulders. There was only one thing that might differentiate him from a dozen other fishermen. Instead of blue jeans or khaki work pants, the suspected PFF man wore a threadbare pair of dark brown slacks.

"Will he get back on the boat or come ashore?" Bolan asked Haili.

The little drunk shrugged nervously. "Don't know," he said. "I've seen him do both."

The soldier turned in his seat. He didn't want to grab the man for questioning on the dock in front of the others if he didn't have to. Word would quickly spread, and it would get back to Benjamin Liholiho and the rest of the PFF. So he'd have to wait, and hope that the big Samoan chose to hit the bars tonight. If he didn't, if it looked like he planned to get back on the boat, Bolan and Susan were close enough to sprint to the docks, show their credentials and take him that way.

But this night luck seemed to be on their side. As soon as the fish were all dumped into the waiting containers, several shadowy forms started away from the fish market toward the street. Bolan handed another Heineken over the seat and said, "Go over there where you can see them. Make *sure* it's him. If it is, throw down the bottle and break it so we'll know."

"Waste good beer?" Haili said as if Bolan had asked him to desecrate a church. "Don't grab him while I'm there...*please*," Haili said. "He'll know—"

"We won't," Bolan said. He pulled a ten-dollar bill from his pocket and handed it to the man. Any more, and Haili would probably drink himself to death that very night.

Haili grabbed the money.

"I'd tell you to go get something to eat but it wouldn't do any good," Bolan said.

Haili was a drunk, not a liar. "No, it wouldn't," he said.

"But I will tell you this. You ID the wrong guy or try to run, and I will drop everything until I see you strapped to a hospital bed and screaming at the ghosts. You got that?"

The man in the back seat nodded as he stared at the beer in one hand, the ten-dollar bill in the other. He got out of the car and crossed the street, sticking the money into a filthy trouser pocket.

One by one, two by two and sometimes in larger groups, men from the fishing boat that had just finished unloading began to leave the docks and walk up the sidewalk toward the bar area. They passed the little drunk, who sat cross-legged on the grass with his bottle clenched protectively to his chest as if it were a baby, without seeming to notice him. Many of the men were large, many looked Samoan and many wore ragged blue chambray work shirts. But only one, who finally came stalking up the sidewalk alone, wore tattered brown dress slacks.

The sound of breaking glass broke the stillness of the night.

Bolan let the man get a block past where they were parked before starting the engine. He drove past him, then cut the Nissan into a fast U-turn and pulled up next to him. With the mammoth Desert Eagle extended through the open window, the barrel pointed at the big Samoan's chest, he said simply, "Get in."

WITH BOTH OGATU and Sielert holding the big Samoan at gunpoint, Bolan drove along the Bayfront Highway until they crossed the Wailuku River. Roughly halfway between Hilo and the city of Papa'ikou, he found a deserted stretch of beach and pulled the Nissan off the road and onto the sand beneath the soft Hawaiian moon.

Ogatu and Sielert kept their guns trained on the Samoan as Bolan exited the driver's seat and drew the Desert Eagle once more. Opening the back door with his free hand, he said firmly, "Get out."

A snarl covered the Samoan's face as he got out of the Nissan. Bolan took a step back as the man rose to his feet. The guy looked tough. He wasn't going to talk easily if he was a die hard member of the PFF, and the Executioner hadn't yet decided exactly how to make the man change his mind.

Still at gunpoint, Bolan forced the man away from the car and toward the waters of Hilo Bay, away from any curious eyes that might pass in cars along the highway. Ogatu and Sielert followed. From behind, the Samoan's arms looked like the trunks of small oak trees; his legs could have been giant redwoods. But he walked with surprising agility and grace for a man so large.

When they were twenty feet from the water, the Executioner said, "Stop right there."

The man did as ordered, turning to face Bolan. "What'd I do, fuck your sister and get her pregnant?" he asked with no trace of fear in his voice.

The Executioner ignored the comment. "I want information from you and I'm going to get it," he said. "I can get it the easy way or the hard way. It's up to you."

The man snarling at him remained silent.

"I want to know where the nukes have gone," he said.

The snarl on the other man's face became an expression of total surprise. If he was acting, he deserved an Academy Award for the performance. "What nudes?" he said.

"Nukes," Bolan repeated. "As in nuclear bombs."

The look of astonishment on the man's face intensified, then he burst into laughter. "What in the hell are you talking about?" he asked.

Bolan stared at the man's eyes, trying to determine whether or not his ignorance was as sincere as it appeared. He couldn't be sure. "I'm talking about the nukes that you and your Polynesian Freedom Fighter brothers unloaded yesterday," he said.

The big Samoan shook his head. "First of all," he said. "I got nothing to do with those PFF sons of bitches. They're a bunch of stupid, idiotic morons who refuse to face reality." He snorted through his nose like a bull. "Gonna take back the islands and we'll all wear grass G-strings over our dicks again. Right. And as far as nukes go, I don't know what the hell you're talking about. In fact, what I think you are is a damn lunatic."

"You had Dicky Haili buy a raft for you a couple of months ago," Bolan said.

"Yeah," the big man said, crossing his thick arms across his expansive chest. "So what?"

"That raft was used to off-load the nukes from a yacht."

"Bullshit," the Samoan said. "A friend of mine who used to be on the boat with me started a private fishing business. He asked me to pick one up for him, and I forgot all about it until it was time for me to ship out. Then I saw the drunk on my way to the boat and promised him a case of beer when I got back if he'd go do it for me while I was at sea."

The Executioner thought about it. The story had the ring of truth, but there were holes in it. "What made you think he wouldn't just drink your money away?" he asked.

"I told him I'd kill him if he did," the big Samoan said. "And he knew I meant it."

"Give me the name of your friend who wanted the raft."

The surprise had worn off the man's face. And he was tired of the questions. His lips moved slowly, forming the two words precisely under the moonlight. "Fuck you," he said. "I've told you all I'm going to. I ain't giving up a friend." He stared at the Executioner, the snarl returning to his lips. "Go ahead and shoot me if you want, you pansy-assed bastard. But you wouldn't be half the man you think you are right now if it weren't for that gun in your hand."

The path to the truth the big Samoan held became clear to Bolan. Slowly, he lowered the Desert Eagle, then turned slightly and handed it to Susan Ogatu. The Honolulu detective seemed able to read his mind, and she stared at him, her face concerned, but didn't say anything.

Bolan jerked the Beretta 93-R from his shoulder rig and handed it to Greg Sielert. The Applegate-Fairbairn combat dagger and its smaller folding companion came out of their sheaths, and Susan took them, too.

The Samoan had figured out that the man who had held the Desert Eagle had accepted his challenge. And he loved the idea. "Only problem I see now," he said, "is that the bitch and your little squirrel of a friend are going to shoot me after I kick your ass for you."

Bolan shook his head. "No, they won't. You've got my word on it."

The Samoan cackled like a banshee. "I'm supposed to trust a guy who just kidnapped me?" he said.

"You have a better offer?" the Executioner asked. When the man didn't answer, he said, "Here's the deal. We're going to fight, and we're going to find out just how big we both are without guns. If you win, you go free. In fact we'll give you a lift back to town."

"Your friends might," the Samoan said. "You won't be in any shape to drive." He uncrossed his arms and laced his fingers together, cracking his knuckles loudly.

"If I win," Bolan said, "you take us to the friend of yours who wanted the raft. Got it?"

The big Samoan threw back his head and laughed again.

"That's not going to happen," he said. "But sure, yeah, just in case, I agree."

Bolan let a hard smile cover his face. "You have a name?" he asked.

The big Samoan quit laughing, and his eyes narrowed. "They call me Kekaha," he said. "Don Kekaha."

The Executioner nodded as he moved toward the Samoan. "Okay, Don Kekaha," he said. "Let's go."

WITH HIS ELBOWS supporting him on the safety rail that circled the platform, Benjamin Liholiho held the shark-tooth club in his right hand, tapping it lightly on the palm of his left, as he watched the fishing boat crest the waves toward him. He and Vladimir Syvatoslav had arrived at the abandoned offshore drilling rig by helicopter thirty minutes earlier, circling the area several times to insure that it was deserted, then finally landing on the helipad next to the saltwater-worn steel of the derrick. Liholiho glanced quickly to the crown block at the top of the tower high over his head. Except for the rusty traveling block attached to the derrick and a few broken parts from the gas lift module scattered around the deck, the site had been cannibalized. All usable equipment had been taken elsewhere, and the platform looked very much like a ghost town in one of the Old West movies the Americans held so dear. Movies in which they stole the land of the Native Americans like they had the Native Hawaiians, thought Liholiho.

He smiled. But the offshore site also looked like a supermarket, appliance store or other business after the Rodney King riots in Los Angeles. The thought brought a smile to his heart. Even on the mainland, the oppressed who had so long been downtrodden by the descendants of the white Europeans were rising up to take back what should have been theirs all along.

The PFF man took another glance around the stripped production platform. It was everything he needed—more, actually. All he needed was something to which he could attach the nuclear bomb, to keep it from drifting.

As the big Samoan continued to watch, one of the boat's

crew—Jonathan Laulau, his most trusted man within the PFF—threw a line around one of the platform's thick steel girders. The girders extended out of sight beneath the water all the way to the ocean floor. Laulau tied the line, then two other men began carefully prying open the wooden crate on the deck of the boat while another pair donned scuba gear. Laulau looked at the PFF leader and grinned.

Liholiho watched the men as they prepared for their tasks. He heard none of the jokes or banter or good-natured insults that usually flew between his PFF brothers when they were together. This day they were silent. They were serious. They knew what they had in the wooden crate, and although the chances of it hurting them at this stage were nonexistent, the capabilities of what they possessed had draped the most somber of moods over them all.

"So," Syvatoslav said next to Liholiho. "When will you contact Washington?"

"Tonight, Vlad," Liholiho replied. "Or perhaps in the morning. As soon as both weapons are in place."

Syvatoslav chuckled. "I'm glad you finally found a suitable spot," he said, looking at the production platform beneath his worn brown shoes. "I myself wouldn't have been so choosy."

"I know, Vlad," the PFF leader said. "You made that clear many times." He glanced at the Ukrainian, then turned his eyes to the boat. He had searched the ocean for months to find just the right spot to plant the smaller of the nuclear bombs. He had wanted a site that was far not only from land but from the shipping lanes, as well. And he needed it to be far enough away that the tidal wave the explosion produced would die down to manageable size by the time it reached land. Liholiho agreed with Syvatoslav that the United States wasn't likely to give in to his demands without proof that he did indeed possess weapons of mass destruction. The first bomb—the one the men slipping into their fins, face masks and buoyancy units would plant just beneath the platform—would have to be detonated. In his heart, he was sure of it. But he had no desire to kill anyone—even white Americans—if he didn't have to do so.

All Benjamin Liholiho wanted was his islands back. And a billion dollars to rejuvenate the Polynesian culture, of course.

Finally ready, the men who had opened the crate were assisted by two more who carefully lifted the water-sealed plastic container from inside the wood. Sweat dripped from their foreheads, and their faces were masks of terror. The way they held the hard plastic case, they looked like four men crowded around a newborn infant, all worried that the baby might fall and injure itself.

Jonathan Laulau looked up from the boat again. "Ready?" he asked.

Liholiho smiled and nodded. Laulau had studied nuclear fission and had activated the bomb while they were still on the fishing boat. Then it had been sealed into the container. The PFF man knew little about nuclear fission himself—but he knew dropping the case wouldn't detonate the reactor. Only a series of complex entries into the remote control device in his pocket would do that. And the code was long and complicated enough that the chances of the bomb exploding prematurely were nonexistent.

The two men in scuba gear slipped carefully into the water, then pulled their face masks up from around their necks and placed them over their eyes. They stuck their breathing regulators into their mouths, then looked at the platform.

Liholiho nodded. The scuba divers turned to the boat and gave the signal to the men holding the plastic case.

The case was lowered carefully into the water, and a moment later it disappeared beneath the waves with the two divers.

The leader of the PFF turned to his Ukrainian friend. "When this is over," he said, "you will receive your two million dollars. But I would like to make you another offer, too."

Syvatoslav's thick eyebrows lowered. "Yes?" he said.

"It is true you are white," Liholiho said. "But you have given me a new perspective on white men. Some of them, at least. In your part of the world, Caucasians turned on fellow Caucasians."

Syvatoslav pulled the familiar handkerchief from his pocket and mopped his forehead as he nodded. "This is true," he said. "But I don't understand—"

"Lasso," Liholiho said, "I'd like you to stay in Hawaii. Without you, none of this would have been possible." His eyes fell to the water below the platform, where the divers had disappeared, then looked up to stare the shorter man in the eye. "If your part in this operation for freedom should come out—"

"And it will come out," Syvatoslav said. "Just as I told you the American intelligence network would learn you obtained the bombs, eventually they will learn that I played a part in it."

"*When* it comes out, then," Liholiho said. "You won't be safe anywhere else in the world, Lasso. You *must* take me up on my offer."

A thin smile crossed Syvatoslav's face, but only for a second, before the frown returned. "I have thought of this," he said. "But I have made arrangements to go into hiding. Correct me if I am wrong, but it was my understanding that white men wouldn't be welcome in the new Hawaii."

Liholiho chuckled. "The new Hawaii will actually be a return to the old Hawaii. But regardless of what it is called, I offer you sanctuary here. I'll find a place of importance for you in my government. And you will be revered as a hero of the Polynesian people. The *one* white man who understood the theft of our homeland and the enslavement of our people."

A look of shock covered Syvatoslav's face. "I don't know what to say," he said. "I'm honored beyond words." His hand rose to his chest, and he patted it. With a sly grin, he asked, "Are you sure you aren't just trying to get rid of me by giving an old man a heart attack?"

Liholiho laughed openly. "No, my friend," he said. "If that was my wish, there are far easier ways to get that done." He continued to smile as he raised the shark-tooth club in one hand and tapped the Raging Bull in the other. "I want to put you to work, Lasso. You have a tremendous mind and many more good years in you before we put you out to pasture on one of our cattle ranches.''

An expression of humbleness covered Syvatoslav's face. ''Again, I am honored. And I accept. Without reservation.'' He mopped more sweat from his face, then said, ''But before that takes place, there is one minor problem I see in the operation that will make it all possible.''

''Yes?'' Liholiho said.

The scuba divers surfaced and removed their masks.

''It is done,'' one of them yelled.

''Perhaps we should discuss the problem as we fly,'' Syvatoslav said, turning toward the helipad behind them. ''There is little sense in staying here now. And however unlikely it might be, there is always the possibility of being spotted from the air by the wrong set of eyes.''

Liholiho followed the Ukrainian as the old man limped toward the helipad where their pilot sat in the chopper. He had thought everything was all ironed out, and now Syvatoslav's mention of a problem brought a sick feeling to his stomach. ''Is it serious, Lasso?'' he asked nervously as he helped the Ukrainian board the helicopter. ''This problem?''

Syvatoslav turned to face the PFF man as he sat. ''Yes,'' he said. ''I believe it is.'' Then, seeing the worried look on Liholiho's face, he laughed and quickly added. ''But don't worry. I have already devised a plan to circumvent it.''

DON KEKAHA had walked smoothly and gracefully for such a big man when Bolan had watched him earlier. Now he proved what the Executioner had seen wasn't a fluke. Kekaha's jaw tightened as he began to circle the Executioner. They were ten feet away from each other. Kekaha's arms hung loosely at his sides. He rolled his shoulders, then snapped his elbows, loosening the muscles.

A puncher, Bolan thought.

Kekaha shifted his weight to his right leg and snapped his left at the ground in more preparation for battle. Then, shifting to his left leg, he repeated the motion on the opposite side.

Bolan nodded. *And* a kicker.

Kekaha continued to circle, gradually working closer to the soldier. When roughly five feet separated the two men, he raised his hands in a classical boxing pose, fists clenched. The Executioner saw the subtle shift in balance a hundredth of a second before Kekaha charged.

Yes, the big Samoan was a puncher and a kicker. But he was also a grappler, and because of his weight advantage he hoped to take Bolan to the ground. And he was smart—he had done everything except hand paint a sign to tell the Executioner that he planned to fight on his feet.

Bolan held his ground until the last possible microsecond, stepping to the side just before big Samoan arms reached out to engulf him. He brought his knee up to the side, catching Kekaha just under the armpit. But the knee glanced off, doing little damage.

The sudden movement shocked the Samoan more than it hurt him. He spun in the sand, stopping in place and staring at the Executioner. Then, he smiled. "You're smarter than you look," he said.

Bolan smiled back. "You, too," he said. "But not smart enough."

"We'll see, won't we?"

"Yes. We'll see."

Kekaha raised his arms again, this time with the fingers spread. He turned slightly sideways, shifting into a cat stance with most of his weight on his rear leg. He was doing his best to telegraph a kick with his front leg. Bolan wasn't surprised when it came. But he was even less surprised when it was thrown halfheartedly, then followed by another charge.

The Executioner stepped to the other side, throwing a left hook as the big Samoan passed. His fist caught the man on the ear, but again, much of the power was lost as Kekaha passed by. Kekaha stopped suddenly in the sand, shooting his leg behind him in a back kick that could have split a four-by-four beam, had it struck one.

Bolan didn't intend to let that happen. He swept it to the side with the palm of his hand, letting the force of the kick spend itself in thin air.

Don Kekaha's breathing came a little harder as he turned. "Tell me when you're ready to get serious," Bolan said.

The big Samoan's eyes narrowed. In the dark brown orbs, the Executioner read several emotions. Surprise—Kekaha had probably easily whipped every man he'd ever fought. At least easier than now. But Bolan saw a trace of fear enter the Samoan's eyes, as well. If the Samoan had never lost a fight, that meant he didn't know how to lose. And that scared him. But most of all, what Bolan saw in the eyes squinting in the moonlight was rage.

Don Kekaha was mad.

The big Samoan charged again, this time snorting like an angry bull. He kept his head down and his eyes up. For the third time, Bolan waited until he was within arm's reach, then stepped to the side. Reaching out, he grabbed the man's chin with one hand, the hair on the top of his head with the other. The Executioner twisted, and Don Kekaha went twirling off to land on his back fifteen feet away.

Bolan moved in quickly, but Kekaha returned to his feet like a panther. The fall had knocked the anger out of him— or at least brought him to his senses and reminded him that losing control of his temper in a fight usually meant losing altogether. He crouched slightly, facing the Executioner head on, his open hands held in front of him. The man had trained in a variety of fighting styles, Bolan decided.

A little light sparring followed, with Kekaha throwing punches and kicks and Bolan blocking and countering. But Kekaha was no rookie, and he knew how to protect himself, too. A front kick to the groin forced the Executioner back a pace, and the big Samoan immediately followed with a side-thrust kick from the opposite side. Bolan took another step back, suddenly knowing what had to follow.

Don Kekaha twisted out of the side kick, turning his face away from the Executioner. His right leg came up at the knee in preparation for another of the furious back kicks Bolan had seen earlier. But this time, instead of sweeping the kick to the side, the Executioner stepped inside it before the kick could be launched. The movement jammed the Samoan, breaking his balance.

Bolan's right cross to the kidney broke that balance even further.

Kekaha dropped to his knees but twisted to wrap his arms around the Executioner. He still had enough strength to pull inward, and Bolan found his legs leaving the ground. Throwing all his weight backward, he flew away from the Samoan, landing on his back in the beach. He scrambled to his feet as Kekaha crawled toward him on hands and knees through the flying grains of sand.

Bolan brought his knee up, catching Kekaha squarely under the chin as the man tried to stand. The impact would have knocked any normal man senseless. But Don Kekaha was no normal man, and while the blow caused his head to quiver, it seemed to help propel him to his feet.

The Executioner stepped forward.

It was time to end this game and get on with the mission.

The two men circled each other again. Kekaha threw a left, then a right. Bolan countered. Then, faking a left jab, he stopped suddenly and twisted into a hook that caught the big Samoan on the same ear he'd hit earlier. A right cross followed, striking Kekaha squarely in the nose and sending blood flying from both nostrils. Bolan lowered his target, attacking the midline as the Samoan's hands rose instinctively to his face. Another left hook caught the man in the ribs. Then a right uppercut lifted the big Samoan off his feet an inch before dropping him onto his back in the sand.

Bolan stepped cautiously forward. Don Kekaha had proven he could take tremendous punishment and still come back swinging, and the Executioner intended to take no chances that he was playing possum. He looked at the prostrate form covered in sand. The Samoan's eyes were open. But they seemed to be gazing without sight at the stars.

"You awake?" Bolan asked.

The dark brown eyes fluttered. Then, slowly, they cleared. They moved slightly to look at the Executioner. With blood pumping from his nose and dripping down his cheeks, a grin broke across Don Kekaha's face. "When do we leave?" the big Samoan asked.

Bolan frowned. Kekaha sounded as if he were still half giddy

But he wasn't. Reaching up, he extended a hand toward the Executioner. "Help me up, you big son of a bitch," he said.

The Executioner extended his hand.

"I promised to take you to my friend if I lost," Kekaha said. "And a promise is a promise."

8

With Don Kekaha sitting where Dicky Haili had been earlier, the back seat of the Nissan looked a lot more crowded than it had. The big Samoan's wide shoulders seemed to stretch all the way across the seat to where Dr. Greg Sielert was crushed against the opposite window.

Bolan followed Kekaha's directions, guiding the Nissan into Hilo Bay, then turning inland onto Waianuenue Avenue. In the rearview mirror, he could see the big Samoan watching him. Kekaha's eyes held a mixture of curiosity and respect. "I've never lost a fight before in my life," he finally said. "At least not against just one man." A light rain began to fall as he asked, "Where'd you learn to fight like that?"

The Executioner shrugged. "Here and there," he said.

Kekaha nodded. "Well, it wasn't all in dojos and boxing gyms. You've had your share of real world experience, is my guess."

Bolan didn't respond.

"I used to be in the Marines," Kekaha went on. "Every place I was stationed, I'd try to find the best school. Okinawa, Manila, you name it. Never got much rank in anything but picked up a little bit of each system and made it my own."

"You look like you did a good job of it," said Sielert, who never seemed to tire of his interest in combat. "What did you do in the Marines?"

Kekaha shrugged. "Beat people up and shot them," he said.

"You make it to the Gulf?" Sielert asked.

Kekaha nodded. "And Panama," he said. He leaned forward in his seat. "There," he told Bolan. "Turn there." He pointed at a street sign.

The soldier made the turn, and Kekaha directed him half a block down the residential street, then to the curb in front of a split-level lower-middle-income house. "What's your friend's name?" Bolan asked.

"Yates," Kekaha said. "Nathan Yates. Everybody calls him Nate, though."

"Cute," Susan Ogatu said. "Nate Yates. An Anglo?"

Kekaha nodded. "White as Wonder bread," he said.

Bolan killed the Nissan's engine. The lawn and flower beds in front of the house were well kept, and except for a couple of overturned tricycles in the front yard, everything was in place. Several lights were on inside the dwelling and glowed eerily through the closed curtains and the steadily increasing rainfall. "Okay, Don," he said. "Stay here. No sense in your friend finding out it was you who fingered him."

The big Samoan threw back his head and laughed the way he had when Bolan had implied that he might take a beating on the beach. "Like he's not going to figure it out?" he said. "No, I'll go with you. I want to find out what's going on as much as you." He paused, clenched one massive fist, then opened it again. "Like I just told the lady, this guy's an Anglo so he ain't gonna be part of the PFF, either. But he's still got some explaining to do—to us both." The fist closed. "One way or the other, he's going to explain. I don't like getting used. Especially by a friend."

Bolan turned to look at Sielert. "Greg, stay here and guard the car," he said. "It could get stolen in a neighborhood like this."

Sielert took a quick glance around and frowned. The neighborhood might not have been Knob Hill, but it wasn't East L.A., either. He understood the real reason Bolan wanted him to stay—so he wouldn't be in the way. He looked a little sad when he nodded.

Exiting the car, Bolan led the way to the front porch. His knock was answered by a small, frail-boned white woman with a baby in her arms. She had the pale, drained look of a woman who spent twenty-five hours a day cleaning house, washing clothes and chasing rug rats all over the neighborhood.

Don Kekaha said, "Hi, Mary. Need to talk to Nate."

The woman he'd addressed as Mary didn't speak. She just turned and disappeared into the house.

A moment later, a Caucasian man of medium height and weight, clad in a white undershirt, worn-out OD fatigue pants and rubber thongs opened the screen door and stepped onto the porch. He nodded to Kekaha, ignoring Bolan and Ogatu. He didn't speak. The expression on his face made it clear he didn't know what to say—didn't know what the visit was all about, but knew the strange combination of people on his front porch couldn't be good news.

Kekaha didn't waste time. "You told me you needed a raft," the big Samoan said. "I didn't ask you why—just guessed it was for your new business. I don't demand explanations from my friends when they ask for a favor, Nate. I just do it." He paused, and his face held a combination of pain and anger. "Did I make a mistake, Nate? In thinking you were my friend?"

Yates stared at the man for a moment. Suddenly, all the energy seemed to drain from his limbs. He looked at the concrete porch and his legs gave way. He wound up sitting cross-legged on the concrete with silent tears pouring out of his eyes. "I'm sorry, Donnie," he said. "I didn't have any choice."

Kekaha had proven he could be tough. Now he showed another side. Sitting next to his friend, he draped a massive arm around the smaller white man's shoulders. "Just tell me, and these people, what happened," he said.

Between tears, Yates said, "A guy contacted me. Said he'd kill Mary and all the kids if I didn't do it."

"Do what, exactly?" Bolan said, dropping to a squatting position in front of the man.

"I had to supply him with a raft. He paid me a thousand bucks over the cost. But the stipulation was I couldn't buy it myself—had to get somebody else to do the paperwork."

The Executioner nodded. He wondered how many other layers Benjamin Liholiho had built between the actual purchase

of the raft and the PFF. Such layers could always be tracked
down. But each additional step took time. And even though
the PFF hadn't yet contacted the U.S. with their demands, he
knew time was running short.

Now that he'd spoken, a dam in Nate Yates's heart seemed
to burst, with the spillover coming out his mouth. "The guy
said he'd kill my family if I didn't do it, Donnie," he repeated.
"And he would have. I could see it in his eyes. And I needed
the money. The new fishing business isn't working worth a
shit. We're behind on the house payment, the car—" Another
huge sob racked his chest. But he seemed calmer when it was
over. "I knew it was going to be used for drug smuggling,"
Yates said. "But what could I do, Donnie? What could I do?"

The Executioner saw no reason to tell the man what the raft
had been used for—it would only make him feel worse. Compared to blowing up millions of innocent people, drug smuggling was on a par with the grade-school kid who chewed gum
in class. "Do you know the man's name?" he asked Yates.
"The man who contacted you?"

Nathan Yates shook his head. "No," he said. "I never
asked. Didn't want to know."

Bolan felt his jaw tighten. He believed the man. But did
that mean the trail ended here? "Okay, Mr. Yates," he said.
"But is there anything else you can tell us that might help us
find him?"

Yates looked into the eyes of the Executioner. "Well," he
said, "I don't know if it would help. But I could take you to
the place where I delivered the raft."

AS IT TURNED OUT, there was no reason for Nathan Yates to
leave his family and take them to the spot where he'd delivered the raft. Don Kekaha knew the area well.

Yates had been ordered to follow a specific route, and he
had done so to the letter, fearing for the lives of his wife and
children. He had been sent to a launch point just on the other
side of where the yacht had been abandoned.

Bolan set his jaw as he drove along the Chain of Craters
Road, dodging the larger of the huge depressions that had

given the path its name. He was surrounded by lava flows and an electrifying ocean view in the distance. A sign on their left announced the Pu'u Loa Petroglyphs. They drove toward the water.

They had ridden silently much of the way, the quiet broken only now and then by Sielert's need to fill the air with speech. As they passed the sign, the scientist said, "You know, Donnie, you take up a lot more room back here than Dicky Haili did."

"But he smells better," Ogatu said from the front seat.

Reaching the shoreline, Bolan stopped the Nissan. He didn't need to get out of the car to see where the raft, and many other rafts and boats over the years, had been launched into the sea. The tracks of vehicles and skid marks through the lava gravel were evident.

Bolan threw the Nissan into park and closed his eyes, thinking. Was there anything here to learn? He already knew where the raft had gone after being launched—up the coast to where the yacht had been anchored. Was he at a dead end?

There's something along the road, he thought. *Something near the...*

Bolan opened his eyes, threw the Nissan into reverse and backed onto the Chain of Craters Road. Maybe driving it once more would let the thought surface.

"Going back?" Sielert asked.

No one answered, and the scientist picked up on the fact that he should remain silent, too.

Bolan drove slowly the way he had come. Rather than focus on any one thing in his field of vision, he tried to take the scenery in whole rather than in parts. They passed the sign pointing to the petroglyphs, and the uneasy feeling intensified. He drove another half mile, and it began to lessen. He reversed direction again. He didn't know what it was he'd seen, but it was near the sign.

The Executioner dropped his speed, dodging the holes in the pitted road and watching the horizon. Thirty feet from the Pu'u Loa sign, the feeling came over him again. He stepped on the brake. The Nissan's engine idled as he stared at the sign. Finally, he said, "You know anything about the petroglyphs, Donnie?"

"Sure," Kekaha said. "Big tourist spot for hikers. There's a whole field of etchings…done by some of my ancestors, is the guess."

"Lots of tourist traffic?" Bolan asked. If so, it didn't make sense to take the nuclear bomb there.

Kekaha wasn't stupid. "Too much for what you're thinking, would be my guess. Unless, of course, you want to follow that old saying about hiding in plain sight."

Bolan hesitated. That was always possible, but his instincts told him it wasn't the case. He stared at the sign. He hadn't decided what it was that had registered in his subconscious.

The Executioner pulled out his cellular phone. Sometimes, when you tackled a problem too directly, the answers slipped away. It was often better to think about something else for a while. Sometimes, when you did, the little voice in your brain suddenly shouted the answers unexpectedly. He tapped in the number to Stony Man Farm. When Price answered, he said, "Hi, Barb. Anything new?"

"By that, I suppose you want to know if the PFF has contacted the U.S. yet. The answer is no."

"Well," Bolan said, "it can't be much longer. They've got the bombs, and they've had time to set them up wherever it is they're going to. Anything from the Bear?"

"Yeah," Price said. "Hang on."

As the Nissan continued to idle, Bolan listened to the line connect to Kurtzman's computer room. A moment later, Kurtzman lifted the phone. "Striker?" he asked.

"Go. What've you got?"

"Okay. Vladimir Syvatoslav," the computer genius said. "Born in Vinnitsa, Ukraine, 1932. Flew for the Soviet air force, and it looks like he was certified to fly almost as many different birds as our own beloved flyboy, Mr. Grimaldi. From the air force he went to the KGB. Made it to colonel. You mentioned his nickname was Lasso, I believe?"

"That's what I was told."

"Well, he didn't get it from watching old Gene Autry movies. He'll use any weapon to get the job done but, according to this, he *likes* strangling people. Particularly with ropes."

"Sounds like a nice guy," Bolan said.

"Oh, yeah, life of the party." Kurtzman took time for a breath, then went on. "Anyway, another KGB man—Leon Kishinev—supposedly hung the moniker on him and it stuck. When the Soviet Union went, Syvatoslav disappeared into thin air for a while. Resurfaced in a few intel reports doing contracts for the Russian Mafia. Interpol and other intel nets suspect him in international smuggling ops, and I'd say that's not only possible but probable—he has links to other criminal organizations around the world." Kurtzman paused, then added, "I think he's your man."

The Executioner's face tightened. "Then you must know more."

The man called the Bear chuckled on the other end of the line. "There was a mass murder near Odessa last week. Among the dead—who all had Soviet military or KGB backgrounds, by the way—was Syvatoslav's old chum Leon Kishinev."

"Sounds like a smuggling deal gone bad," Bolan said.

"I tapped into Ukrainian intelligence," Kurtzman said. "They think Syvatoslav did a deal with Kishinev, then turned on him. They suspect drugs."

"Everyone always suspects drugs," Bolan said, his mind flitting from the DEA man on the yacht to Donnie Kekaha's friend Nathan Yates. "What do *you* think, Bear?" Bolan wanted to know.

"I think it was your nukes," Kurtzman said without hesitation. "Syvatoslav is getting up there in years, and my guess is he's ready to retire. To do that, he needs one last big score. So he takes the money to buy the nukes for the PFF but kills his old friends and keeps the cash. Then he delivers the bombs to Hawaii and also gets whatever commission he was promised for his services on top of that. After that, who knows? Maybe he plans to retire to Tahiti where the women go topless."

The soldier didn't answer right away. He agreed with Kurtzman—but only up to a point. This Syvatoslav was undoubt-

edly the man called Vlad, and Vlad was of the right age to be
thinking about retirement. But he didn't think the money for
the nukes and his commission from the PFF was the big score
on which the Ukrainian was planning to retire. Not when there
was an even bigger one he could net.

"Okay, Bear, thanks," Bolan said. "Have Barb get in touch
as soon as Liholiho makes contact."

"Will do, Striker," Kurtzman said.

Bolan hung up and turned halfway in his seat. "Anything
else besides the petroglyphs in the area?" he asked the Samoan behind him.

"Lots of lava." Kekaha chuckled. "But nothing else of
interest. Unless religious nuts interest you."

"Religious nuts?"

Kekaha shrugged. "Never seen them myself," he said.
"Supposed to be a sort of a commune or something around
here somewhere. They worship the ancient Polynesian gods.
Hell, I don't know—Jim Jones in a hula skirt or something."

"Where are they?" Bolan asked.

Kekaha turned to face the sign. "Like I said, I don't know.
Just heard about them. But they're supposed to be somewhere
in the area of the petroglyphs."

The Executioner followed the man's gaze to the sign, and
suddenly his subconscious screamed at him. It wasn't anything
about the sign—it was what was just below the sign.

Bolan looked at the small turnout parking area where vehicles could be left while the petroglyph explorers hiked along
the narrow trail to the etchings. Like the coastline at the end
of the road, it was made up of dirty black-gray lava gravel—
a substance that wasn't going to show distinct tire tracks. But
the gravel should at least have been uneven and shown some
sign that tires had crossed and disrupted it. In some places, it
did. But along one stretch of the gravel—a wide area big
enough for a larger vehicle to enter, turn around then leave—
it didn't.

The parking area had been raked. Recently.

Why? Bolan asked himself. Parked cars were to be expected. Hikers arrived in them, left their cars while they ex-

plored the petroglyphs, then came back and drove away. Why would anyone go to the trouble of raking out a specific set of tracks?

The answer the Executioner knew, was both simple and complex at the same time. Simple in that the specific set of tracks that had been raked away showed something distinctly different than the others. Complex in what that something might be.

Bolan pulled the Nissan off the road onto the gravel. "Let's go," he said.

"Where?" Sielert asked as they got out of the Nissan.

"We're going to get some religion, is my guess," Ogatu said.

IF IT WAS a religious commune, it was the most well-armed religious group the Executioner had ever seen. And if the men dressed in camouflage were worshiping the ancient Polynesian gods, they had a funny way of doing it.

From the top of the tall lava formation they had just climbed, Bolan stared through the binoculars. The terrain was as rough and craggy as any he had seen, and to call the encampment a clearing was to stretch the term to its fullest. But the area he saw in the distance did lighten up somewhat compared to the harsh topography he, Ogatu, Kekaha and Sielert had crossed since leaving the trail that led to the petroglyphs. It was a well-hidden area, enclosed by higher lava formations on all sides and invisible.

Bolan dropped the binoculars from his eyes. He had seen men moving about the encampment carrying rifles. But the uneven configuration of the land caused them to appear momentarily, then disappear again. Which made it impossible to estimate how many men there were. And even more impossible to guess whether the nuke that had come ashore on the Big Island might be hidden in the camp.

No, the Executioner thought, as he pulled the binoculars from around his neck and stuck them in the case on his belt, he'd have to get closer if he wanted to know more.

Bolan stared into the distance. A soft probe into the camp

was needed. But soft probes, the Executioner knew from long experience, had a way of turning hard all of a sudden. There was a better than fifty-fifty chance that he'd be discovered during some part of the probe. Which meant shooting would be the name of the game. Forget the fact that he couldn't get an accurate read on the number of enemy. Exact numbers weren't important. Regardless of how many PFF men he was about to face, he was outnumbered, even with his backup.

Bolan let his eyes fall on Ogatu. She had proven herself in battle and would be a benefit to have along. But anyone who hoped to penetrate the camp would have to disguise themselves as one of the men in cammies. And in spite of all the skill and courage Ogatu had demonstrated, the woman had failed miserably when it came to passing herself off as a man.

No, Bolan thought, shaking his head. Susan Ogatu was out.

The Executioner's gaze shifted to Dr. Gregory Sielert. The scientist's spirit was certainly willing. But his flesh was weak—in a different sort of way than that old proverb was usually used. Sielert's personal insecurities would force him to try to do what had to be done, even though he knew he lacked the skill. He'd be willing to die in battle. The problem was, he *would*. And he'd be of little help to Bolan along the way, leaving the Executioner with no one capable of neutralizing the nuclear bomb after his death. If one of the nukes did lay ahead, Bolan would have to figure out a way to get Sielert to it after it had been located. But it made no sense to risk the man's life until he was sure.

No, Sielert was out, too. He'd have to stay with Ogatu.

Bolan's eyes rested finally on Donnie Kekaha. The big Samoan had proven he was one tough hombre when it came to unarmed combat. But this was different. If the soft probe went hard, it wouldn't turn into an episode of *Walker, Texas Ranger*. There would be shooting, not flying fists and feet. But there was another problem to consider, as well. Could the Executioner trust the big Samoan to stand by him, to back him up? Since Bolan had gained the man's respect by whipping him on the beach, Kekaha had done nothing but help them in every way he could. He wasn't part of the PFF. Rather, he was just another in a long line of pawns unwittingly used by them.

But could the man's courage be trusted under these conditions?

The Executioner's instincts said it could. He looked the man in the eye. "You as good with a gun as you are with your fists?" he asked.

"No," the Samoan said honestly. Then he grinned. "But you got to remember, I'm exceptionally good with my fists. So the fact that I'm not as good with a gun as my fists doesn't necessary mean I'm not damn good with a gun." The grin spread. "And I am."

The Executioner couldn't suppress a smile of his own. There were bumps and bruises all over his body that reminded him that while he had beaten Donnie Kekaha, the man was nobody's wimp. If he was even half as good at pulling the trigger as he was at unarmed combat, he'd do.

Bolan looked to Susan Ogatu. "You have both of your Glocks?" he asked.

She nodded.

"Give one to Kekaha," he said, and saw the first wrinkles of resistance begin to form on the woman's face. "Don't argue. Donnie and I are going to sneak into camp, and to do that, we've got to look just like one of the boys. You're great at the things you can do, Susan, but you've proven that looking like a man simply isn't one of them."

"But—"

"No."

Ogatu pulled out one of her Glocks and handed it to Donnie Kekaha.

"This all I get?" the Samoan asked, looking at the polymer weapon. It seemed small in his huge hand.

Bolan looked to Sielert. "Give him your Gold Cup, Greg," he said. Knowing that the wannabe warrior would feel emasculated, he quickly added, "Susan will have her Glock until you both get back to the car. You shouldn't run into any trouble along the way. Once you reach the Nissan, get a pair of the M-16s out of the trunk." He reached into his pocket, pulled out the car keys and flipped them through the air to the scientist.

Sielert caught them, then handed his Colt and two extra magazines to Kekaha.

Without further ado, the people in the group went their separate ways.

A PERIMETER GUARD had been set up roughly an eighth of a mile around the camp in a circle. Bolan had spotted two of them with the binoculars. But as he and Donnie Kekaha made their way over the jagged lava shore, forced to drop to their hands and knees half the time, it was the Executioner's well-trained battle sense that warned him they had neared one of the sentries.

Bolan crept forward with Kekaha at his heels. A few minutes later, the Executioner held up a hand behind him. Kekaha halted on hands and knees.

Bolan crept forward, silently crawling around a lava formation. He caught a glimpse of camouflage and pulled back.

The sentry was on the other side of the formation, sitting on the ground, his back pressed against the lava.

Slowly, half-inch by half-inch to avoid the telltale sound of steel sliding against Kydex, the Executioner drew the six-inch blade of the Applegate-Fairbairn combat dagger from its sheath. He took a deep breath, then stood and turned the corner around the lava formation. As he moved, he cast a quick glance toward the camp.

He could see only two men in the distance, and neither appeared to be looking his way.

The sentry was shocked to suddenly see the big man standing over him. He was even more shocked when the knife came down through the top of his head. The sharp dagger point crunched sickeningly as it penetrated the skull and entered the brain. Bolan pumped it twice, then pulled the dead man back with him as he dropped out of sight. He rolled the body onto its side.

He had chosen the head for his attack to keep from soaking the man's cammies in blood, and the wound in the top of the head hardly bled. But it took both of the Executioner's hands, and a boot against the back of the dead man's neck, to get the firmly wedged blade out of the skull. When he did, blood mixed with gray matter poured forth onto the ground.

As the sentry bled out, Bolan leaned around the lava and waved Kekaha forward.

The big Samoan crawled to his side.

Bolan took off his shirt and wiped the blade of the Applegate-Fairbairn on it, dropping it to the ground and replacing his shoulder rig over bare skin. He wouldn't need the clothes he'd worn. The only problem he saw was that the sentry was bareheaded. And while Donnie Kekaha, with his unmistakable Polynesian features, might be able to get away with that, Bolan would need something to conceal his face when they entered the camp.

Like all Samoans, the dead man was big. Both his camouflage pants and matching BDU shirt fit Kekaha perfectly.

As soon as Kekaha had changed clothes, Bolan lifted the sentry's .30 caliber M-1 carbine. The weapon was a light version of the Garand—an old design. But still a useful one. The Executioner handed it to the Samoan.

"Damn popgun," Kekaha muttered under his breath.

"So shoot straight," Bolan advised. He knew from vast years of combat that shot placement was far more important than caliber.

Bolan led the way through the lava. He hoped to encounter another of the guards along the way, but this time Lady Luck wasn't with them. They reached a spot near the camp where to continue meant exposing themselves to sight. And with the Executioner's wrong clothing and obviously Caucasian features, to do so would have been suicide.

On hands and knees again, Bolan turned toward Kekaha and dropped to a sitting position. "You're going to have to go on alone," he said. "Pick the first man you come to and lure him back out here where I can get his cammies."

Kekaha understood. He grinned as he looked at the Executioner. "What if he's a little guy?" he asked.

"One of the few advantages I've had on this mission," he

said. "There *aren't* any little Samoans." He paused. "Just make sure the man has some kind of headgear."

Kekaha nodded. "I'll be back," he said in a poor imitation of Arnold Schwarzenegger.

The Executioner shifted to watch as Donnie Kekaha stood and strode confidently toward the camp. He had taken no more than a few steps when one of the men from the camp appeared, walking toward him. He wore a floppy hat of the same camouflage pattern as his shirt and pants.

"Hey," Kekaha said. "You got a minute to give me a hand with something?"

The cammie-clad Samoan nodded. "Give me a second first," he said. "I got to take a leak."

The man took several steps into the lava beds, then slung his .30 caliber carbine over his shoulder and began unbuttoning his fatigue pants. Bolan retreated behind the lava to keep from being seen.

A hissing sound echoed through the lava beds, then stopped.

"You finished?" the Executioner heard Kekaha ask.

"Yeah," came the voice of the man who had urinated.

"Good," Kekaha said. A split second later, there was a loud thumping noise.

Kekaha immediately appeared behind the lava with the man hung over one shoulder. He dropped the Polynesian Freedom Fighter on the ground. "I waited for him to piss," he whispered. "Didn't figure you wanted to wear wet fatigues."

"That is greatly appreciated," the Executioner whispered back. He stared at the man on the ground. His eyes were still open. Bolan pushed a finger into his throat but found no pulse. "What did you hit him with?" he asked Kekaha.

The big Samoan held up a fist the size of a softball.

Quickly, Bolan changed into the PFF man's fatigues and pulled the floppy hat over his head, hiding his face with the brim. "You ready?" he asked Kekaha.

"And willing," the big Samoan said.

Both men stood and walked boldly past the final lava formations into the camp.

The ground was still rough in the encampment. But some

effort had been made to make it livable. Bolan saw picks and shovels stacked up inside small lava caves, and a wooden box with no lid had Dynamite stenciled across the side. Evidently, they had blasted out the area, then cleared it with the hand tools.

But why? Bolan wondered. Why go to so much trouble when so many other parts of the Big Island were already habitable?

There could be only one answer. Benjamin Liholiho had wanted this encampment hidden in a spot that was hard to reach if the authorities ever discovered their location. Which, while it didn't assure that the bomb would be hidden there, at least made it an attractive place to cache the device while he negotiated with the United States.

So, where was it?

Bolan counted close to thirty men inside the camp as he and Kekaha made their way over and around the cragged lava formations. Most of the men were lounging in canvas folding chairs or on makeshift seats of hand-smoothed lava. One PFF man had made a hammock out of a bed sheet and olive drab rope, and suspended it between two of the taller lava growths. He lay snoozing in the makeshift bed as they passed.

Other PFF men seemed intent on tasks and moved through the camp with purpose. It was the latter Bolan hoped to fade in with, and he walked with design and authority as he and Kekaha circled the area, looking for any signs of the bomb. He also made sure to keep the hat over his eyes and his face pointed toward the ground.

It appeared to work. None of the PFF men paid them any attention.

The camp appeared to have been built in three tiers, with each level utilizing a natural set of steps made by the lava as a means of access. Wooden platforms had been attached with bolts to the second and third floors of the unusual bivouac, and there were PFF men at all three levels. Unless he found the bomb at ground level, the Executioner knew he would have to check them all before determining that neither of the nukes were in camp. And each level to which he and Kekaha rose would isolate them further from escape if they were discovered.

The single set of ragged lava steps leading to the higher levels was the only way up. And the only way down.

The search on the ground didn't take long, and Bolan risked a quick glance from under the brim of his hat toward the second and third tiers. The second level appeared to be a storage area—as they had done on the ground with the shovels and picks, the PFF had taken advantage of the natural cave formations formed by the lava to store goods. Some of the boxes he could see were large enough to contain one of the nukes. Some were marked on the outside with letters or words, and he saw MRE on several. But other boxes and crates were bare. In any case, it made little difference.

The nuke could be in any of the boxes, regardless of how they were marked. Terrorists weren't likely to write Nuclear Weapon on a crate containing a contraband bomb.

Shifting the .30 caliber to his shoulder on the sling, Bolan walked to the lava staircase and took the first step up. Two more steps up the jagged staircase and he had reached the wooden platforms. He motioned for Kekaha to take the lead, and the big Samoan nodded his understanding. Although there were fewer PFF men on the second tier, the ratio of area to population was more dense. Direct contact was going to be unavoidable.

With Kekaha taking the lead, the two men began working their way around the second tier in a clockwise direction. Kekaha nodded, grunted or said, Hello each time they encountered one of the PFF men. Bolan continued to keep his face down and shield himself from view behind the Samoan's bulky frame. They stopped at each nook and cranny they came to, quickly lifting box lids and letting their eyes skirt the area for anything suspicious. They found nothing. The MREs were just that—Meals Ready to Eat.

The third tier was smaller than the second, with only a few of the wooden platforms bolted to the lava. It appeared to have been designed as a sleeping area for the higher ranking PFF men, and sleeping bags and a few cots were all that would be seen from the second level. But as they climbed the steps, the tan color of a pine crate caught the Executioner's eye just inside one of the larger cavities in the lava.

Several men were napping in their sleeping bags. A card table had been set up. Four men sat around it, playing what looked to be poker. All four had rifles either propped against the table or on the ground beside their chairs.

Were they a special guard unit designed to keep the others away from the nuke? Was it the nuke he saw ahead, in the large pine crate? Bolan didn't know. But he knew they were going to have to pass directly by these men to find out.

Reaching ahead of him, he grasped Kekaha's arm. The big Samoan turned. "There's no BS story we can come up with that's going to hold water," the Executioner whispered. "Can you take out two of them?"

Kekaha nodded. "Sure," he said. "Completely, I suppose?"

The Executioner nodded. "Unless you like the idea of standing here in the open and getting shot at," he said. "Take the man with his back against the lava, and the one to his right. I'll get the two closest to the plank. But don't do anything until you see me move."

"You got it," he whispered. He turned and led the way toward the card table.

Bolan followed, keeping his face down but letting his eyes skirt the two levels below. The men on the second tier weren't a problem—they were directly below, and he and Kekaha would be out of their field of vision. But those on the ground, particularly the ones directly across from them, had a clear view of the card table. And that was the exact spot about a dozen of them had chosen to sit on the ground. As the Executioner followed Kekaha, he could see them talking, laughing and drinking cans of soda pop.

All it would take would be a casual glance upward at the wrong time.

Ahead of him, Kekaha reached the card table. Bolan watched him take a step to the side, moving into a position between the two men who were his targets before saying, "Hey, guys, who's winning?"

"Me." A voice laughed in response. "They're going to be broke, naked and in debt when I get through."

"Yeah, in your dreams," said another man.

Bolan continued to look down as he walked past the table, then stopped between the two men he planned to take out. He wanted to take a quick glance to the ground to insure no one was looking up.

He never got the chance.

Before the Executioner could look down, one of the men at the table said, "Hey, who the hell are—"

Bolan didn't let him finish his sentence. A right cross shot out from his shoulder, smashing into the face of the man to his left. He felt the jawbone splinter beneath his knuckles even as he pivoted on the balls of his feet, bringing his other hand around in a no less devastating left hook.

Across the table, Donnie Kekaha had used a hammer fist to the top of one man's head and a huge forearm strike on the other. All four men were unconscious, and Bolan and Kekaha quickly straightened them in their chairs. Everything appeared normal again.

From the ground, a voice cried out, "Hey, you!"

9

A bombardment of .30 caliber rounds hit the lava walls behind Bolan and Kekaha, sending sharp chips of rock flying. A black cloud of dust rose from behind, covering them and the unconscious card players at the table like a layer of soot.

Bolan and Kekaha hit the platform on their bellies with a combined weight of close to five hundred pounds. The wood swayed like an ocean wave beneath them as the Executioner snapped his Desert Eagle from his hip and Kekaha produced Sielert's Gold Cup.

Bolan had to time his first shot with the oscillation of the platform. As the sights of the Desert Eagle moved across the chest of a PFF man below, he pulled the trigger. A 240-grain hollowpoint round spit from the Eagle, drilling through the terrorist's chest and dropping him to the ground.

Bolan heard two pops from the Colt in Kekaha's hand and saw another man fall. A hard smile curled his lips as he pulled the trigger once more.

Kekaha hadn't lied. He was a good shot.

Swinging the hand cannon slightly to the side, the Executioner squeezed the trigger once again. A huge Samoan—bigger even than Don Kekaha—took the round squarely in his barrel chest. He plummeted to the ground like a felled oak tree with a force that seemed to shake the camp.

More rounds popped to Bolan's side, and he saw another of the PFF men fall against the lava wall on the other side of the camp. The soldier took aim on a man who would have been large by normal standards but was small for a Polynesian.

Again, the Eagle roared. It snatched the top of the terrorist's head off.

Kekaha ran the Gold Cup dry, dropped the magazine and inserted one of the spares Sielert had given him. He turned to the Executioner. "We're going to run out of ammo long before we run out of targets," he said.

Bolan pulled the trigger, driving another .44 Magnum slug into the heart of a PFF man charging toward them. "You forget the carbines?" he asked.

Kekaha had taken aim. He pulled the trigger and another of the enemy bit black lava dust before he chuckled. "You know, I had," he said.

Bolan glanced at the rifle slung across the Samoan's back. More men kept appearing. Each one the Executioner shot seemed to give birth to two more.

Jamming the big hand cannon into his holster, Bolan reached over his head and pulled the M-1 carbine from his back.

The .30 caliber weapon had been designed as a lightweight shoulder weapon to replace the pistol in some areas of military action. That hadn't worked particularly well, but the short rifle had proven to be an adequate weapon anyway. It was fast and easy to maneuver, and the recoil wasn't much worse than a .22 Long Rifle.

Bolan proved that as he laced round after round at the men below.

But the return fire continued in spite of his efforts. In fact, it grew more dense. The men seemed to multiply rather than diminish. The thirty or so men Bolan had counted appeared to have doubled. And he and Kekaha had dropped a good two dozen.

Bolan fired the 15-round magazine in the carbine dry, then rolled to his side. Each of the men who still sat around the card table had a rifle. Grabbing the closest one, he rolled over as he pulled the bolt back slightly.

The chamber was empty. Bolan pulled the bolt the rest of the way back and watched the brass round slide into the barrel as he released the handle. Returning to the prone position, he began to drop the enemy once again,

Kekaha suddenly cursed. Bolan turned to see the man pulling the trigger of his carbine to no effect. The weapon had jammed. The Executioner watched Kekaha try to pull back the bolt, but not even the tremendous strength in the big Samoan's hands could budge the jam. In frustration, Kekaha threw the carbine off the platform to the ground and drew Susan Ogatu's backup Glock. He began pulling the trigger.

Bolan wondered what had become of the men on the second tier of the lava wall. Suddenly a hand gripped his rifle barrel, freezing it in place as the man's other hand brought a .45 caliber pistol toward the Executioner's head.

Dropping his left hand from the grip of the carbine, Bolan reached forward and swept the pistol to the side as the man pulled the trigger. The pistol exploded, the residual powder stinging the skin of his hand as the bullet crashed harmlessly into the lava behind him. But the PFF man didn't relax his grip on the barrel of Bolan's rifle, and in the awkward position in which the Executioner found himself, he had no leverage to rip the weapon away.

The pistol was still in recoil as Bolan reached beneath himself with his left hand. The first weapon his fingers fell upon was the Applegate-Fairbairn, and he ripped it from its Kydex sheath. With the fighting knife held in a saber grip, he lunged forward, pulling hard on the carbine with his other hand. The PFF man's grip on the rifle barrel held firm, and the Executioner pulled him into the knife as he thrust it forward.

The tip of the blade hit the right place.

As the dagger entered the PFF man's right eye socket, he screamed and let go of the carbine barrel. Bolan shifted the rifle slightly and blew the man off the second tier of the compound onto the ground.

The gunfight continued. Kekaha killed as many of the enemy as he could with Ogatu's Glock, then crawled around Bolan to the card table, returning a moment later with two more carbines. Round after round from all sides pummeled the lava. Hot brass casings sparkled under the Hawaiian sun like small golden birds in flight. At first, the return fire from the men in the ground had been frantic, scattered and panic-driven. Bolan had taken note, however, that they'd all been careful not to throw stray shots in the direction of the crate in the crevice at the other end of the plank walk. Was that because it contained a nuclear weapon? Maybe, even if they knew a direct hit wasn't likely to ignite a nuclear bomb.

But as the gunfight had continued, many of the men who had fired wildly had gained control. And as more PFF terrorists emerged from hidden holes in the lava, all of the men's confidence, and with it their marksmanship, improved. The bottom line was that Bolan and Kekaha were still exposed. And the return fire that had missed them by feet earlier was missing them by mere inches now.

Sooner or later, one or more of the PFF men was going to find his range. When he did, it would be all over.

Bolan sighted in on a PFF man who had sprinted from behind one tall lava formation toward another. Before he could reach cover, he had taken two rounds and fell facedown on the ground. Bolan sighted on the top of a head above the black rock and fired. He didn't miss.

Bolan fired the carbine in his hands dry and rolled to grab the last weapon propped against the card table. He realized Kekaha had been right about running out of ammo. The Samoan had just been a little premature in his prediction.

Taking his time, making each shot count, Bolan aimed and fired with precision. With every pull of the trigger, another PFF terrorist went down. And it appeared that the Executioner and Donnie Kekaha were beginning to make a dent in the superior forces.

But would they destroy the remainder of the PFF men at the camp before all their guns ran dry? It didn't look like it.

What kept Bolan going, aiming and firing, wasn't his own survival. What fueled the Executioner in the face of what appeared to be insurmountable odds was the fact that if he died here, millions of innocent men, women and children were likely to be blown to pieces within the next few days.

The Executioner sighted on a running PFF man and started

to pull the trigger. Before he could do so, the man jerked, then fell. Bolan glanced to his side to see if Donnie Kekaha had made the shot. But the big Samoan was in the process of switching from the rifle he'd been shooting to the last carbine.

Bolan looked down and saw another PFF man fall to the ground. The man's elbows were behind him, his shoulder blades trying to touch, just before he fell. The Executioner had seen such a reaction to a bullet many times before, and it meant only one thing.

The man had been shot in the back.

Bolan's eyes rose, skirting the rim off the rock wall that formed the other side of the compound. His eyes caught a slight movement, and a small explosion came from the spot. Below, another of the PFF men fell. The tiny form at the top of the lava wall was far too small to be a Samoan.

A glimmer of light caught the corner of his eye, and the Executioner glanced toward it. The bright Hawaiian sun was shining off something slick and reflective roughly fifty yards away from where Susan Ogatu stood firing. As he watched, Bolan saw another slight movement and heard another roar. Then a hand reached up and wiped sweat from the top of the gleaming object that had first caught his eye.

The Executioner had ordered Ogatu and Sielert to return to the vehicle and wait. Those orders had been disobeyed. But he was glad they had been.

The fighting went on with men dropping from the guns of Bolan and Kekaha on one side of the camp, Ogatu and Sielert on the other. The Honolulu detective and the scientist raised their aim slightly, and below him, Bolan began hearing grunts and groans as their rounds took out the men on the second level. On the ground, more of the men died with rounds in the back. Others caught bullets when they realized there were shooters behind them as well as in front and rose to change positions.

Gradually, the gunfight began to die down as fewer participants remained to take part in it. Bolan ran the last carbine dry and switched to the Beretta 93-R. Finally, the explosions became sparse enough that a voice could be heard from the ground.

"Stop! We give up!"

The voice had the ring of one that had been shouting for a long time without being heard.

"Cease fire!" the Executioner yelled, and suddenly the encampment's only sound was the hollow ring as the explosions died down. Looking downward, he said, "Throw out your guns! Stand with your hands in the air!" He paused, then added, "Anyone we find hiding will take a bullet through the head with no questions asked!"

A half dozen or so rifles flew through the air and fell to the ground. Two of them came from the second tier, just below the Executioner and Kekaha. A moment later, two big men in camouflage stepped to the edge of the platform below them. A few others stood in the lava bed below.

The men around the card table had been unconscious through the entire gunfight. With Kekaha covering the men below, Bolan checked them. Two of the men were never going to wake up. They'd taken stray rounds—one in the heart, the other in the brain. The Executioner slapped the other two awake, then herded them toward the lava steps.

Bolan and Kekaha prodded the two men down the steps, picking up the other pair on the second level. By the time they had descended to the ground, Ogatu and Sielert had the four men there sitting on the lava with their hands clasped behind their heads.

"Keep them covered," Bolan said. "I'll be right back." Turning, he jogged up the lava steps to the third tier, passed the two dead men at the card table and walked across the plank leading to the wooden crate in the lava's hollow cavity.

The Executioner saw that the lid was nailed shut. Returning to the spot where he and Kekaha had lain on the platform, he grabbed the nearest empty carbine by the barrel and slammed it against the lava like a baseball player hitting a home run. The wooden stock splintered away, and he walked across the plank to the crate.

Using the Applegate-Fairbairn first, Bolan worked the

wooden lid up high enough and wedged what was left of the
carbine between it and the crate. It wasn't the best pry bar
he'd ever used, but it worked. Finally, with a loud splintery
sound, the nails in the lid broke free. Bolan removed the lid
and looked into the crate. Finally, he could see why the PFF
men had so studiously avoided shooting in that direction.

No, the crate contained no nuclear bomb.

Inside the box, the Executioner saw smaller cardboard
cases. Each of the boxes read, Jack Daniels.

RICKY KING hated Honolulu's Chinatown—hated every damn
thing about it. He shifted the backpack over his sweat-soaked
T-shirt and stepped off the Waikiki trolley onto Maunakea
Street.

Of course, Ricky King hated everything and everyone.

King went to work immediately, shifting the worn canvas
backpack straps across his shoulders once again and staring
down the street. He watched a car pull up to a stop sign. A
man pushed his back away from the building he'd been leaning against and reached into his pocket. When he got to the
car, he handed something small through the window to the
man in the passenger's seat. His hand came out holding
money, which quickly disappeared into the same pocket.

King ignored the man as he walked by, his eyes skirting the
sidewalks for a likely candidate. The big Samoan who had
hired him was nuts—of that he had no doubt. What was his
name? Lililili or Lolololo? Not that it mattered. But he was
crazy. He wanted King to get him a whole mess of cellular
phones. And he insisted that nobody get hurt in the process.

Two blocks ahead, King saw a cab pull to the curb. The
passenger who got out and paid the driver caught his eye. She
was a small woman—Chinese or Japanese—and wearing an
expensively tailored striped business suit as she fumbled in
her purse with one hand and kept talking into the cellular
phone pressed against her ear with the other. King smiled as
he quickened his pace. She had what he wanted.

Finishing with the cabby, the woman began walking down
Maunakea away from him. Ricky King broke into a jog as she

turned the corner and started toward the O'ahu Market area. He frowned. She didn't look like she worked there—not the way she was dressed. More likely, she worked in some office somewhere around there.

King had closed within a block of the woman by the time they reached the market. He followed her past the stands displaying fresh fish, fruits and vegetables and through rows of pigs' heads hanging from wires.

On the other side of the market, Ricky King saw his chance. The woman in the expensive suit cut left out of the market area and started down a side street. He broke into a jog, timing it so he caught up to her as soon as she was out of sight of the market.

The woman heard his footsteps as he approached and turned. She started to smile but never finished. King had taken his cellular phone from the case on his belt as he ran, and he brought it down on top of her head.

The woman fell to the sidewalk unconscious.

Ricky King took a quick glance around, saw no curious eyes on the street and lifted the woman into his arms. A moment later, he laid her to rest on the concrete ground of an alley. He looked at her. She'd need a few stitches when she woke up but she'd be okay otherwise.

Quickly, King rummaged through her purse until he came to the cellular phone. It was zipped into a neat little leather case, which he opened only long enough to be sure the ringer was turned off. Last thing he needed was a bunch of phones ringing in his pack. With his luck, he'd be walking right past a cop when the phones rang.

King tossed the woman's phone into the backpack, then searched the purse until he found a credit card case. The woman only had twelve dollars in cash. But all twelve went into the pocket of his jeans with the credit cards.

The cell phone on his belt rang. He knew who it had to be—only one person had the number. Angrily ripping the instrument from his belt, he punched the answer button and said, "Yeah?"

"You were supposed to make your delivery half an hour ago," the Samoan said. "I'm waiting."

"Look, Benjamin," King said, remembering the man's first name. "Two dozen cell phones off the street ain't that easy to come up with." He paused. "Specially when you ain't supposed to hurt nobody getting them."

"How many do you have now?" the Samoan asked.

He thought for a moment. "About eighteen, nineteen, I guess," he said.

"Get them to me. Now. You can get the rest later." The line went dead.

VLADIMIR SYVATOSLAV loved watching Benjamin Liholiho work. It was refreshing. The man had to be close to forty— Syvatoslav had never asked his true age. Liholiho believed, truly believed in the Polynesian Freedom Fighters' cause. What was even more remarkable was that he truly believed that the PFF could force the United States of America, the one and only superpower in the world now that the Soviet Union was gone, to leave Hawaii and give him a billion dollars to return the islands to the pristine Utopia he thought they had been before the white man invaded.

That, among other things, Syvatoslav thought as he watched the leader of the PFF guide the car down the Ala Wai Boulevard in Waikiki, was what made him so amusing. Clowns were always amusing.

As he drove, Liholiho pressed a cellular phone to his ear, waiting for the call he had just made to connect. Syvatoslav had to work hard to keep the smile off his face. The man was such a naive buffoon.

As they waited, the Ukrainian glanced at the shark-tooth club on the seat between them. He remembered an earlier conversation in which Liholiho had explained its symbolism to him. According to Liholiho, the club was an icon that represented the future freedom of Hawaii's native Polynesians. The memory brought a smile to Syvatoslav's face. The ridiculous weapon had been of no more than Stone Age caliber even when it had been made over two hundred years ago. Now it was even more silly. It was symbolic, however, Syvatoslav had to admit. But it didn't symbolize any future freedom. It symbolized the stupidity and blue-sky dreams of Liholiho and his PFF followers.

Finally, as they neared the intersection with Kalakaua Boulevard, Liholiho said, "Yes? Mr. President?" Syvatoslav watched him frown and saw his face turn a harsh red as he listened to the response on the other end. Then the big Samoan's voice boomed in anger. "I told you I would speak only to the President himself!" he screamed into the phone. "My name is Benjamin Liholiho, and I represent the Polynesian Freedom Fighters. I have two nuclear reactors in my possession, and if my demands are not met, I will activate them and destroy what you call your fiftieth state!" Again, Syvatoslav waited as Liholiho listened to the response. Suddenly, the big Samoan jumped as if bitten by a snake. He pulled the cellular phone away from his ear, held it in front of his face and stared at it in awe. "They hung up, Lasso," he said quietly.

Syvatoslav shrugged. "They get crank calls every day. You must do something to make them take you seriously."

Liholiho turned onto Kalakaua and headed north toward Kapi'olani Boulevard. Rolling the window down, he cast the third of the cellular phones he had just picked up from Ricky King out the window. The use of multiple cellular phones, recently stolen and with no connection to him or the PFF, had been his idea. It sounded as if no one at the White House was taking the threats seriously yet. But who knew? The American agents who had boarded and destroyed the decoy ship might have learned more by now. Perhaps the Americans were stalling while they tried to triangulate and position the calls.

That would happen eventually. But all they'd learn would be the route the caller had driven while making his calls. And he and Liholiho would be long gone.

"I will try one more time," Liholiho said. "Perhaps I will get someone who isn't such a low-level bureaucrat."

"Good luck," Syvatoslav said, shrugging. "But it's my guess you won't get through until you do something dramatic to demonstrate you are more than a mere madman.'' He paused. ''And we both know what that must be.''

Liholiho stopped at a red light and reached behind him, pulling another phone from the filthy backpack the street criminal had stored them in. He studied the face of the instrument—each make and model operated a little differently, it seemed—as he waited for the light to change. This was a more expensive cellular than the one he had just used, and included a speakerphone feature. He pointed out the fact to Syvatoslav as they waited.

''Please use it,'' the Ukrainian said. ''I would like to listen.''

Liholiho nodded. He adjusted the tail of the shirt hanging outside his pants, and for a brief second Syvatoslav got a glimpse of the black and red rubber grip on the Raging Bull hidden in the Polynesian's waistband. He glanced at the shark-tooth club, then turned to hide a new smile. Oh, yes, my dear Polynesian terrorist, he thought. Forgive me, I had forgotten— you're no longer in the Stone Age for you have progressed from mere clubs to the revolver, an invention merely a century and a half old.

Liholiho had tapped the White House number into the phone when the red traffic light disappeared and the green began to shine. He switched his foot from the brake to the accelerator and started through the intersection.

''Good afternoon,'' said an official-sounding female voice on the speakerphone. ''And welcome to the White House of the United States of America. How may I direct your call?''

''This is Benjamin Liholiho,'' the big Samoan said. ''Of the Polynesian Freedom Fighters. I must speak with the President immediately.''

''Excuse me, Mr. Liholiho,'' the voice said, sounding slightly irritated. ''But didn't we speak about half an hour ago?''

''We may have,'' Liholiho said. ''This is the fourth time I have called. And either every one of you there is too lazy to connect me, or too stupid to recognize that I am serious when I say I'm about to blow up the state of Hawaii.''

The voice from the White House sighed. "Mr. Liholiho, the President is a very busy man. He can't be bothered by nonsense such as this. Please, Mr. Liholiho, don't call back. Your name has already been turned over to the FBI and Secret Service. I'm sure if you are actually in Hawaii, as you claim, they will be contacting you soon."

"You don't believe me?" Liholiho asked.

"We take all threats seriously here at the White House, Mr. Liholiho. And you will be investigated, of that you may be sure, Mr. Liholiho—if that's what your name really is. And your tone of voice now is hardly furthering your cause to get me to take you seriously. Please, don't call back anymore and bother—"

"So!" Liholiho shouted. "It is proof that you want? Proof that you demand?"

"Mr. Liholiho—"

"I'll give you proof, then!" Liholiho shouted. He pulled the car off the street into a parking lot on the corner of Kapi'olani Boulevard and Beretania Street and rolled down the window. "As you love to say yourself," he said sarcastically into the phone, "please hold."

Syvatoslav knew what was about to happen. He loved watching the Polynesian Freedom Fighter's hypocrisy. Oh, no, Benjamin Liholiho didn't want to hurt anyone if he didn't have to. He didn't want to blow up the islands if he didn't have to. The PFF leader made such a show of his humanity, even making the street maggot who had procured the many cellular phones promise that no one would get hurt in the process.

The Ukrainian wondered how many people had died so Liholiho could get his untraceable phones, and a snort of contempt blew from his nostrils. But Liholiho was too preoccupied with his own anger to notice. Syvatoslav continued to watch as the Samoan pressed the phone to his ear and said, "Are you still listening?"

"Yes," said the bored voice in the White House. "But, Mr. Liholiho, I can't waste all day with—"

"Then listen closely!" Liholiho screamed. He extended both the cellular phone and the remote detonation device out the window of the vehicle, pointing them toward the Pacific Ocean. Syvatoslav couldn't see him punching the code into the transmitter.

But he heard the explosion a few seconds later, far in the distance.

Liholiho turned toward the Ukrainian with a leer that made even the hardened former KGB man's blood run cold. The Samoan might be naive and he might be a true believer. But all traces of the classic noble savage were gone from his face. He was naive, yes, Syvatoslav thought. But he was a naive monster.

The Ukrainian settled in his seat. In other words, Benjamin Liholiho was the perfect pawn to be moved at Syvatoslav's will and assist him in achieving his personal goal.

THE EXECUTIONER looked at the eight PFF men who had survived the battle. They all knelt on the ground, their hands clasped behind their heads. Three of the faces looked frightened. Three more tried to snarl with a courage their eyes didn't support. The final pair were openly weeping, awaiting what they believed to be imminent execution.

Bolan studied the men as he considered the situation. Benjamin Liholiho, advised by former KGB officer Vladimir Syvatoslav, had proven so far to be a competent leader. Part of that role was the incorporation of the need-to-know-only theory of information distribution among the troops. What that meant was simple.

The Executioner would be surprised if these men knew anything that might lead them to the nukes. They had been stationed here as a regular PFF outpost or as another of the decoys like the *Nakinka Melaniya* in Honolulu Harbor.

But there was a third possibility.

Bolan leaned in, picking the face that looked most frightened and shoving the barrel of the carbine into the throat beneath it. "Stand," he ordered.

"But I—"

"Now!"

The man on the ground had a strange reddish twinge to his

hair, as if one of his ancestors might have been an Irish sailor. His features looked only part Samoan. He shot to his feet as commanded, and the Executioner prodded him away from the other PFF men with the carbine barrel. "Susan," he said. "See what you can get out of them." He turned to the other two men. "Sielert, you and Kekaha keep them covered. If any of them so much as blinks, put a bullet between their eyes."

The Executioner drove the part-Polynesian toward one of the natural caves formed by the lava. To Bolan, Kekaha had proven to be a good man. And it was clear he had no use for fellow Polynesians who used terror to achieve their goals. In fact, Kekaha seemed to take it as a personal affront.

As soon as they were inside the small aperture, Bolan swept a boot across the ground behind the man, knocking his feet out from under him. The terrorist hit the ground on his back. "Sit up," Bolan ordered. The man had complied. Bolan asked bluntly, "Where are the nukes?"

"I don't know," said the man, and the answer cost him both his front teeth as the wooden stock of the carbine struck him squarely in the mouth. Blood flew from between his lips in a spray of red, and the teeth sailed through the air like popcorn escaping an air popper.

As soon as the man had spit a few times, the Executioner said, "Want to try another answer?"

The PFF man held up both hands defensively. "Look," he said. "I'm telling you the truth. I swear." With his two front teeth missing, the last word came out *thwear.*

Bolan started to move the rifle butt again, and the man cringed and shrieked. The Executioner stopped. "Then you better tell me something," he growled.

"Okay," the man seated on the ground said. "The nuke— I mean one of the nukes—was here. But only for a few hours." He spat again. "They took it away."

"Who took it away?" Bolan demanded.

"Liholiho and the Russian," the man said as he spit another mouthful of blood.

Bolan saw no reason to confuse his prisoner with the actual ancestry of the former KGB officer. To many people, anyone who had been part of the old Soviet Union was Russian. "Where'd they take it?" he demanded.

"That, I don't know," said the part-Polynesian and held his hands in front of his face in anticipation of another blow.

The Executioner surprised him. Instead of striking him with the stock, he held the barrel slightly to the side of the man's head and pulled the trigger.

The explosion threatened to deafen them both as it drilled through the porous lava just behind the PFF man. He screamed again.

Bolan waited until the scream had died down, and the fact that he hadn't been shot sank into the part-Polynesian's brain. Then he said, "That was your last chance. Your last free one. Tell me where the nuke went or the next one's not a practice round." He jammed the bore of the carbine between the man's protective arms and into the center of his forehead.

The terrorist's horror-stricken eyes looked past the tangle of arms, gunmetal and wood in front of him to the Executioner. "If I knew, I'd tell you," he said in a soft voice resigned to doom. "But I don't know. Liholiho didn't tell any of us where he was taking it."

Bolan was about to lower the .30 caliber when a series of shots exploded outside the cave. Swinging the carbine in another arc, he caught the PFF man on the chin. The man's eyes closed and he fell to his side on the ground.

The Executioner turned and sprinted out of the cave. He was just in time to see Kekaha draw a bead on the last of the seven PFF men who was sprinting away from where they'd been sitting. Another round boomed through the encampment, and the man looked like a diver going off the high board as he flew through the air.

Bolan glanced into the cave, assured himself the man on the ground was unconscious, then hurried forward. "What happened?" he asked Kekaha.

The big Samoan shook his head. "They heard the shot inside the cave and figured you'd killed the guy," he said. "Guess they thought a last-ditch attempt at escape was in order."

The Executioner turned toward Susan Ogatu. "You get anything out of them?" he asked.

The detective shook her head as Kekaha had done. "They didn't know anything," she said. "I'm sure of it."

Sielert nodded in affirmation. His face and the bald spot on top of his head were both a lighter shade than usual but not as pale as they had been after similar incidents. The scientist might not ever make the all-time-greatest-warriors list but he was getting more accustomed to the real world outside laboratories and think tanks.

Ogatu stepped toward Bolan. "Your man say anything worth hearing?"

Bolan was about to shake his head when the island beneath him began to vibrate as if an earthquake would split the ground open. A second later, a dull boom sounded from far out to sea.

The Executioner turned and raced toward the entrance to the camp, exiting where he and Kekaha had snuck in earlier and entering the smaller lava formations. Picking a cluster of lava a little taller than the others, he took two leaps to the top.

Far in the distance, across the peaceful waves of the South Pacific, the mushroom cloud was beginning to form.

Bolan stood watching it. At least he now knew where one of the nuclear bombs was.

The others stood frozen as the Executioner pulled the cellular phone from his pocket and tapped in the number.

Barbara Price didn't waste any time with formal greetings. "We just got word of it," the Stony Man mission controller said. "Kurtzman picked it up on one of his magic machines. It was several hundred miles away from any of the islands, and not close to the shipping lanes, but the tidal waves have already formed." She paused, and Bolan heard her take a deep breath. "It was for demonstration purposes only, Striker. But I'm afraid that's the good news."

"Let's hear the bad," Bolan said into the instrument.

"Benjamin Liholiho's on the phone to the President right now," Price said. "He and the PFF want a total evacuation of the islands by anyone without Polynesian blood. And they want a billion dollars in cash to boot.''

"That's it?'' Bolan asked.

There was a momentary pause on the other end of the line. Then Price said, "No. Benjamin Liholiho has assured the President that the nuke that just went up is the smaller of the two.''

10

Vladimir Syvatoslav knew there were logistical problems to the transfer of all extortion or ransom payments. They had to be exchanged quietly and safely. The authorities would try to use that moment of vulnerability as their best chance of apprehension. But with the bulk of the package demanded by one billion dollars in small and medium bills, the problems were magnified by almost that number of times.

Or so he had assured Benjamin Liholiho. And once that fact was established in the mind of the gullible PFF leader, convincing Liholiho that former KGB Colonel Vladimir Syvatoslav was the only man who could pull it off had been mere child's play.

Syvatoslav sat in the metal folding chair watching the waves break across the Pacific. The men, women and children playing on the sands of Waikiki looked happy as they threw beach balls and Frisbees back and forth, sipped cool drinks with fruit and tiny umbrellas floating at the top and worked on their tans so they would be complimented when they returned home. *If* they returned home, the Ukrainian mused, and the thought brought a chuckle to his chest. Only the people who had flights leaving the islands within the next few hours would be going home. The rest would soon be nothing more than vapor.

Syvatoslav reached into his pocket and produced a handkerchief, wiping sweat from his aging face. He glanced at his wristwatch. Yes, it was time. He lifted one of the cellular phones from the dirty backpack at the side of his chair and tapped in the number.

It wasn't the only call he had made from the beach that

morning. Earlier, he had contacted some friends. He had learned the name of the American, but nothing else.

The phone rang twice in Syvatoslav's ear. Then a voice on the other end said, "Yes?" Syvatoslav paused. He couldn't be certain that the man who answered was the big American agent who had boarded the *Nakinka Melaniya* with the female Honolulu detective and the scientist. But he suspected it was. And his curiosity demanded satisfaction. So he said, "Good day, Mr. Belasko."

The voice on the other end didn't sound shocked or even surprised. "Good day to you, Lasso," it said.

The use of his nickname by the American sent an electric shock surging through Syvatoslav's chest. The jolt he had hoped to induce in the American had been reversed on him. But the feeling passed quickly. As he had told Benjamin Liholiho so many times, the Americans were hardly stupid— they would learn certain things during the course of the operation. It was, in fact, one of the few truths he had told the leader of the PFF.

Recovered from the shock, the Ukrainian said, "Let's get down to business."

The man on the other end of the line remained silent. Syvatoslav went on. "You have followed the directions which were given to your President?"

"Yes."

"The money is packaged as I ordered and ready for transfer?"

"I said yes."

"Very good," the Ukrainian said. "Then the game can begin."

"It's not a game, Vladimir Syvatoslav," the voice on the other end of the line said in a tone that brought a chill to the Ukrainian's chest. "And you know I'm going to kill you."

"Perhaps you will," Syvatoslav said. "But if you do you will also be killing millions of other people." He drew a deep breath. "Go immediately to the intersection of Alohea and Twelfth Avenue. It is in Kaimuki. Just north of Diamond Head."

"I know where it is," said the American.

"Good. You'll see the phone booth and be contacted there. You have thirty minutes."

"I'm in Honolulu, Syvatoslav," the American said. "I can't make it that fast."

"I suggest you do," said the Ukrainian. "If you don't answer by the fifth ring, I'll hang up. The next sound you hear…" Syvatoslav let the sentence trail off, then said, "Actually, you aren't likely to hear the next sound. Or any other sound ever again." He disconnected the call and glanced at the water once more. A quick glance up and down the beach told him no one was watching. He dug a hole in the sand with his shoe and dropped the cellular phone into it. The same shoe swept sand over the phone, and he grabbed the backpack and rose to his feet.

Leaving the chair where it was, the Ukrainian headed toward the sidewalk that ran along the beach. As he did, a beautiful young bikini-clad woman in her early twenties ran toward him chasing an airborne Frisbee. She was looking the other way, and Syvatoslav's aging bones and muscles refused to follow orders when he told them to get out of her path. A moment later, they both lay in the sand.

A young man of the same age came running forward. The woman was already on her feet and apologizing profusely. "I'm so sorry," she said, trying to help Syvatoslav to his feet. "I didn't see you. Are you okay?"

The Ukrainian nodded. The man joined them and together the two young people pulled him to his feet. Both began brushing sand from his slacks and shirt. "I can't tell you how sorry I am," the woman said again.

Syvatoslav smiled. "It doesn't matter," he said. "I'm not hurt."

The young man caught his accent and grinned. "Russian?" he asked.

The former KGB officer saw no reason to confuse them with the fact that he was Ukrainian rather than Russian. Considering the level of American education these days, these two weren't likely to know the difference. He nodded.

"Wow," said the man. "Come a long way, huh? Glad to have you. I'm glad to have you guys as friends these days instead of enemies."

Syvatoslav smiled.

"Can we buy you a drink or anything?" the man asked.

"We're on our honeymoon," said the girl.

"No, a drink won't be necessary," Syvatoslav said. "But congratulations on your marriage. Are you honeymooning in Hawaii long?"

"Two weeks," the man said.

"How unfortunate," said the Ukrainian.

Both the young man and woman were looking at him quizzically as he walked away.

BOLAN PULLED the car into the parking lot with a squeal of rubber. He slowed only slightly as he twisted the steering wheel toward the phone bolted to the brick wall of the convenience store. He glanced at his wristwatch as he pulled up to the building and threw the transmission into park. It had taken him twenty-nine minutes and thirty seconds to blast past, around and through the angry drivers and honking horns that had separated him from the phone. Now, as he killed the engine, he heard the phone ring through the closed glass of the window.

The Executioner reached for the door handle and pulled. A soft click sounded, but the door remained closed. His eyes shot to the door. The orange rectangle that indicated the door was unlocked wasn't visible, and when he pushed the sliding latch to reveal it he found it frozen in place.

Bolan cursed softly under his breath as the phone rang again. His hand moved to the locking system's master control on the arm rest, but it failed, as well. Lifting the remote device attached to the car's keys, he punched the button.

The door remained locked as the phone rang for the third time.

The Executioner drew the Desert Eagle from under his sport coat and slammed it into the window. Glass shattered over and around him, and a moment later he was pulling himself through the opening as sharp shards still attached to the window frame cut through his clothing and into his flesh. The fourth ring came as his feet hit the pavement, and the fifth had just started as he ripped the receiver from the wall.

"Ah," Syvatoslav said in Bolan's ear. "So you like to cut things close, eh?"

"I just got here," the Executioner replied. "The door lock stuck."

The Ukrainian laughed into the phone. "How ironic," he said. "To think that millions of people might have died because of some lazy automobile worker." He laughed again, then said, "The money is in the sealed containers I ordered?"

"I told you it was before."

"Very good," Syvatoslav said. "And they are chained together as I instructed?"

"They will be. I don't intend to try to carry them around that way."

"But they are in the Ryder rental truck?"

"Yes, Lasso, your billion dollars are all sealed up and in the truck."

"Do you know why I demanded a *Ryder* truck, Mr. Belasko?"

"No, Vlad, why don't you tell me?"

"It was to remind you of your Oklahoma City bombing, of course. Which will seem like nothing more than a firecracker compared to what will happen if I find you have lied about anything."

"That's very cute and clever on your part, Vlad," Bolan said. "But can we get on with it?"

"Certainly. Now, let me instruct you as to the rest of the rules of the game. They are not elaborate, and even someone such as yourself can follow them, Mr. Belasko."

Bolan ignored the childish insult.

"You will drive the truck yourself," Syvatoslav went on. "Alone. You will proceed to Honolulu International Airport, to the runways used by Mahalo Airlines. Clear so far?"

"Crystal."

"If your President has also followed my orders, the runway

and terminal will both be deserted except for one plane. Mine." Bolan heard him take a breath. "If there is any sign of deception, Hawaii will go up in a mushroom cloud. I need only make one quick phone call. Or not report to my confederates on time."

"You'll go up with it," Bolan said.

"Yes, and so will you," Syvatoslav said. "But what does it matter, eh? I am growing old, and if I can't spend my remaining years in the manner I choose, I don't choose to spend my remaining years at all."

"Go on."

"You'll load the containers onto the empty plane. There is to be no tampering with the controls or any other equipment. Is that understood?"

"Yes."

"I'll then arrive to inspect the plane. If everything has been done as I ordered, we will shake hands, and I will fly away. If not, we all go boom."

"And you expect the United States to just clear out of Hawaii at that point?" he asked.

"Of course not," the Ukrainian said, laughing. "What happens from there will be between you and Benjamin Liholiho and will no longer concern me. I want only the money. The future of the Hawaiian Islands—if there *is* a future for the Hawaiian Islands—is of no interest to me whatsoever."

Bolan nodded. It was as he had suspected ever since Kurtzman had mentioned his theory that the man called both Vlad and Lasso was in actuality Vladimir Syvatoslav, and that the aging former KGB man wanted one last big score. That theory was now fact. Forensic expert Becky Foreman had lifted several latent fingerprints and a partial off the raft. Most of the prints belonged to Benjamin Liholiho. The partial had gone unidentified so far, but Kurtzman was running it through all the AFIS identification systems in his computers and cross-referencing it with other suspected PFF men.

One thumb print, however, had led them directly to Vladimir Syvatoslav, and the man's identity had been confirmed. The Executioner knew that the money Syvatoslav had kept after killing his friend Kishinev and his cut from the PFF weren't the big score Kurtzman had had in mind. However much those two amounts totaled, they had to be mere peanuts compared to the cool billion of which he soon planned to be in possession.

"Is everything clear in your mind, Mr. Belasko?"

"I won't forget you, Syvatoslav. Keep that in mind."

"I will," the Ukrainian promised. "Now, I suggest you get the truck and proceed to the airport. You have one hour."

Bolan started to respond. But the line had gone dead in his ear.

BOTH the Mahalo Airlines terminal and the interisland flight company's runways had been evacuated, Bolan saw, as he pulled the twenty-four-foot Ryder moving van onto the service road leading that way. The human purge had been swift, with Susan Ogatu running the show over the objections of the Honolulu police chief. But Ogatu had been the Executioner's choice in that role, and a phone call from the White House had insured the female detective's place at the top.

The Executioner pulled the truck off the service road and onto the apron next to the terminal. He circled the deserted building, not seeing the plane until he reached the side. But there it stood, ready and waiting. Just like Vladimir Lasso Syvatoslav had said it would be.

It wasn't a new plane but a time-proven model. The Helio Stallion H-550A was a general-utility aircraft with seating for eight to ten passengers and a crash-resistant cabin structure. Some of the armed versions had been flown by American pilots in Vietnam during close air support and other special missions, and others had been furnished to the Cambodians by the USAF. The soldier wondered briefly where Syvatoslav had come up with the craft, but pushed the idea to the back of his brain. It didn't matter much at this point. A man who could shut down an entire area of Honolulu International could certainly procure an aircraft.

The H-550A stood on the taxiway leading to the runway in the distance. Bolan pulled the truck in next to it, then backed around until the rear bumper stood four feet from the closed cargo hatch. Climbing from the cab, he wasn't surprised to find the hatch unlocked. Nor was he surprised to see that all the seats had been ripped out of the body of the plane to enlarge the storage area.

The soldier lifted the back door to the Ryder rental truck and let it roll up over his head. He began lifting the large watertight containers from the truck, setting them in the plane, then pulling himself on board to stack them against the walls. Glancing at his watch, he saw that he still had fifteen minutes left to complete the task. More than enough time. His eyes made a quick inventory of the inside of the plane. Bare, except for four storage lockers bolted along one wall. He saw nothing to indicate where Syvatoslav might be heading after he took off.

After his final trip with the last of the money boxes, Bolan ran the heavy-duty plastic-coated cable chain through the handles of each box, binding them together. He had wondered why Syvatoslav had insisted on such an arrangement, but the man had hung up before he could ask. Not that he'd have expected an answer, anyway. Making sure the water-sealed hard plastic boxes were bound together obviously had something to do with his escape plan.

Bolan snapped the ends of the cable together, then turned to the lockers. He found nothing inside the first two. But in the third, he saw a packed parachute at the bottom. Frowning, he knelt on the floor of the plane and pulled it forward to inspect it. As he did, Syvatoslav's plan became clear.

The Ukrainian had insisted the cash be packed in waterproof containers. At first, the Executioner had guessed that was because he planned to hide them somewhere within the humid tropics. Now he knew better. If you combined the waterproof boxes with the cable connecting them and the parachute, Syvatoslav's general scheme, if not the specifics of it, became clear.

Bolan continued to stare at the parachute. The former KGB man knew he would be followed on radar as soon as he took off in the H-550A. There was nowhere in the world he could land without officers waiting to take him and the money into custody. So he planned to jettison the boxes from the plane at some prearranged coordinates. He wasn't going to hide the cash where it was humid, he planned to hide it where it was *wet*. Deep within the ocean.

The Executioner slid the parachute into the locker. Syvatoslav was no youngster anymore. But as the man hoped for one last big score, he was willing to risk one last big parachute jump to get it. Bolan guessed he planned to put the Helio Stallion on autopilot and make his jump into some isolated location while the plane flew on until it ran out of fuel. Then, when the heat had cooled down, he'd go back to the coordinates with a dive boat and search for the cash.

Syvatoslav's plan had become clear in Bolan's mind in a microsecond. As he prepared to stand up, the Ukrainian seemed to appear by his side just as fast. The door of the fourth locker opened, and Bolan saw a flash of black steel as the collapsible ASP baton came down on his head.

The blow was well-executed, and Bolan fell forward toward the lockers on hands and knees. Something rough and ragged was pressed against his throat.

The rope tightened quickly around the Executioner's neck. Behind him, he heard a grunt. He was pulled to a kneeling position as the oxygen to his brain was choked off. He reached behind his head, clawing, trying to get at hands he couldn't reach. His vision grew blurred, and he felt the blood beginning to build in his face.

The Executioner tried to twist one way, then the other. But he was held in place on his knees by the body he realized was pressed against his back. He felt an elbow at the back of his neck, placed there to increase the pressure as Syvatoslav pushed against him and pulled on the rope at the same time. As his vision clouded, threatening to turn black, he realized he was only a few seconds from unconsciousness. Then death.

With all the oxygen-starved strength that remained in his body, Bolan shifted his weight, getting his feet under him and rising to a squatting position. With what he knew must be his final act on earth, he thrust back with all his might. The man behind him stumbled. The noose slackened for a moment, and the Executioner gasped for air. But the rope tightened again.

On his feet, Bolan leaned back, giving in to rather than fighting the force pulling against his throat. He felt the man behind him lose his balance, and when he did the Executioner backed up hoping to drive Syvatoslav against the wall of the plane and jar him loose.

The drive in the Executioner's legs took them both across the aircraft and through the hatchway. Bolan landed on top of the man on the taxiway and heard another grunt. The rope around his neck went suddenly slack, and when he reached up, he found he could pull it free.

Choking and coughing, the Executioner rolled off of the Ukrainian and to his side on the ground. Next to him, he saw Vladimir Syvatoslav flat on his back. The Ukrainian's mouth was open in a silent plea for help.

Reaching down, Bolan grasped the man's hair and lifted his head. The back of Syvatoslav's skull had split open like an overripe peach. Dropping the head, Bolan jammed a finger into the man's neck. There was no pulse.

Wobbling slightly, the Executioner rose to his feet and stared at the rope in his hand.

It looked very much like a cowboy's lasso.

"WE'VE GOT to figure Liholiho still doesn't know Syvatoslav double-crossed him," Bolan said. He could hear his voice in his ears. It was scratchy and a full octave deeper than usual. He looked across the office to where Susan Ogatu sat in the chair she had wheeled from behind her desk. Greg Sielert was on the end of the couch, and Don Kekaha, who was every bit as big and Polynesian as Buck Kalakaua had been, was sitting in the spot Kalakaua had taken a few days before. In fact, in many ways, Ogatu's office was the same as when they'd first begun the search for the nukes.

The mood had been somber then, too. But it was even more so now.

"Yes," Ogatu agreed. "Liholiho was duped by Syvatoslav

all along. But it's just a matter of time before he figures it out.''

Bolan nodded. ''Syvatoslav assured me on the phone that the bomb would blow if he failed to make contact. I believed that then, and I believe it now.''

''Liholiho will really push the button?'' Sielert asked. The reality that it might actually happen seemed not to have sunk into his mind until that moment.

''Oh, he'll do it, all right,'' said Don Kekaha. ''He'll see himself and his men as martyrs.''

''We don't know exactly what Syvatoslav told Liholiho,'' Bolan said. ''But he had to have promised to meet him somewhere with the money. At some prearranged time. Which means we have some time left ourselves. How much? I don't know.''

''And the nuke could be anywhere in the islands,'' Sielert said.

''It could be,'' the Executioner said. ''But it isn't. They've brought it from the Big Island to Oahu.''

Three faces turned his way.

''How do you know that?'' Susan asked.

Bolan straightened slightly in his chair. ''It only makes sense. Liholiho keeps threatening to blow Hawaii off the map. Well, maybe he can actually do that, and maybe he can't—stop and think about it.'' He turned to Sielert. ''Greg, how many nuclear devices did the Soviets have that were capable of *that* big an explosion?''

Sielert frowned in thought. ''I don't know for sure. But from one end of the islands to the other...no, you're right. One bomb isn't very likely to get them all.''

''Not that it's a big consolation,'' the Executioner went on. ''Because he can still kill millions of people. But doesn't it make sense that he'd want the most bang for his buck? Do the most mass destruction he can?'' He didn't wait for an answer. ''That means Honolulu. The island of Oahu. He's brought the bomb right here.''

Bolan saw Ogatu force a grin. ''Well,'' she said. ''That narrows it down to only a few million suspects.''

"Do we have anything to go on?" Don Kekaha asked. "Anything left at all?"

Bolan turned to the Samoan. He had brought Kekaha to Oahu from the Big Island after the man had proven his value in the battle at the lava beds. It never hurt to have an extra gun along—a gun you could trust. Particularly when the man who wielded that gun could blend in with the PFF so well. He was about to answer Kekaha's question when the cellular phone in his jacket pocket rang. He pulled it out, tapped the answer button and said, "Yes?"

Aaron "Bear" Kurtzman's voice said, "Striker? I've got an ID on the partial print. Jonathan Wesley Laulau. Also an address."

Bolan grabbed a pen and notepad from the top of Ogatu's desk. "Shoot it to me, Bear," he said. The Executioner wrote while Kurtzman talked, getting Laulau's address as well as taking down several other notes. A few minutes later, he stood.

"Let's go," he said. "We've got the name and address of the PFF man whose partial print was found on the raft. Jonathan Wesley Laulau."

The other three rose to their feet, as well.

"Think he'll take us to the nuke?" Sielert asked as they hurried out the door. "Think he'll even know where it is?" When Bolan didn't answer, he said sheepishly. "Okay, stupid question. No way of knowing. But who knows? We're due some luck."

"I think we may already have it," the Executioner said as he led the way out of the Honolulu police headquarters building and across the parking lot toward the Bonneville.

"How's that?" Ogatu asked.

"My man on the other end," Bolan said. "As soon as he got the ID, he made a couple of phone calls to the guy's neighbors. Pretended to be a concerned relative who hadn't heard from Laulau in a while."

"And?" Ogatu said as they all got into the car.

"The neighbor told him not to worry. Jonathan Laulau is just fine. In fact, he seems to have been having some kind of party at his house for the last couple of days. Lots of people coming and going."

Sielert had gotten into the back seat. "Not that I'm questioning your judgment," the scientist said. "But isn't that a little thin?"

"Maybe," the Executioner said. "But it's all we've got. And the fact that the neighbor is irritated that Laulau's new flatbed truck is blocking his driveway helps some, too."

DARKNESS HAD FALLEN and the Hawaiian moon had risen high in the tropical sky by the time Bolan parked the Bonneville across the street and a block down from Laulau's house. Through the car's broken window, he had listened to the sounds of the island as he sped along the highways and streets, hearing the surf and birds and the laughter of children as he raced toward the spot where he prayed the nuclear bomb had been hidden.

He knew that all those sounds and the people and animals who made them could disappear into nothingness at any moment.

The Executioner turned in his seat. "Stay here," he told Ogatu and Sielert. "Don, I want you to go down there and check it out. You aren't going to be noticed the way we would be. Find out if—" He was interrupted by the cellular phone, which once again rang in his pocket. Pulling the instrument out, he said, "Yeah?"

"Striker," Barbara Price said in a voice so calm he knew something had to be wrong. "The President just got off the phone with Liholiho again. The man knows something's up. And he threatened to detonate the nuke in five minutes if he hadn't made contact with Syvatoslav by then." She paused briefly. "That was two minutes ago."

Bolan let the phone fall to the floor of the Bonneville as he threw open the door. There was no time now for Kekaha's recon. No time to plan at all. The only course of action was a direct assault. He'd have to hope he could get inside and neutralize the situation before anyone had a chance to touch off the explosion.

For that matter, he'd have to pray the bomb really was at Jonathan Laulau's house.

The Executioner heard Ogatu's soft footsteps directly behind him as he sprinted across the yards. Behind them came the heavier footfalls made by Sielert and Kekaha. He hadn't even had time to tell them what had occurred. But none of them were stupid. His sudden actions had told them the clock had just run out.

Two houses away, Bolan drew the Desert Eagle and cut across the street. He passed the flatbed truck parked out front, leaped up onto the front lawn and raced for the door.

The Executioner took the three porch steps in one leap. As his feet landed on the concrete, he saw a broad Polynesian face in the window. The face saw him, as well, and turned into the room to shout something. A split second later, Bolan lowered his shoulder and struck the door. The lock snapped and the door flew back on its hinges, smashing into the wall behind it. The knob crashed through the wallboard, trapping the door open.

Bolan raced into the room, all doubts that he might have the wrong house suddenly evaporating. The living room was filled with men—all big, and all of Polynesian descent. They had begun to lunge for the weapons scattered around the room.

The Executioner pointed the Desert Eagle at a man trying to flee into a rear hallway. A 240-grain hollowpoint round took off the back of his head. Another .44 Magnum slug struck the chest of a PFF man diving for an M-16, and a third burrowed into the sternum of a terrorist who had lifted an Uzi. Behind him, Bolan heard the familiar pops of Ogatu's Glock and the louder roars from Sielert's Gold Cup. More PFF men bit the carpet.

Bolan took a step to the side to make room for Don Kekaha. The Samoan had borrowed Ogatu's Remington pump-action riot gun, and the room exploded with 12-gauge buckshot. Bolan pulled the Desert Eagle's trigger again and again, and more men fell. A huge man who looked to be around forty threw a club with some sort of spikes embedded in it, and the Executioner ducked under the strange weapon. The man's big hand fell to a huge revolver holstered on his belt. As it came out of the holster, Bolan could see it was a Taurus Raging Bull .454 Casull—a round even more powerful than his own .44 Magnum.

But only if it reached its mark first.

Bolan lifted the Desert Eagle, and a double-tap of .44 Magnums crashed into the man's chest. He flew back against the wall with a scream, then slumped to the ground in a sitting position as blood poured from a gaping chest wound. His hand disappeared into his pocket and came out with what looked very much like a remote control for a television.

Before he could push any of the buttons, another round drilled through his brain. The remote control fell harmlessly to the carpet.

Suddenly, the living room was filled with silence.

Bolan walked forward, lifted the remote device and pocketed it. He drew the Beretta and holstered his near-empty Desert Eagle. Holding up a hand for the others to remain motionless, he walked cautiously toward the hallway where the man had tried to escape. Stepping over the body on the floor, he let the 9 mm lead the way as he searched the rest of the rooms. They were empty.

At least of human beings.

In the rear bedroom, the Executioner stopped. Calling into the hall, he said, "Greg! Come here!"

Sielert, followed by Kekaha and Ogatu, answered the call and appeared inside the bedroom door. Bolan pointed the Beretta toward the large wooden crate in the corner next to the bed. "Greg," he said. "I think it's show time. Check it out."

Sielert moved quickly to the crate, stopping and checking the sides and top for trip wires. Satisfied that none existed, he lifted the lid. The scientist stared into the crate for a few seconds, nodding silently.

"Is that it?" Bolan asked.

Sielert turned and nodded again.

"Not another decoy?" the Executioner asked.

Sielert let a thin smile cover his lips as he stared inside the box again. "Oh, no," he said. "This baby's for real. But we might have been wrong about something."

"How's that?"

"They really might have been able to leave it on the Big Island and still take out the whole Hawaiian chain." Before Bolan could respond, Sielert turned and walked across the room. His cheeks were slightly flushed with excitement, but he was as calm as a priest after Mass. Gone was the wannabe warrior and the insecure man who spoke simply to fill silences. Addressing Bolan, Ogatu and Kekaha, the nuclear expert said, "Gentlemen...and lady...if you would be so kind..." With his hand, he indicated that they should move out of the bedroom.

Don Kekaha, who had faced death over and over with the Executioner during the last two days, showed far more alarm than Sielert. "Er, Greg," he said. "Should we, er, like, evacuate the neighborhood or anything?"

Bolan watched Sielert suppress a smile. But the man's eyes glowed with humor as he said, "If you'd like to, Don. You might want to relocate them somewhere on the other side of Kansas City."

"Let's get out of the man's way," Bolan said. As he holstered the Beretta and began to shepherd Ogatu and Kekaha away from the bedroom, he saw Sielert reach into his vest pocket, pull out a small leather tool case and unzip it.

Bolan, Ogatu and Kekaha returned to the living room and took seats on the couches and chairs. The recognition of how ridiculous his question to Sielert had been seemed to have forced some of Kekaha's usual composure back. "Well," he said as he sat and eyed the bodies on the floor around them. "At least we've got company while we wait to find out if we're going to get blown up."

As is so often the case with warriors forced to wait, dark humor followed to ease the tension. Seconds became minutes. Finally, a long silence ensued. Then Ogatu suddenly looked up at Bolan and said, "There's a good chance we're about to die, isn't there?"

Bolan nodded.

"Okay," Ogatu said, her eyes boring into those of the Executioner. "Normally, I don't say what I'm really feeling. Don't ask me why. Maybe it was the way I was raised. Maybe it's because I don't want to look soft to the other cops. In any case, I've learned to hide my feelings." The beautiful woman glanced at the floor in embarrassment, then suddenly looked into Bolan's eyes. "But just in case, there's something I want to tell you, Mike," she said. "Something I've wanted to tell you almost from the moment we met. Mike, I—"

Greg Sielert's footsteps coming down the hallway cut her off and caused all three of them to rise to their feet and turn toward him. The scientist appeared at the doorway, zipping his tools into the leather case. He looked at them and smiled. "Relax," he said. "It's over."

Ogatu let a rush of relief escape her lips. Kekaha let out what Bolan could only guess was some ancient Polynesian war whoop of victory. The Executioner smiled.

Kekaha shook his head. "I've faced a lot of things in my time," he said. "But I don't mind telling you, that scared the hell out of me. I might just need to go change my drawers."

The comment caused Ogatu to laugh. "Better get an extra pair for me," she said. Then, frowning slightly, she studied Sielert. "Greg," she said. "Donnie and I are wiped out. But you look as fresh as a daisy. And you're the one who had all the pressure on him."

Greg Sielert grinned, finally acknowledging he was a scientist, not a warrior. Then, turning toward the Executioner, he winked. "It's what *I* do best."

**A journey through the dangerous frontier
known as the future...**

JAMES AXLER

DEATHLANDS®

Zero City

Hungry and exhausted, Ryan and his band emerge from
a redoubt into an untouched predark city, and uncover a
cache of weapons and food. Among other interlopers,
huge winged creatures guard the city. Holed up inside
an old government building, where Ryan's son, Dean,
lies near death, Ryan and Krysty must raid where a local
baron uses human flesh as fertilizer....

James Axler

OUTLANDERS®

TIGERS OF HEAVEN

In the Outlands, the struggle for control of the baronies continues. Kane, Grant and Brigid seek allies in the Western Islands empire of New Edo, where they try to enlist the aid of the Tigers of Heaven, a group of samurai warriors.

Book #2 of the Imperator Wars saga, a trilogy chronicling the introduction of a new child imperator—launching the baronies into war!

On sale February 2001 at your favorite retail outlet. Or order your copy now by sending your name, address, zip or postal code, along with a check or money order (please do not send cash) for $5.99 for each book ordered ($6.99 in Canada), plus 75¢ postage and handling ($1.00 in Canada), payable to Gold Eagle Books, to:

In the U.S.	In Canada
Gold Eagle Books	Gold Eagle Books
3010 Walden Ave.	P.O. Box 636
P.O. Box 9077	Fort Erie, Ontario
Buffalo, NY 14269-9077	L2A 5X3

Please specify book title with order.
Canadian residents add applicable federal and provincial taxes.

GOUT16